"He ___ ing int ___ will fi ___ powers. And I'm not a witch," she added. "Although some of my best friends are witches. All dead, of course."

I sighed. It was exactly the opposite of what Grandma had assigned me to do. If we really did find Rellik, it would mean the end of Grandma's matchmaking business, which was unthinkable. Like Ruth's Tea Time, Grandma's Matchmaking Services was an institution in town, and her whole life. I didn't think she could be happy without her vocation.

Spencer ran his fingers through his hair and walked over to Luanda. With Spencer's back turned, Remington let his hand travel up the side of my body from my hip to under my arm, his fingertips grazing my breast. My core melted like a chocolate lava cake. I moaned.

"You okay, Gladie?" Ruth asked.

"Yes," I croaked. "Just tired."

I was happy for the darkness. I took a step back and allowed him to press his body against me. His hand slipped around to my belly and then lower. It occurred to me that Luanda might not be the only crazy person out here. Letting myself get fondled by a hot Trekkie not ten yards away from Spencer was pretty wackadoodle.

"Probie!" Spencer called, as he walked into the grove of trees with Luanda.

Remington leaned over and surreptitiously kissed the side of my neck. His face was rough with an end-of-the-day beard, but his lips were baby soft. I looked down to make sure my body hadn't burst into flames. Good news: I was still intact.

But one thing was certain. I was playing with fire.

By Elise Sax

*An Affair to Dismember*
*Matchpoint*
*Love Game*

Books published by The Random House Publishing
Group are available at quantity discounts on bulk pur-
chases for premium, educational, fund-raising, and special sales use. For details, please call 1-800-733-3000.

# LOVE GAME

*The*
**Matchmaker
Series**

## Elise Sax

BALLANTINE BOOKS • NEW YORK

A Ballantine Books Mass Market Original

Copyright © 2014 by Elise Sax
Excerpt from *An Affair to Dismember* copyright © 2013 by Elise Sax

Published in the United States by Ballantine Books, an imprint of Random House, a division of Random House LLC, a Penguin Random House Company, New York.

BALLANTINE and the HOUSE colophon are trademarks of Random House LLC.

ISBN 978-0-345-53226-8
eBook ISBN 978-0-345-53227-5

Cover design: Caroline Teagle
Cover photograph: Claudio Marinesco

Printed in the United States of America

www.ballantinebooks.com

9 8 7 6 5 4 3 2 1

Ballantine mass market edition: March 2014

*For Max and Sam*

# Chapter 1

**✦ ♥ ✦**

*E*veryone talks about the calm before the storm, but nobody warns you about the calm after the storm, bubeleh. I know, I know—storms are scary. All that wind blows you to hell and gone and can turn you upside down. Drown you. But in love, dolly—and in matchmaking—drowning can be a good thing. Things should be stirred up. Things should be moving. Chaos is love's friend. You know what I mean? So if your matches are drowning, if they are having their kishkes blown to smithereens, that might be a good thing. Be happy for storms in your matches' lives. Be happy for the couples who are holding on for dear life. But if the wind changes and it becomes dead calm, dolly, be afraid. Be very afraid.

**Lesson 57,**
**Matchmaking Advice from Your Grandma Zelda**

I SCREAMED and threw a bucket into the corner of the shed. I heard Grandma's designer heels *click-clack* toward me on the stone walk.

"Don't worry, there's nothing poisonous in there," she called in my direction. "Not since the end of rattlesnake season."

I didn't know there was a rattlesnake season in

Cannes, California. I had moved to the small mountain village only five months earlier to live with my grandmother and work in her matchmaking business. If I had known there was a rattlesnake season, I might have stayed in Denver to work on the cap line at the plastic-bottle factory for more than the six weeks I was there.

I raised the can of bug spray above my head as a warning to all the creepy crawlies in Grandma's shed. There were a lot of them.

"Are you sure rattlesnake season is over?" I asked as she opened the door wider and peeked her head inside. She was decked out in what I suspected was a Badgley Mischka wedding dress, two sizes too small, her flesh threatening to burst out of the seams.

"Normally it's over by the beginning of October," she said, adjusting her lace bodice. Grandma was a lot of woman, but she had style and was never caught out of her house without full makeup and at least a fake designer ensemble. Not that she ever got past her property lines. She was a homebody, what people uncharitably described as a shut-in. It didn't matter, though—the town came to Grandma, as she was the indispensable matchmaker and all-around yenta. And she knew things that couldn't be known.

"*Normally* it's over?" I asked, peering into the corners of the shed.

"The last one slithered out of here at least a week ago," she said, certain of herself.

I screamed and sprayed the wall. "There's spiders the size of Rhode Island in here."

"If you don't like spiders, don't open your red suitcase, dolly," she told me, shaking her head. "There's some nasty ones in there."

My sweaters were also in the red suitcase. And my good coat. The weather in Cannes had turned cold with the arrival of apple season, and I had been wearing the same Cleveland Browns sweatshirt every day for the past week and a half. It was time to unpack my winter clothes, but I didn't know if I was brave enough to fight off nasty spiders for a wool coat.

"You could borrow something of mine," Grandma told me, seemingly reading my mind. "I have a lovely velour jacket with feather detailing that's very warm, and it's just attracting moths in my closet."

"Hold your breath, Grandma," I said. "I'm going in." I took a gulp of fresh air and resumed spraying. I made it to the red suitcase, doused it with the last of the poison, grabbed the bag by the handle, and shot out of the shed like a bullet.

Grandma looked down at the dripping suitcase. "Yep, there are some nasty ones in there," she said.

I TOSSED the suitcase into the trunk of my Oldsmobile Cutlass Supreme and closed it successfully after three tries. The rust had overtaken my old silver car, making it look two-tone, with large red rusty patches. I had never minded the rust, but now it had infected the lock on the trunk, making it nearly impossible to shut.

"I'll have Dave open the suitcase," I told Grandma. Dave was the owner and operator of Dave's Dry Cleaner's and Tackle Shop. He was both fastidious and a lover of bugs. My suitcase was right up his alley, and I would have my winter clothes back clean and pressed within twenty-four hours.

But Grandma wasn't paying attention to me. She stood in the driveway, ramrod-straight, her head raised, and her eyes closed. A cool breeze blew against her bouffant hairdo, making it stir ever so slightly.

"Something wrong?" I asked her.

"The wind has shifted," she said, flustered.

"Don't I know it. What a relief." September had been chaos. The whole town had gone crazy. But now we were a week into October, and it was calm and relaxed. Cannes had settled into its Apple Days events, and apple cider and apple pie were being sold at just about every store in the historic district. Everyone was in a good mood, including me.

In fact, I was in the best mood I had been in since my three days as a cashier at a medical-marijuana dispensary in Monterey. My bank account was finally in the black, and I was starting to think I might have the hang of the matchmaking business. My last match was working like gangbusters. Even though it had been years since I'd settled down in one place for more than a couple of months, Cannes was starting to grow on me. It was beginning to feel like home.

"An ill wind," Grandma muttered.

I turned my face to the breeze. I could smell the fires coming from the neighbors' fireplaces, nothing else. Nothing out of the ordinary.

"Isn't it time for the Dating Do's and Don'ts class?" I asked.

"Nobody's coming."

"What?" Grandma's house was usually Grand Central, with no end to singles coming to her in their journey to find love.

"Not today. Nobody."

"Did you cancel it?" I asked. "Are you feeling all right?"

Grandma ignored me and walked up the driveway to the front door. I could hear the rustle of her pantyhose as she walked, her thighs rubbing against each other. It was unusual behavior for my grandmother, and I had begun to follow her into the house when I heard a car horn.

The sound got louder, until finally the most beautiful Mercedes I had ever seen barreled around the corner and up onto the curb at the bottom of the driveway. Without turning off the motor, my friend Lucy Smythe hopped out.

"Help! Now! Come!" she shouted in my direction. Despite her panic, she was impeccably dressed, not a hair out of place, her face made up to perfection.

"Wow, is that a new car?" I asked her.

"Don't just stand there, darlin'. Get in the car."

"What's the matter?"

Lucy stomped up the driveway and tugged at my arm. "No time to talk. Come along."

"I'm on my way to Dave's. I have spider clothes that need to be cleaned."

Lucy seemed to notice me for the first time. My hair was tied in a frizzy ponytail on the top of my head. I was wearing my threadbare Cleveland Browns sweatshirt, torn jeans, and slip-on sneakers.

"What's that smell?" she asked.

"Bug spray," I said. "I might have gotten some on me."

"You smell like citrus death." She waved her hands in the air. "No time to change."

She pushed and pulled me until I was sitting in the calfskin-leather passenger seat of her salmon-colored Mercedes. "My butt is warm," I noted.

"There's also a massage setting." She pressed a button on what looked like the control panel of a fighter jet, and my butt started to vibrate.

"Oh, that's nice," I said.

"Bridget says Mercedes has made a leap toward women's sexual independence," Lucy told me. Bridget was our friend, my grandmother's bookkeeper, and a militant feminist.

Lucy raced down the street, driving erratically and nearly clipping a garbage can as she turned the corner. I snapped my seat belt into place.

"Is someone dying? Has someone been murdered?" I asked Lucy. It wasn't a stretch. Since I arrived in Cannes, I had come across a few dead bodies. I was getting a reputation.

"No, why? Have you heard something?"

"No. Should I have heard something?"

Lucy was sweating, and she hadn't blinked since she started to drive. It was out of character for her, to say the least. She wasn't the erratic kind of woman. She was a very successful marketer, whatever that was. She was a Southern belle who had traveled the world and was calm in every situation.

In fact, I had seen her flustered on only one occasion.

"Lucy, does this have something to do with Uncle Harry?" I asked. Uncle Harry wasn't really Lucy's uncle. He was a magnetic man a few years older than

Lucy with a fortune from a questionable source. He lived in a giant house east of town with man-eating Rottweilers, a gate, and a security man named Killer. Okay, I didn't know the security guard's name, but he looked like a Killer.

At the mention of Uncle Harry, Lucy's eyes glazed over and her hands slipped off the steering wheel. She let out a squeak, as if she were a Kewpie doll and someone had given her a hard squeeze.

"Coffee!" I shouted in warning, but it was too late. Despite Lucy coming to her senses and slamming her foot down on the brake pedal, the front door to the Tea Time tea shop sped toward us, or at least it seemed that way. Actually, it was Lucy's car that sped toward Tea Time's front door, but in the end it was the same thing. The salmon-colored Mercedes with the warming vibrator tushy seats pulverized the massive wood doors of Tea Time and took large chunks of the walls with it.

Tea Time used to be a saloon, back when Cannes was a gold-rush town in the late 1800s, but now it was all lace tablecloths, yellow painted daisies, porcelain teapots on every table, classical music piped in at a respectable level, and a rack of crocheted tea cozies for sale at ludicrous prices. It was owned by eighty-five-year-old Ruth Fletcher, a crotchety old lady who despised coffee drinkers. Despite Tea Time's name and Ruth's demeanor, the shop had the best coffee in town.

I stumbled out of the car, past the deflated air bags and the debris. Miraculously, no one was hurt. The shop had been experiencing a lull in the day, and there were only two people inside. Ruth and her danger-prone grandniece, Julie, stood behind the intact bar, their mouths hanging open, the sunlight filtering past the dust through the gaping hole in the wall and onto their shocked faces.

Lucy opened her car door and hobbled out. One of her sling-back heels was broken, making her limp. Besides that and her toppled hairdo, she was unscathed.

I saw red. "My coffee!" I yelled at Lucy. "You killed my coffee!" I couldn't live without my coffee, and Ruth made the best lattes on the planet. I needed Ruth's lattes.

"I didn't do it!" Julie squealed, waking Ruth out of her stupor. Ruth threw down her bar towel and stomped over to us.

"This building has been in existence since 1872," she spat at me, her words coming out in clipped consonants as she gestured to Tea Time's destroyed front wall. "Had! Had been in existence!"

"Strictly speaking, I wasn't driving," I said.

"You're just like your grandmother," she accused. "Wackos think they know everything. I bet she didn't guess this little event, did she?"

She had a point. Besides saying the wind had changed, Grandma could have warned me not to get into the car with Lucy.

I pointed at Lucy. "She did it," I said.

Lucy swiped her hair out of her eyes. She climbed over the debris and hobbled toward us, riffling through her purse as she limped closer. She pulled out her wallet.

"I've got five hundred dollars here. Do you think that will cover it?" she asked Ruth.

I thought I saw steam come out of Ruth's ears. "This is a historic building in the historic district of a historic town," she said. "It will take at least a month to fix the damage, during which I will be out of business. There is no wall here!" she shouted, pointing at the hole that used to be Tea Time's front door.

"You have five hundred dollars in your purse?" I asked. For the first time in months, I was up-to-date on my bills, but I had only $7.50 on me. Marketing sure paid well. Whatever that was.

"I'm in a hurry," Lucy said. "I don't have time to stand here and chat, Ruth."

"Well, then maybe you shouldn't have taken a detour into my shop!" Ruth said, stating the obvious.

"Here's my insurance card. I've got to get to Uncle Harry. He's waiting. Come on, Gladie, let's go."

"Are you serious?" I stammered. "I'm not getting in a car with you!"

"Gladys Burger, did I not save your life not one month ago?"

And there it was, the trump card. Lucy and Bridget had come to my rescue a few weeks back, and I owed her one, to put it mildly.

"Okay," I agreed. "But not without coffee. I need coffee."

"Don't look at me!" said Ruth. "I'm not about to make you coffee."

I stared Lucy in the eye. "Not without coffee."

IT TURNED out we couldn't start the car with the deployed air bags, and Lucy insisted we leave it there for the Mercedes dealership to tow away. We had to walk back to Grandma's to pick up my car. I remembered that my red suitcase was in the trunk, but my desire for coffee far outweighed my desire for spider-free clothes, and I didn't think Lucy would take the time to stop at the dry cleaner's.

Lucy said Cup O'Cake had fabulous coffee, and it was on the way to Uncle Harry's, just on the edge of the historic district.

"Can you make this jalopy go any faster, darlin'?" she asked me as I chugged down Main Street.

"Are you kidding me, Mario Andretti?"

"Sorry, I'm in a hurry."

"Yeah, I still don't know why. Can you tell me what's going on?"

Lucy dusted off a piece of my car's upholstery, which had dropped from the ceiling onto her lap. "Uncle Harry called me and said to get over there right away and to bring you. He was very agitated, Gladie. I've never heard him like that. Flustered."

"Flustered" must have been the adjective of the day. First Grandma, then Lucy, and now Uncle Harry. Three people who were never flustered had suddenly turned flustered. So much for my relaxing Apple Days.

But the flustered stopped at the historic district. Despite the car accident, the ill wind, and whatever trouble Uncle Harry had, the town was calm, quiet, and doing what it did best. An influx of sedate tourists sat eating apple pie at the outside tables of Saladz, a favorite hangout for Bridget, Lucy, and me.

Cannes was a small village in the mountains east of San Diego. It had had a couple of years of prosperity during the gold rush, more than a hundred years before, but the gold ran out quickly, and the town settled into a relaxed state after that. Besides growing apples and pears, it welcomed tourists with its beauty, charm, and antiques shops. It was usually very quiet and everyone got along. Not much flustering here.

"Take a right," Lucy instructed.

I turned onto Gold Digger Avenue. Cup O'Cake was on the corner in an old, small Victorian house. It took up the bottom story, and there were apartments on the floor above. The building was painted a bright cobalt blue with blood-red trim. A sign out front read CUP O'CAKE in green letters, with the letter "O" replaced by a big cupcake. That cupcake looked damned good.

"I'm supposed to be on a diet," I said aloud, more to myself than to Lucy.

"Again? Darlin', you are on more diets than any skinny bitch I know."

"You think I'm skinny?" I asked, sucking in my stomach. I had put on a few pounds since moving to Cannes, regularly eating junk food with my grandma. I was actually looking for a new diet, something that worked. So far, I hadn't had any luck losing a pound.

"How many calories do you think are in a cup-cake?" I asked Lucy.

"Fourteen thousand," she said, opening the door. A bell announced our entrance. Inside were serenity, bliss, and nirvana, all wrapped in an odiferous cloud of chocolate, vanilla, sugar, and yeast. And there was another smell, something really familiar.

"Coffee," I breathed in relief.

Cup O'Cake was laid out more like a large living

room than a bakery. Big overstuffed chairs took up most of the floor space, all in bright colors, as if they were cupcakes themselves. Little coffee tables dotted the floor, as well, covered in pretty tablecloths and books. There were books everywhere. The walls were lined with shelves bursting with them. The mantel over the fireplace was stacked high with books, too.

Hardbacks, paperbacks, reference, literature, and pulp. Books everywhere.

A tiny thirtysomething woman with gorgeous long jet-black hair, wearing a brown sweater dress that practically swallowed her whole, picked up a book I had been eyeing.

"That's a good one," she said. "Funny romantic mystery. You can borrow it if you wish."

"I'm not much of a reader," I said. Not since a failed one-week stint as a speed-reading teacher in Austin. I hadn't gotten past the training, and my migraine had lasted three days.

Her face dropped in obvious disappointment. "Oh."

"But, sure, it looks great," I said, taking the book from her. I'm really bad about disappointing people. I'd rather move to another town than disappoint someone. Perhaps I needed therapy.

Or a cupcake.

"Let me know how you like it." Her frown had turned into a smile. "We can talk about it tomorrow, if you wish."

Drat, now I actually had to read the thing. It was about two inches thick. I wondered if I could find CliffsNotes online.

"I'm Felicia," she told me. "Felicia Patel. I help

Mavis run Cup O'Cake. You look like you could use a cup of coffee."

I almost hugged her. I was so used to Ruth yelling at me every time I ordered a coffee. Since Ruth only liked tea drinkers, I had to submit to abuse every time I wanted a latte. All I had to do for coffee at Cup O'Cake was read a book.

"We're in a hurry," Lucy said, adjusting her hair. "Make it to go."

"No problem!" Felicia was still smiling. "It will take just a second."

Instead of a counter, there was a series of tables with assorted pastries and a large table with espresso machines.

"Give her the apple spiced latte, Felicia," an old lady standing at one of the tables told her. She was around my grandmother's age, smelled like White Shoulders and chocolate, and had an air of fatigue about her.

"How are you, Lucy?" she asked. "Haven't seen you in a while."

Lucy looked at her out of the corner of her eye while she reapplied her lipstick in a hand mirror.

"Hi, Mavis. Running late. You know Gladie Burger?"

"Zelda Burger's granddaughter?" Mavis asked.

Everybody knew my grandmother, but I was pretty new in town, and I didn't know everybody. In fact, I didn't even know about Cup O'Cake.

"The matchmaker," Lucy said.

Mavis nodded. "Sure. Sure. You live in this town awhile, you hear about Zelda."

Felicia handed me a red-and-blue to-go cup and a red-and-blue polka-dotted box. "A little surprise for you," she said, with a wink toward the box. "See you tomorrow?"

"Sure," I said, smiling. Sweat rolled down my back. I was having flashbacks to high school—I had dropped out. Suddenly the book felt like it weighed twenty pounds.

I tried to hand Felicia a five-dollar bill. Mavis waved it away. "On the house," she said. "First-time customers get special treatment."

Lucy pushed me out of the store. "We're really late now," she grumbled, trying to open the locked car door. I unlocked it for her and took a sip of the latte.

"Holy crap, this is the best thing ever," I said. "It's not coffee. It's coffee candy."

"Drive!"

Halfway there, I convinced Lucy to open the box for me. She was afraid I would slow down to eat whatever fabulous thing they had given me, but I assured her I could eat while doing just about any activity.

It *was* fabulous. Some kind of apple cupcake with a crumble-icing concoction that almost made me crash the car when I took a bite. Even better, there were three cupcakes.

"How come I never heard of this place?" I asked.

"It's pretty new," Lucy said. "A couple years. Mavis Jones is a doll. Felicia's a little odd, though—with all those books, I mean. But Mavis doesn't seem to mind. They're there all the time. You can buy cupcakes late into the night. They live upstairs in two of the apartments, and they'll open up for anyone with a craving."

It was dangerous information. What would I do with the knowledge that I could have coffee candy and cupcakes anytime I wanted? "I won't fit through the door," I said. "Let's throw the rest out the window. My waistband is digging into my belly."

"Too late, Gladie. You ate all of them."

UNCLE HARRY lived farther up in the mountains, in a relatively new gated community of McMansions. His house was one of the biggest, with its own gate and security guard. It wasn't anything like Cannes. There was nothing quaint or old about it, but it was gorgeous.

We were stopped at Harry's personal security shack in front of his house. The guard didn't seem too happy to see us. "We're expected," Lucy said, leaning toward my open window.

"You one of them?" the security guard asked, gesturing to our right. A small group of elderly people stood on the sidewalk. They were talking among themselves and looking at their watches.

"We're expected!" Lucy said again. She was clearly agitated and, I thought, not above taking on the guard.

"We should be on your list," I pointed out.

We were. He waved us in, and that's when we saw the two police cars and another car that I was more than familiar with.

"What the hell?" Lucy asked. "Should I call my attorney?"

Uncle Harry was standing on his front porch, surrounded by police. A very tall old lady stood over him, wagging her finger in his face. Uncle Harry appeared unconcerned as he took long drags of his cigar and blew them out at her.

I recognized all of the police officers. Unfortunately, I had had more than my share of dealing with law enforcement since moving into town.

"Lord have mercy, the cops," Lucy said. "Gladie, you distract them, and I'll get Harry to safety."

I rolled my eyes. "Uncle Harry looks fine, Lucy. Besides, how am I supposed to distract them?"

"Take your shirt off. Use your feminine wiles."

"I'm not going to use my feminine wiles." I wasn't sure I had any wiles, and if I did, I wasn't sure what I would do with them. Besides, wiles could be dangerous, and there was one person present I needed to keep my wiles far away from.

Lucy jumped out of the car and ran toward the group. I followed her, wishing my suitcase had been spider-free and that I wasn't dressed like a homeless person.

Spencer Bolton, Cannes's chief of police and a womanizing, hottie hunk, turned sharply toward me as I approached. His mouth dropped open in surprise, and his chest inflated as he gulped air. He made my blood pressure rise and my pulse race. I didn't want him to know how much I wanted to watch him strip naked while I ate chips, but I suspected he already knew. The familiar car was his.

"Uncle Harry, I'm here," Lucy said, stating the obvious. Gone was the sophisticated, sure-of-herself Southern belle I had grown to know during the past five months, and in her place was a quivering five-foot-eight mass of Jell-O. Six foot even in her heels. Well, the unbroken heel, anyway.

Uncle Harry stood no taller than five foot four, his balding head reaching Lucy's sternum. Lucy giggled wildly when he said hello to her. I squidged my eyes, trying to see what she saw.

"Mr. Lupino, this development is an eyesore," the tall lady said to Uncle Harry. "A blot on the historic nature of our town. You are a cancer on this land. I cannot allow you to spread."

She sounded like Katharine Hepburn, with a wobble in her voice and a slight English accent. She was formidable even in her age and, I imagined, a force to be reckoned with. Even so, I took a cowardly step back in case Uncle Harry decided to shoot her or let loose his dogs.

"Mrs. Arbuthnot, would you excuse me?" Spencer asked the woman, and walked quickly toward me.

"I'm only here for moral support," I said, trying to duck behind Lucy.

He grasped my arm and pulled me down the driveway, away from the group. "Move!" he ordered the security guard, and closed us in the guard's shack. There wasn't quite enough room in there for two. Spencer placed his hands on the wall above my shoulders and leaned in close.

"You have been avoiding me for weeks," he said. His breath was minty fresh and made me wish for Christmas so I could eat him like a candy cane.

"Have I?" I croaked.

"Yes. You know we have to talk about what happened."

"Forget about it, Spencer. Let's pretend nothing happened."

He leaned in closer, his lips almost touching mine. "I don't want to forget it," he said.

# Chapter 2

✦ ♥ ✦

*The people that come to us, dolly, are looking for serious relationships. If they only wanted a hoochie mama or a good-time Charlie, they would go out to Bar None at closing and find a warm body for the night. But sometimes we get a client or two who think they want a serious relationship, think they're ready, but they couldn't be more wrong. They're not ready or suited for a serious relationship. They might not even understand what a relationship is. We're not in the teaching business, bubeleh. We're in the matching business. Sometimes a client isn't ready to be matched. So we need to know when a match should happen or not happen. We need to be selective. An ounce of wisdom on our part can save them a pound of heartbreak.*

**Lesson 98,**
**Matchmaking Advice from Your Grandma Zelda**

I TRIED to squirm away, but Spencer pinned me to the wall of the security shack with his body.

"You smell nice," he said.

"Bug spray."

"I'm not sure what you're doing with your hair here, though." He ran his fingers over my frizzy ponytail, making it flop over my face and sending my blood racing through my veins.

"I was in my grandma's shed," I explained.

He traced the lettering on my sweatshirt. "This outfit is working for me. I like when you're into sports."

"I found this sweatshirt when I was working at the morgue." I had never worked at the morgue, but I needed all the help I could get in turning off Spencer Bolton.

"Morgue. Interesting," he mumbled, his lips tracing the curve of my neck.

"Off a dead . . . off a dead . . . corpse." My traitorous arms wrapped around Spencer's back and pulled him even closer. Geez, he was talented with his lips, like he had been trained as a lip ninja or something.

"Lip ninja," I moaned.

"I'm all kinds of ninja," he said. That was the truth. Spencer had lip-ninja'd his way through town and probably farther than that. The thought sobered me up. I tried to push him away again.

"Shouldn't we get back to Uncle Harry and Mrs. Arbuthnot?" I asked. "We're in a security shack. This is probably illegal."

"Since when did you worry about what's legal or not?" But he had sobered, too. He stood up straight, creating space between us. "Time to talk about what happened."

"Nothing happened."

"Exactly," he agreed. "Exactly!" His face dropped, an expression of agony. I almost felt sorry for him, but it was difficult to feel sorry for Spencer. He had more than his share of ego, and it was comforting to see him deflate to normal.

"You look nice," I said, changing the subject.

He smirked his annoying little smirk and straightened his jacket. "You like it? Armani. I got a whole new wardrobe. My credit cards will never be the same."

The month before, a crazed former lover had cut up all of Spencer's clothes. He deserved it, of course, and it was a fitting punishment for a confirmed metrosexual.

But, damn, Spencer looked good in a fitted suit.

"Pinkie, you're going to find yourself naked in this shack if you look at me like that another second."

I blinked. "What's the deal with Mrs. Arbuthnot? Grandma says she's been a lemonhead ever since she moved here a couple years ago." Grandma was pretty dead-on with that description. Mrs. Arbuthnot pursed her lips—even when she spoke—as if she had just sucked on a lemon.

"Harry is working on a new development, and she's head of the Cannes Responsible Growth Commission. Nothing too serious."

"Responsible growth? Sounds dermatological."

"Why are you here?" His expression had changed as he finally realized I was meddling where I didn't belong.

"I'm with Lucy. Uncle Harry wanted us," I said, before he could yell at me. My interfering in police business was Spencer's number-one pet peeve. Not that I ever wanted to get involved in police business. It just so happened that I found myself in more than my share of murder and mayhem.

"All I want are spider-free clothes that will keep me warm," I explained.

"I'll keep you warm."

I stepped around him and opened the door. "Don't worry about it, Spencer. It wasn't your fault. Nothing happened for a reason. I made a mistake going to you that day. It was for the best that nothing happened."

I was halfway back to Harry's porch when Spencer caught up to me. "But that's never happened to me before!" he announced loudly.

Mrs. Arbuthnot, Harry, and the others standing on Harry's porch gave Spencer their undivided attention. Waiting, I figured, for him to give a few more details on what exactly had never happened to him before. The moment Spencer realized he was the center of attention registered on his face with a blush of embarrassment.

I was surprised that such a little thing would embarrass him, and I was about to tell him so when the attention shifted to me.

"Darlin', were you feeling a bit warm?" Lucy asked me. I followed her gaze and glanced down. My sweatshirt and undershirt were rolled up, revealing my Walmart white cross-my-heart bra. Somehow, Spencer had bared my torso without me noticing. I quickly pulled my shirts down and shot Spencer a nasty look. This seemed to perk him up, and his irritating smirk reappeared.

"Mrs. Arbuthnot, you can file a complaint at the town hall," Spencer told her, his cop demeanor back in full force. "Meanwhile, this is private property and you have to leave, or I will have Officer James arrest you."

"Listen, Sparky," she spat. "Complaints go nowhere. I need action."

"Yeah, Sparky," I said. "What are you going to do about it?"

Spencer shot me a dirty look, and I cowered behind Uncle Harry.

Lucy got in Mrs. Arbuthnot's face, growling, "Back up, woman, this is private property." She was like one of Uncle Harry's Rottweilers: protective, frothing at the mouth, and not above biting.

Spencer stepped between the two women. "Take it to local media," he suggested.

"You mean the Cannes circular?" Mrs. Arbuthnot asked him. He was a good five inches taller than her, but she had a way of looking down her nose at people that made her seem seven feet tall.

And then it was over. Satisfied or not with Spencer's suggestion, Mrs. Arbuthnot turned on her thick, square heel and left Uncle Harry's porch. She maneuvered her Prius through the gate to retrieve her little group of elderly people and drove off.

"Hi there, Legs," Uncle Harry greeted me when the Prius drove out of sight. "What a nice surprise."

"What do you mean 'surprise'?" Lucy asked. "You called me and told me to bring her."

"Did I?"

I shot daggers at Lucy with my eyes. I was wasting half the day on this field trip when I should have been de-spidering my winter clothes. And then there was the minor fact of her destroying my coffee supply with her car and forcing me into an unwanted discussion with Spencer.

"I swear, Gladie, I got a call from a man saying he was Uncle Harry. It sounded exactly like him," Lucy whined.

"Well, are we done here?" I asked. "I have just enough time to drop off my clothes." I envisioned the spider eggs hatching in my sweaters. I imagined them weaving their tiny legs into the threads of my favorite light-blue V-neck acrylic sweater—which I had passed off for cashmere on more than one occasion—and growing to full size as I slipped it over my head. I shivered. I needed to get professional cleaning fast or I would have to dump my winter clothes. And there was a noticeable chill in the air.

"I can't afford real cashmere, Lucy," I said, slightly panicked.

"Are you all right?" Lucy asked Uncle Harry, totally ignoring me. Her sudden neediness where the no-neck Uncle Harry was concerned was starting to turn my stomach.

It was either that or the three cupcakes I had eaten on the ride over.

With the army of elderly, antidevelopment hippies gone, the police hopped into their cars, but Spencer was rooted to the spot in the driveway, standing with his hands balled into fists at his sides and eyeing me with a definite sense of purpose. If I didn't know better, I would have thought he was working on his courage.

Uncle Harry ignored Spencer, and with the front porch cleared of everyone except him, Lucy, and me, he changed his attitude.

"I'm fine," he whispered, looking around nervously. "Come inside, quick." He opened the door and pushed Lucy and me into the house. We were greeted by his two Rottweilers, fearsome creatures with snapping teeth and what I imagined to be a hankering for the tasty flesh of single girl. I smashed my body up against the wall and shut my eyes tight.

"Quiet," Uncle Harry said, and, just like that, the dogs scattered. I took a deep breath and clutched my throat. Yep, it was still there. No Rottweilers attached to my jugular. Phew. I didn't want to die like that, eaten by dogs. It was way down on my list, in fact. Below Ebola but a notch above flesh-eating bacteria.

Lucy and I followed Uncle Harry through the house. It was huge, a mansion. I had been there before, but it still impressed me. The living room had high ceilings and wood paneling, a lot like Hearst Castle, with a view of the mountains through a wall of glass.

Uncle Harry's butler/manservant came into the room with a full tea service in his huge hands. He was a dead ringer for Lurch, and I expected him to say, "You rang?" but instead he reminded Uncle Harry that his poker buddies would arrive momentarily.

Harry hosted a regular poker game for a group of old cronies, who resembled the cast of *The Sopranos*. His game room was at the back of the house, with a King Arthur-like round table and erotic tapestries on the walls. He had invited me to play once, but the stakes were too rich for my blood.

Sure enough, the doorbell rang, and Lurch went to welcome in the first player. Uncle Harry motioned for me to sit. "I'll make this quick," he said. "I did ask you to come here. I want to hire you."

I looked behind me to see who he was talking to. Nobody was there.

"You want to hire *Gladie*?" Lucy's voice came out an octave higher than normal.

"You want to hire *me*?" I asked.

"As a *matchmaker*?" Lucy asked, as if it was the craziest thing in the world to hire me as a matchmaker. She had a point.

"I *am* a matchmaker," I reminded her. "As a *matchmaker*?" I repeated to Uncle Harry.

"Sort of, Legs," he said. "It's complicated."

We were interrupted by an old man tugging a portable oxygen tank behind him, the wheels squeaking loudly. "Where the hell is everybody!" he yelled. "I don't have all day, you know."

"Blow it out your hole, Marty," Uncle Harry shot back. "You have all day and you know it. All day, all week, all year, if you live that long. Grab yourself a scotch in the game room."

"If you only got that single-malt crap, I'm never coming back," he spat, but he turned down the hall toward the game room.

"I got a problem, and I need you to fix it," Uncle Harry told me when the squeaking receded into the background. "Luanda has her hooks in me, and I need you to unhook me."

"Who is this Luanda?" Lucy asked in my direction. She raised her eyebrows to just under her hairline. Her face turned purple, and she rooted around in her clutch purse for what I hoped wasn't a firearm. Lucy was scarily protective over Uncle Harry.

I racked my brain. Who *was* Luanda? Grandma knew so many people, but I was terrible with names.

"I don't know Luanda," I assured Lucy.

"She's one of you people. Another crazy matchmaker. You know," Uncle Harry said, making a circling gesture with his finger against his head. "Screw loose," he added, as if that explained it all.

As far as I knew, Grandma was the only crazy matchmaker in town. It was a small town. Crazy or not, she was the only matchmaker in Cannes, if you didn't count me, and practically nobody counted me.

"You're speaking Greek," I said.

"The Indian woman with the clothes, the one who speaks to dead people. She wants to fix me up with Ruth Fletcher. You got to get her to stop."

"Ruth Fletcher!" Lucy screeched. "That woman! I will not stop killin' her."

"Hold on, Annie Oakley," I said. "First of all, you almost did kill her today, if you remember, and second of all, what are you talking about, Uncle Harry? Dead people?"

"She's very persistent, and it's bad for business," he said, pulling a cigar out of a box on the coffee table. "You get me? The matchmaker Indian is calling nonstop, coming over and bothering me. Blathering about soul mates. This is a place of business. I can't have crazy people traipsing around my place of business."

"Where the hell is the toilet! Harry, a place is too big if you can't find the damned toilet." The old man was right behind me. I hadn't heard him coming, because he'd left his squeaky oxygen tank in the game room, and I now noticed that he was wearing slippers, the kind the hospital gives you.

"There's a toilet in the game room, Marty," Uncle Harry told him.

"That's a toilet?" Marty asked.

"What did you think it was?"

"How the hell should I know? I've never seen that much marble before."

"It's a toilet!"

Marty grunted and shuffled back toward the game room. Uncle Harry lit his cigar, puffing rapidly.

"So what do you want me to do?" I asked.

"Convince Luanda that Ruth is not my soul mate."

"Of course she's not your soul mate, darlin'," Lucy announced.

The doorbell rang again, and I heard the front door open and close. "Let me get this straight," I said. "Instead of matching you, you want me to *unmatch* you?"

Grandma wouldn't approve. It would be against the matchmaker code or something. Besides, I had no idea who Luanda was, and if Ruth Fletcher had her sights set on Uncle Harry, I wasn't about to block her. After all, she already blamed me for destroying Tea Time and her livelihood. And she could be ornery, to say the least.

"I'll triple your normal fee, whatever that is," Uncle Harry offered.

"Done," I accepted.

I got a whiff of expensive cologne, a cloud of familiar yummy manliness that shifted my estrogen production into high gear. Obviously, Spencer had finished working up his courage.

"What's done?" Spencer asked. He walked into the living room and took a seat next to me on the couch. He put his arm around my shoulders. "What's done?" he whispered into my ear.

I sucked in air, and my hair curled. Spencer had a

bad effect on me. He made me want to get naked right there between cigar-smoking Uncle Harry and green-eyed Calamity Jane. But he was poison. An Olympics-worthy womanizer. He was the Usain Bolt of players. But I wasn't going to let him catch me.

"The toilet is in the game room," I said, for no apparent reason.

Uncle Harry pulled three hundred dollars out of his wallet and handed it to me. "Here you go, Legs. A down payment. I'd appreciate it if you got on it quick-like."

I clutched the money in my hand. Cash. It was the most money of my own that I'd seen in one place in forever. I mean, in my whole life. I could afford real cashmere now. I was almost a one percenter. I was Donald Trump with better hair. A tear threatened to roll down my cheek. I tucked the bankroll in my pocket.

"We'll get on it immediately," Lucy announced, standing. She tugged at my hand to leave.

"We?" I asked, but there was no way I could get rid of Lucy. She wanted first dibs at shooing away any of Uncle Harry's potential suitors. Attraction is a weird thing. There's no accounting for it.

"Hold on." Spencer pulled my arm away from Lucy. "We need to talk. It will just take a second."

He led me out to the balcony. I got a rush of vertigo and turned away quickly from the view of the canyon below us. I clutched Spencer's arms and closed my eyes, willing the world to stop spinning.

"We need to talk," he repeated. I opened my eyes. He had leaned down, and his face was inches from mine. He smelled good. Better than good, and he was focused on me. Earnest. He absentmindedly slipped his hands around my back and caressed me with slow, circular movements.

He wasn't going to leave me alone until we cleared the air. "You had a concussion," I said.

"I had a concussion."

"They didn't catch it at the hospital."

Spencer nodded. "I should sue them!"

"Yes, you should. They shouldn't have let you out."

I wasn't lying. Spencer had his skull bashed in by a bad guy, and the hospital let him out the same night. "And you fainted," I said.

"I didn't faint. I lost consciousness."

"You lost consciousness."

"When you were kissing me."

"When you were kissing *me*," I lied. I had gone to him with a clear intention. It was my idea. I wanted him, and I initiated the kiss.

He had let me into his house, and before he could close the door behind me, I slipped my arms around his neck and pulled him down to my lips. I had kissed him once before, and my memory of that first time was fireworks on the level of the Fourth of July. It turned out my memory was dead-on, but the second time the fireworks were accompanied by a passion I wasn't expecting.

The kiss went on and on. We connected so perfectly that I didn't know where he left off and I began. I stepped forward and moaned. He put his arms around my back and let his hands slip lower. I knew we were going to go beyond the kiss, go all the way, as they say at prom.

I was powerless to stop the momentum. My head

was invaded by a buzzing that clouded my judgment, drowned out reality, and disoriented me. To make a long story short, I was lost.

Being lost in Spencer's arms was dumb. He regularly lost women, and they didn't show up again, at least not as themselves but more like lunatic stalkers who couldn't find themselves after the lip ninja had dumped them for the next hapless female in line.

I didn't want to be lost. I had a lifetime of being lost. I wanted to be found. But the buzzing got louder, and I knew I was out of luck.

Then I won the lottery. Just as I began to forget my name, Spencer froze. His lips slid off my face, and his hands dropped to his sides. A second later his knees buckled and he slumped over me. I managed to hold his weight for a moment, confused, but quickly I realized that Spencer was no longer conscious, and we fell together onto the maple-colored laminate flooring in his narrow entranceway.

The hospital kept him for three full days. I sent him flowers, but I stayed far away. While he recuperated at a safe distance, I Spencer-detoxed. I was partially successful. I still heard the low-level echo of the buzzing, but I knew my name and I knew where I was.

Also, I was delighted I had made a man pass out merely through the power of my kiss. He might be the lip ninja, but I had magical lips. As much as I wanted to tell everyone about my magical lips, I thought it was wiser to pretend the whole thing didn't happen. A weak moment. An almost disaster.

"I have magical lips," I told Spencer on Uncle Harry's balcony.

Spencer smirked. "I concur. How about we see

what other body parts of yours have magical properties?"

I sighed and pushed him away from me. "No way. I had a lapse in judgment, but my lapse is over."

Through the window behind Spencer, I could see Uncle Harry and Lucy deep in conversation. I wasn't clear on the parameters of their relationship, and I wondered what they were talking about. Lucy had a major crush on Uncle Harry, but he didn't show much interest in her beyond mild flirtation.

I worried that she was lost, that Spencer wasn't the only man in Cannes who had the power to make a woman forget who she was. I also worried that Lucy would incite a knock-down drag-out fight with Ruth Fletcher, and, despite Lucy's Southern-belle strength, she was no match for the eighty-five-year-old tea enthusiast.

I also worried about Luanda. Could she be the changing wind Grandma spoke about?

I watched as Harry's poker buddies filed into the house. He offered them cigars, and they lit up. Something about that stimulated the anxiety receptors in my brain.

"Other men would call you a tease," Spencer said, drawing my attention back to him.

"Whatever," I replied. "I'm not jumping into bed with you. I'm a relationship girl." If you didn't count the happy-hour incident in February, the Lady Gaga concert in Des Moines, and more or less the entire year of 2010. Besides those indiscretions, I didn't engage in meaningless sex.

"Like your relationship with Holden?" he asked.

Ouch. I hadn't heard from my sort-of boyfriend

and sexy neighbor Holden in weeks. He was out of town, trying to get his life back on track, but his leaving had derailed our relationship.

"Yes, like my relationship with Holden," I told him.

"A relationship you thought you'd take a break from with me? Hey, come to think of it, where is Pretty Boy?"

"He's not pretty; he's gorgeous. He's Adonis. He's Mr. Universe. He's Treetop Lover. He's—"

Spencer raised an eyebrow. "Fine, you win. I can do relationship." He ground his teeth, and his eye twitched.

"What do you mean, you can do relationship?"

"Dating, wooing, courting. You know, the whole bullshit."

"Why, Spencer, I didn't know you were a romantic."

"Call me Nicholas Sparks."

"Doesn't someone always die in his stories?" I asked.

"That shouldn't bother you, Miss Marple. You seem drawn to dead people." That wasn't completely true. I just happened to stumble on the occasional corpse.

I searched Spencer's face for signs. His eyes flashed, dilating and contracting, like he was signaling ships. He really was handsome, sexy, like a Marlboro man without the horse and cigarette. I would have paid money to see him in chaps. The corners of his mouth slowly turned up into his usual smirk. I punched his arm.

"That's what I figured," I said. "Spencer, you are so full of crap. You 'can do relationship.' Yeah, right."

Spencer's mouth dropped open, but he seemed to have stopped breathing. He blinked twice, and then he shrugged. "Yeah, well, you know me."

"After last month, I would think you'd want a break from women." Spencer had gotten in trouble for being involved with too many girlfriends at once. It had been a pretty dramatic situation.

"Exactly," Spencer agreed. "I'm focusing on other things for the foreseeable future. Women are more trouble than they're worth. I was only tying up loose ends where you were concerned."

"Uh-huh." I watched through the window as more of Uncle Harry's friends lit up their cigars and blew out smoke. Again I felt anxiety, but I didn't know why.

"Anyway, I don't have a lot of time to follow you around like a puppy dog," Spencer continued. "I've got to handle all the Apple Days events, I've just hired a new detective, who's on a probation period, and there's a wild rumor about mad cow disease in town I need to squelch."

"Mad what?"

I spotted one of Uncle Harry's friends put a cigar in his mouth, grab the crystal lighter off the coffee table, and disappear down the hall toward the game room. Suddenly I realized why I was anxious.

"I hope Marty found the toilet," I said.

That's when Uncle Harry's house blew up.

# Chapter 3

✦ ❤ ✦

*I love movies. Nowadays I watch movies on my television at home, but I pop some popcorn, rip open a bag of M&M's, and it's just like I'm at the Cannes Regal 4. My favorite part of a movie is the "meet cute." Just as you would expect, that's when the couple meets for the first time in a cute way. Like Cary Grant and Katharine Hepburn. They met-cute in their movies. Every fakakta client who walks through our door wants a meet cute. They're superstitious about the circumstances in which they meet. They figure if they meet under normal circumstances, it can't be true love. Let me tell you something, dolly, it's better to not meet-cute. Sometimes the cute ain't that cute. Sometimes the cute just means trouble. And that doesn't sound good—the meet trouble.*

**Lesson 13,**
**Matchmaking Advice from Your Grandma Zelda**

IT WASN'T a huge explosion. We found out later that it was muted because Marty's oxygen tank was running near empty. Luckily for Marty, he was safely in the all-marble bathroom, halfway through the sports pages, when the explosion happened, taking the poker table with it and making mincemeat of the erotic tapestries. Uncle Harry's other friend miraculously made it out with only burns on his lighter hand, since he had ignited it far from his face.

From outside on the balcony, the explosion was scary enough, and we didn't know the extent of the damage. But it was the fireball we witnessed hurtling from the hall toward the living room that made Spencer throw me to safety—which in his mind was over the balcony, away from the house.

He tossed me like I was a horseshoe at a company picnic, then ran in the direction of the fireball, bent on saving Lucy, Uncle Harry, and the rest, I assumed. Meanwhile, I flew over the railing toward the depths below and my certain death. My life flashed before my eyes. It took two seconds, which reminded me I was way too young to die.

I flailed my arms and legs in a fit of survival instinct and, with a bit of acrobatics worthy of any Cirque du Soleil performer, latched on to a piece of railing that ran along the underside of the balcony, and I hung there like a bat.

I was in shock, surprised that I wasn't lying at the bottom of the canyon with every bone broken, and scared out of my mind that my grip on the rail would fail at any moment. I tried to scream, but I couldn't get sound out.

After a few seconds, I heard footsteps on the balcony above me.

"Oh, my God! Oh, my God! You killed her. You squashed her like a bug," Lucy wailed like her best friend had died. I supposed that was just what she believed.

"Gladie!" Spencer called. He rarely used my name, preferring the nickname he had given me in honor of my pink underpants. He called me over and over before it dawned on me that I should answer.

"I'm here," I squeaked. "I'm here, and I'm going to die," I added, so they would fully grasp the situation and move quicker to my rescue.

"Darlin'!" Lucy cried. "Darlin', I thought you were dead!" I looked up to see Lucy's head hanging over the side of the balcony.

"I'm almost dead," I said, stating what I thought was obvious. "I can't hold on much longer."

"Spencer is on his way down," Lucy assured me.

"Did he get thrown off the balcony, too?"

Spencer tossed over a rope ladder and slithered down it. "I've got you," he announced, wrapping his arm around my waist.

"No, leave me and save yourself," I said.

"Are you kidding?"

"Yes, of course I'm kidding! Get me out of here!" I was losing patience. It had been a hell of a day. A catastrophic car accident was one thing, and I could even handle explosions and fireballs, but hanging one hiccup away from an untimely demise would have tried even the Dalai Lama.

Spencer tugged, but I held on tight to the rail. "Let go, Pinkie," he ordered.

"I am! I am!"

"No you're not." He plucked at my fingers, trying to pry them loose, but they held on tight.

"They've got a life of their own," I said, panicking. "They're not letting me go."

"You are certifiable."

"Says the man who threw me to my death."

"If only," Spencer said. "Dead people don't talk."

"You're a riot, Spencer. I always laugh at men who try to kill me."

Spencer tugged again, but my fingers wouldn't come loose. "I didn't try to kill you."

"You did. You're John Wayne Gacy with a badge."

"You wound me, Pinkie. Gacy was the ugliest of all the serial killers."

"Well, you pissed me off."

"Look," he said. "Why would I want to kill you? I'm not married to you."

My fingers sprang loose like magic, and Spencer caught me, slamming my body against his. My feet found the rungs of the ladder, and I breathed a sigh of relief.

I sank into Spencer, wrapping my arms around his neck for dear life, and allowed him to take my weight and climb up the ladder. He laid me on the balcony and knelt next to me. His new Armani suit had taken a beating. Served him right.

Lucy bent over and studied me.

"You all right, darlin'? I never saw anything like it. You hung on like a bobcat's jaw clamped on Bambi's leg."

"I guess I'm fine. Spencer tried to kill me," I said.

"I was trying to save her life," he growled.

"He tried to save everybody," Lucy told me. "Ran in to clear us all out of the house so we wouldn't be burned alive. It would have been brave if there was a fire, but the fireball didn't catch, just a lot of show. Then he remembered he threw you off the balcony."

I struggled to my feet. I was a little shaky, and I was impatient to get home. Grandma would have a good dinner waiting for me, with mashed potatoes, hope-fully.

"Where's my purse?" I asked. "Oh, no."

I looked over the side. My new lip gloss was about halfway down, nestled in the pointy leaves of a yucca plant. The gloss was the perfect color. I had discovered it at the bottom of the clearance bin at the drugstore. It was the last one in stock.

I scanned the canyon, but my purse had vanished, along with my car keys, wallet, and a half-eaten Hershey bar. Luckily I had put Uncle Harry's three hundred dollars in my pocket.

"We really should hurry, Gladie," Lucy said. "We need to find Luanda."

"I have splinters in my hands," I said.

"I wonder if your Grandma knows where to find her," she said.

"Who's Luanda?" Spencer asked.

"I've got bush in my hair," I said.

Lucy waved off Spencer. "We're on a case, darlin'."

"What case? Pinkie, what are you up to?"

"I lost my car keys," I said. "And my spider clothes are in the trunk."

Spencer crossed his arms in front of him. "Did someone die again?"

I looked at my hands. "Can you get tetanus from splinters?" I asked.

THE FIRE department gave the all clear about an hour later. It turned out Uncle Harry's security guard, Kirk, could start my car without keys. From now on I would have to start the engine with a screwdriver, but at least I could drive it. He also opened my trunk for me, but it would have to be kept closed with a piece of rope.

I was looking less like Donald Trump by the minute.

Spencer gave me a law-enforcement lecture about driving without a license. "You threw me over a balcony," I reminded him. "You tossed me to my death, along with my driver's license."

"So I guess a quickie is out of the question," he said.

"I thought women are more trouble than they're worth," I replied, turning the ignition with the flathead.

"Habit." He shrugged and patted the car.

I shifted it into drive and, against Lucy's wishes, took her to her house, with the promise that we would battle the mysterious Luanda the next morning. I was beat, and the only things I wanted were a hot shower and carbs.

I finally rolled into Grandma's driveway as the sun started to set. Next door, Holden's porch light turned on. It was set on a timer, but the interior of his house was dark, and his truck was nowhere to be seen. I hadn't had word from him since he left town weeks ago. I was trying not to take his silence personally. After all, he was on a mission to clear his name and probably didn't have time to call, but I still checked my phone every few minutes.

I slapped my forehead. My phone. It was at the bottom of the canyon, along with my purse. I'd had a lot of bad luck with my phone in the past few months.

"This has been a hell of day," I said out loud.

"You're telling me." I jumped in my seat. Ruth Fletcher leaned against my car, her craggy face poking through my open window.

I clutched at my chest. "Ruth, what are you doing here?"

"Are you kidding me? My shop is condemned, as is my apartment above it. Since the whole nightmare is your fault, I figured I would shack up with you while it's getting fixed."

"With me? What does Grandma have to say about that?" Ruth didn't have the greatest respect for Grandma, and I didn't know how the two would get along living under the same roof.

"Haven't said a word to her. Haven't seen her yet. I've been waiting for you. If the old bat is so all-seeing, then I don't need to say a word to her. She should just know."

I rolled my eyes. "Fine," I said.

"Why do you have bush in your hair?" Ruth asked.

The front door opened, and Grandma peeked her head out. "What are you two waiting for? Dinner is getting cold. Ruth, I made up the blue room for you."


I TOOK a long, hot shower before dinner, spending a lot of time trying to remove the splinters from my hands and the tangles from my hair. Afterward, I dressed in sweats and thick socks that Spencer had left at the house weeks before. Luanda or no Luanda, tomorrow I would get my winter clothes cleaned. I was tired of looking like a high school gym teacher.

I opened my bedroom door and was greeted by a flood of light. At first I thought the sun had exploded, and I worried that I would die hungry, but then I realized the light was coming from across the street. It wasn't flashlight kind of light. It was Hiroshima kind of light.

"What the hell!" Ruth hollered from below. "Is this how you treat your dinner guest? Am I ever going to be allowed to eat?"

"I'm coming." I skipped down the long staircase and hit the last step just as a horrible grinding noise started. I put my hands over my ears.

"It's worse than Woodstock!" Ruth yelled over the racket. It was a stretch imagining Ruth Fletcher at Woodstock. She wasn't really a love-in kind of gal.

Grandma *click-clack*ed into the entranceway, her hands over her ears, too. We stood there, looking like the hear-no-evil monkey, waiting for the noise to stop.

"It's not stopping!" I said.

"It must be the dolphin across the street," Grandma yelled.

My hands dropped away from my ears. "Huh?"

"The dolphin! The dolphin!" she repeated.

Ruth turned toward me. "This is a nuthouse."

The grinding got louder. I felt my brain bouncing in my skull. "The dolphin that bought the house!" Grandma explained, her voice straining against the noise.

"Woman, you need a padded cell," Ruth said.

"The dolphin that bought the house?" I asked Grandma.

"Yes, he's renovating it, and then he's going to sell it. I hope a young family moves in." She clapped her hands and pointed at me. "Or a single man!"

"Single men don't buy houses, Zelda," Ruth sneered. "Neither do dolphins."

Grandma and I exchanged looks. We were thinking the same thing. Holden was a single man and he had bought the house next door, but that didn't end the way we had hoped.

"It's not necessarily the end, dolly," Grandma said.

My brain clicked into high gear. "Flipper!" I yelled in triumph. "You mean a flipper bought the house across the street!"

Grandma nodded. "That's what I said. Dolphin. He says he's going to turn it around quickly. I bet he's got thirty men working on it."

"Not at this time of day, he doesn't," Ruth said. She walked upstairs and came back down a couple of minutes later with a baseball bat in her hand and a look of determination on her face.

"Uh," I said.

"I'll get them to shut up," Ruth announced, and stormed out of the house.

"I'll put the fried chicken and mashed potatoes in the oven to keep warm." Grandma walked back to the kitchen.

I sighed. I didn't want to run after Ruth in order to protect her from a twenty-five-to-life sentence and to save the dolphin from being bludgeoned to death. I had had bad experiences with the house across the street. As far as I was concerned, it should be given a wide berth. Besides, it didn't take a genius to realize I shouldn't chase after a bat-wielding Ruth Fletcher. She could be cantankerous, was probably a home-run hitter, and five gets you ten she was juicing.

But it was obvious we weren't going to eat until we were all sitting together at the table, and nothing could get me moving like the promise of mashed potatoes.

In order to save time, I didn't bother putting on shoes. I ran out into the night toward Ruth and the earsplitting grinding noise, wearing only Spencer's tube socks on my feet. They were cushy and warm, and I would kill Ruth if they got holes.

The house was bathed in floodlights and swarming with construction workers. They climbed on and over the house and passed in and out of the doors like ants in an ant farm. The grinding noise was actually several grinding noises. And the grinding noises were accompanied by knocking noises that I hadn't noticed before.

Luckily, Ruth was slow. I caught up to her halfway across the street.

"Ruth," I called. "Stop!"

She turned with her bat resting against her shoulder, doing her best Sammy Sosa impression.

"I'll just be a minute," she told me.

"Ruth, you have a bat."

"This isn't a bat. It's a 1928 Louisville Slugger. Where it goes, I go."

"So do I," I said.

It was easy to find the man in charge. The flipper looked shockingly like Abraham Lincoln: tall, ugly, with ratty facial hair. He wore shorts, construction boots, and a puffy jacket, and he held an official-looking clipboard. Ruth spotted him at the same time.

"Shut the hell up! Shut the hell up!" she yelled at him without preamble, lifting the bat high.

He smiled like he was the lunch hostess at Denny's. "May I help you, ma'am?" he asked her.

"Turn it off!"

"Turn what off?"

"The noise! The lights! You can't march into this neighborhood like a panzer division."

"I've got a license," he said, holding up a paper, his smile never wavering. "I can do whatever I want until ten."

"Ten?" Ruth shouted. I stood back out of range of the Louisville Slugger. Her eyeballs glowed red. She was ready to blow.

"Ten," he repeated.

"I'll show you ten, Herr Himmler," she threatened. "I'll show you ten through your fascist skull!"

Time slowed. Ruth let rip with her bat, but I watched it through the eyes of a hummingbird, my reflexes turned lightning-fast. I was the Bionic Woman. I was Wonder Woman.

I was wounded.

I had leapt for the bat, determined to stop it mid-stroke, but my foot landed on a rusty nail, making me scream louder than anything the flipper's team of construction workers could produce. I fell to the ground and gripped my foot, which now had a nail sticking out of it. The flipper had easily dodged Ruth's bat, and she swung all the way around. Strike one, I thought. It was my last rational thought.

I began to hallucinate, because out of nowhere, framed in the light, was Stevie Nicks from the rock group Fleetwood Mac, her hair long and thick and wild and filled with colorful feathers, her clothes flowing in layers to the ground.

"I am Luanda," Stevie Nicks announced. "And I see dead people."

"Boy, do you," I said, and passed out.

# Chapter 4

✦ ♥ ✦

*Hey, kids, keep off my lawn! That's the old man's battle cry, bubeleh, and sometimes you can learn a lot from cranky old men. Like keeping people off your lawn, and you keeping off other people's lawns. You get what I'm talking about? Sometimes it's better to stay home, stay on your own territory. It's called the home-field advantage, dolly. So you'll have clients tell you to come to them. Sometimes that's okay, but other times it's not okay at all. If they insist on their home-field advantage, they want to control the match, and control and love don't go together. If you feel that uh-oh feeling deep in your belly, that's when you should stay home. Let them come to you. But don't let them trample the lawn. Make them stay on the path.*

**Lesson 62,**
**Matchmaking Advice from Your Grandma Zelda**

LUANDA PERSUADED the EMTs to let her ride with Ruth and me in the ambulance, telling them she was my spiritual guide and had to realign my chakras to speed healing.

Ruth said, "Oh, for Christ's sake," and moved over to let Luanda take a seat next to me. Joe the paramedic put a needle in my arm. A warmth filled my body, and suddenly I didn't care a thing about Luanda, my chakras, or the nail poking out of my left foot.

"I am never going to get my dinner," Ruth muttered.

I didn't care. I wasn't hungry. I was chasing the dragon in the best possible way, with pharmaceutical-grade narcotics. "Dragon," I gurgled.

"She's calling the mystic mother, Morgana's dragon," Luanda said, her voice all singsongy, which was appropriate since she was dressed like Stevie Nicks. "She's communing with the goddess. She's enlightened. She's a fairy."

"She's stoned," Ruth said. "She's flying higher than the Goodyear blimp."

"Who are you calling a blimp?" I said, affronted.

"She's not stoned," Luanda told Ruth. "She has the gift. She's transcendental."

"Sing 'Landslide,'" I urged her.

Ruth presented her arm to Joe the paramedic. "Kevorkian me," she said. "Light me up. Put me out of my misery."


IT WASN'T until we'd arrived at the hospital that I remembered I didn't have health insurance. My COBRA had run out. I was tempted to make them leave the nail in my foot, but I knew I would change my mind once the morphine wore off.

Even if I matched the entire town, I wouldn't be able to pay the hospital bill. I lay on the gurney in the ER, and a tear rolled down my cheek. Ruth figured my crying meant I was in pain and, much to her credit, bullied a young intern into pushing another dose of happy juice into my IV.

With the narcotic running through my veins, I flew right to the ceiling and hovered there. I had a great view of the ER from my position overhead, which was a smallish room with only three beds, separated by light-blue curtains. Only one bed was occupied, by a woman who was surprisingly a dead ringer for me, except that her hair was a mess and a nail was stuck in her foot.

Oh.

I watched as Luanda waved feathers over me. Ruth stood with her arms crossed, tapping her sensible shoe on the linoleum.

"Can we hurry this up, people?" Ruth yelled. "It ain't brain surgery." She leaned over and whispered in my ear, "You want me to pull it out with pliers? I've done it before."

I was half-tempted to let her yank it out with her teeth, if it would save me from a monster hospital bill, but I couldn't get my mouth to work. Not from my position flying in the air. I tried to rejoin my body, flapping my arms like a bird.

Luanda studied her feathers, probably marveling at her own magical powers. A man in a polo shirt and fitted slacks approached the bed. He had an uncanny resemblance to The Rock except that he had a Bruno Mars haircut and big black square engineer glasses. He held a pad of paper in the palm of one hand, a pen poised over it with the other. He reminded me of Clark Kent, and I hoped he would pull his cape out and fly up to the ceiling and keep me company.

"Is she having seizures?" he asked. His voice was

deep and smooth, like thoroughly macho velvet. Just like that, I stopped flapping my arms and floated down until I rejoined my body. He looked even better from that angle.

"You got a pliers, kid?" Ruth asked him.

He shook his head. "I'm Detective Cumberbatch. I'm here to take Ms. Burger's statement."

"Nice to meet you," I tried to say, but it came out like I was gargling mouthwash. He smiled at me, a slow, relaxed smile, like he never had to exert himself, like the world had a habit of coming to him.

Luanda handed the detective her business card. "I'm Luanda Laughing-Eagle. I could scrub your aura for you if you want."

"Uh," he said.

A doctor appeared and started to work on my foot, seemingly happy to ignore the people in the room. A moment later, my best friend, Bridget Donovan, stormed into the ER and pushed the detective out of her way. "There's a nail in your foot!" she yelled.

Bridget hugged me and then hugged Ruth, Luanda, and the detective. She didn't usually hug people. She usually just protested injustice. She was anti most everything, a strident feminist, and so far left of center that you couldn't find her on a political map.

"I'm doing a hugging cleanse," Bridget explained. "A full year of hugs."

"Isn't there an easier way to catch tuberculosis?" Ruth asked.

"I'm searching for inner peace," Bridget said. She had recently gone through a crisis of faith and was trying to find her balance.

"I need to take Ms. Burger's statement," the detective tried again.

"Did you read her her rights?" Bridget asked. "Have you provided an attorney?" Bridget was a crusader for the little guy, and I was as little of a guy as you could get.

"There we go. All better," the doctor announced. "Just have to dress it, and you can go home."

"I need to take her statement," the detective said again. He was the epitome of patience. He stood ramrod-straight, but he was so comfortable with himself that he looked like he was leaning back. He was cool. He was smooth jazz, Cary Grant, and expensive whiskey all rolled into a good-looking mass of masculinity.

"Perhaps I can be of help. I'm Michael Rellik." The flipper had arrived and joined our little group. He was still smiling, but he gave the detective what I would call serious attention.

I pointed at the flipper. "He did this to me," I said uncharitably and clear as day, my mouth working again. I was pleased to be able to speak but sorry the drugs were wearing off.

"An accident," Rellik said. "But I'd be more than happy to pay the medical costs."

I almost wept with relief. The flipper pulled out some legal papers, and I grabbed the detective's pen to sign them.

"I wouldn't recommend signing anything until you have an attorney read it," the detective suggested.

"It's fine, Detective Cabbagepatch," I said. I was thrilled my bills would be paid. I would have signed anything.

"Cumberbatch," he corrected. "Remington Cumberbatch."

"That's a mouthful," Ruth said. The room fell into silence, as we were all thinking the same thing: Remington Cumberbatch was a mouthful, a yummy, tall, dark, and massive mouthful.

"You need to clean up your work site, Mr. Rellik," he said.

"Indeed. Indeed. Already done. It's going to be the nicest house on the block."

Grandma would be so pleased. She took neighborhood beautification seriously. But I had doubts about the house across the street. Not that I believed it was cursed, but, yes, I believed the house was cursed.

Rellik clapped his hands. "I have an idea! Why don't you all come tomorrow for a VIP tour of the house? Several other Cannes residents are coming, too. Then you can see for yourself the wonderful things we're doing with the property."

"And I can bless it!" Luanda was oozing excitement.

"Hallelujah," Ruth said.

Bridget hugged Rellik. I wanted to hug him, too, when he pulled out his Gold Card and paid my bill.

It occurred to me that I had both Ruth and Luanda in the same room, and I could unmatch Uncle Harry right then and there and earn my money, but the drugs were wearing off, and even though I was not in pain, the reality of having a hole in my foot was gnawing at the edges of my awareness, and I was starting to freak out.

The doctor had wrapped my foot in layers of gauze and a nylon boot, with instructions on how to care for it, and he gave me a vial of antibiotics to take three times a day for ten days. Then I was wheeled outside to the curb.

Bridget's phone rang, and she took the call.

"Yes," she answered. "Excuse me? I'm wearing a skirt, a top, and a cardigan. Who is this? What did you say you were holding?" She looked at her phone. "They hung up," she told us. "That was an odd conversation. Why would they want to know what I'm wearing?"

"Goddamned telemarketers," Ruth said.

The wind blew, and I shivered, which reminded me that my winter clothes were still in the broken trunk of my car, sheltering an army of breeding spiders. I felt a welcome wave of warmth as a heated blanket was placed over my shoulders. I turned around to see Remington Cumberbatch.

"I didn't want you catching a chill," he said through his suave smile. He was nerdy with his big glasses and wonky haircut, but he had piercing brown eyes that reached down into my soul. It struck me that he was very sure of himself but not in an egomaniacal way. He was sure of himself in an attractive, protector way. I wanted to crawl into his arms and let him rock me to sleep. I wanted to crawl into his arms and let him do whatever he wanted to do with me.

Maybe I needed therapy. It wasn't normal to be attracted to so many men at once. But Holden was away, trying to fix his life. Spencer was detoxing from his gaggle of females. Maybe I was lonely. Maybe I was a whore. Maybe Remington Cumberbatch was a stud muffin.

"Hey, stud muffin, how about you give Gladie and

me a ride back to her grandma's house?" Ruth asked him.

"Sure," he replied.

"I think Bridget is taking us," I said, but Bridget was on her phone again.

"What do you mean, am I coming? Coming where?" she asked into the phone.

"I think your friend is busy," Remington noted.

"If I don't eat, I'm going to bite someone's head off," Ruth warned.

"All right," I said. "Please take us home."

THE DETECTIVE sat Ruth in the front seat, after she complained about claustrophobia. He helped me into the back, tenderly lifting my foot to rest on the seat.

"You doing all right?" he asked me.

I nodded. The morphine had pretty much worn off, but my foot was numb from the shot the doctor had given me. "Your boot is dope," he said, grazing my nylon medical boot with his fingers.

A zing of electrical horniness shot from my foot up to my eyeballs. I blinked.

He winked and shut my door, then went around to the driver's seat. "Let's boldly go where no man has gone before," he said, and turned the ignition with the key on his *Star Trek* key chain.

"You're one of those nerdy fellas, aren't you?" Ruth asked him.

"We nerdy fellows prefer the term 'geek.'"

He drove slowly away from the hospital. I watched out the window as we got closer to the historic district—and then spotted the colorful Cup O'Cake sign. It seemed to be calling my name.

"Stop!" I yelled. "Stop now!"

The car screeched to a halt. The detective turned to me and arched an eyebrow.

"I want coffee," I said.

"She always wants coffee," Ruth explained. It was true. I had a coffee problem.

"I might want a cupcake, too."

"The most overrated pastry ever," Ruth grumbled. "But get me a tea. Earl Grey. I'm in the mood for no-nonsense tea."

"You're not coming in?" I asked her.

"Are you kidding? I'm not going in there." She shot the house a nasty look. Cup O'Cake was Ruth's competition, and now her tea shop was out of commission and she was forced to get her Earl Grey fix from her kindly, coffee-sympathizer rivals. I felt for her.

"I'll bring you a to-go cup," I told her. The detective helped me out of the car and wrapped his arm around my waist to help support me.

"Thanks, Mr. Spock," I told him. He raised an eyebrow.

"Ms. Burger, don't hate," he said, gently squeezing my waist. "Appreciate." He smelled of soap and fresh air. Clean.

"Okay," I breathed.

"And my name's Remington."

"Remington," I repeated.

Ruth opened her car door. "Oh, what the hell," she grumbled. "It doesn't look like much from the outside. Besides, I could go for a cupcake, even though it's just icing on a dry bit of cake."

Inside, the shop was warm and inviting, with a roaring fire in the fireplace and candles lit on every surface. It smelled wonderful.

Mavis Jones greeted me with a big smile and a latte. "I saw you walk up the path," she said, handing the mug to me. "I'm so glad to see you so soon. You smell that? Fresh cinnamon buns. I'll get you and your friends some, hot out of the oven."

They were not mashed potatoes, but cinnamon buns were a close second. We sat in the armchairs by the fire and took deep breaths. Cup O'Cake was nothing short of blissful. Even Ruth, who was disdainful of just about everything, looked around with obvious appreciation. She sighed, deflating into the cushy chair. I took a sip of my latte.

"Not as good as yours," I said to Ruth, trying to appease her.

"Well, what'd you expect?" she said with obvious pleasure.

Mavis appeared with a pot of tea, two mugs, and a plate piled high with iced cinnamon buns. I think I moaned.

"We are so excited to have you here, Ms. Fletcher," she said. "I hope our tea meets with your approval. I must say we are a bit nervous to have the owner of the best tea shop in the world here."

It was the right thing to say. "Call me Ruth," she said. "I'm sure it's fine. For what it is."

"And who is this young gentleman?" Mavis asked.

"Remington Cumberbatch," he said, standing. "I'm the new detective in town."

"He's giving us a ride home," I explained.

Felicia Patel joined us, and my heart skipped a beat.

I had forgotten all about the book she had given me, and now it was lost, somewhere in the canyon behind Uncle Harry's house.

"Felicia," I started. "About the book—"

"Didn't you just love it?" she gushed. "I thought it was hilarious."

"Well, here's the thing—"

"You gave a book to this one?" Ruth laughed, pointing at me. "I've never seen her read anything more than a menu."

"That's not true. I love books," I said. I liked looking at books. I especially liked books in bookstores attached to coffeehouses. But I wasn't thrilled about reading books. After all, most good ones are made into movies.

Ruth harrumphed loudly.

"I kind of lost the book," I told Felicia, looking down into my latte mug. "It sort of fell into a canyon."

Remington's eyes slid slowly toward me, and he arched an eyebrow. The man never said much, but he communicated boatloads.

"I was thrown off a balcony," I explained.

Felicia began to say something, but Ruth stopped her. "It's better not to ask questions, girlie. Just roll with it. Didn't you know Gladie is our town's troublemaker?"

"I wouldn't say troublemaker," I said. More like trouble-finder. Since I had arrived in town, I found more trouble than Lindsay Lohan on a bad day. "Felicia, let me pay you for the lost book."

"Not necessary," Felicia said, although I could tell

she was troubled by the loss. "I'll give you another one. What are your feelings on steampunk?"

I had no idea what steampunk was, but I took the book from her, again promising to read it and give her my report the next day. I sighed and took another sip of my coffee. I would do a lot for coffee and cinnamon buns.

"You were thrown off a balcony?" Remington asked me. "Should I arrest someone?"

"For sure," I said. "Can you do that?"

The door to the shop opened, and Mrs. Arbuthnot walked in like she was Ethel Barrymore on opening night on Broadway.

"Mavis, get me a bear claw and a cup of coffee. I've had a day that would try Job," she said, unwrapping a long shawl from her shoulders and tossing it on a nearby chair. She noticed us and then, deciding we were not important, turned away, sitting delicately. Mavis and Felicia scattered like ants, forgetting us altogether, anxious to do Mrs. Arbuthnot's bidding. Wow, that old lady had a lot of sway in town. I wondered just how much trouble she could make for Uncle Harry's development plans.

"Old biddy," Ruth muttered. "Goes around like she owns the world. Not an ounce of humility."

I thought Mrs. Arbuthnot was scarily similar to Ruth, but the irony was lost on her. I finished a second cinnamon bun and the last sip of my latte and glanced down at the book Felicia had given me. It was a hardback, thick, at least three hundred pages. No way could I read the whole thing by tomorrow. I opened the first pages, hoping for a really big font size, but it was normal. There was a stamp inside the front cover saying it belonged to a school in Irvine. I wondered if Felicia had forgotten to return it or if her book collection was really ill-gotten gain. Perhaps sweet Felicia was a notorious international book thief. I shrugged. I didn't care too much about book thieves.

"Planning to throw it into another canyon?" Remington asked me. He had caught me staring at the book with what had to be a look of dread on my face. He was sipping his tea and had forgone the cinnamon buns. I didn't understand how he could resist them. I counted his self-control as a strike against him. Then I was surprised that I was counting his attributes.

"It was an accident," I said.

"It's always an accident," Ruth said. "The girl is more trouble than she's worth."

"Well, I don't remember inviting you, Ruth," I retorted. "You didn't have to come to the hospital with me."

"Listen, Gladys Burger," she said. "If I weren't homeless, I would be in my bed, watching *Cagney and Lacey* reruns. *If* I weren't homeless."

She leaned forward and stared me straight in the eyes. What was it with old ladies in this town? They were all dead ringers for *What Ever Happened to Baby Jane?*

"It wasn't my fault," I insisted. "I wasn't driving. And don't call me Gladys."

Ruth put her teacup on the table. "Gladys," she repeated.

"I'm surprised you didn't go to Uncle Harry's house to stay after the accident," I told Ruth.

"Have you been sniffing glue?" she asked. "What are you talking about?"

"You know what I'm talking about," I said, my voice rising an octave.

"The minute I know what you're talking about, I'm going to have my head examined."

"Well, then, get Freud on the phone now, Ruth, because you know exactly what I'm talking about. Uncle Harry. Smooch. Smooch." I made kissing noises, pursing my lips at the air.

"No-Neck Harry, the mobster?" she asked. "What did Mavis put in your coffee? Are you one of those ketamine freaks? Should I call a doctor? Quick, someone get a net!"

"I know you hired Luanda to fix you up with Harry," I said. Which wasn't exactly true. I knew that Luanda was trying to fix them up, but, come to think of it, I couldn't imagine Ruth hiring anyone to do anything, let alone match her. Suddenly I felt ridiculous. Of course Ruth didn't hire Luanda.

I leaned back in my chair and lowered my voice. "My foot hurts."

"Harry Lupino is a good thirty years younger than me, Gladie, but that's not why you're ridiculous. You're ridiculous because Harry is a Republican, anti-union, and he has NO NECK!"

"What mobster are we talking about?" Remington asked softly. I had forgotten he was there.

"He's not a mobster," I said.

Mrs. Arbuthnot stood up and stomped over to us. "He is too a mobster, little girl," she said to me, sounding just like Queen Victoria. "He's a mobster and a thief and a crook, and he's trying to rape this town until it looks like Los Angeles. Los Angeles!"

Ruth pointed at her. "See? Even the old biddy agrees with me."

"A person would have to be a fool to get in bed with him," Mrs. Arbuthnot continued. I didn't know if she meant "bed" literally or figuratively.

"Well, the only bed I want to get in is my own, but that ain't gonna happen," Ruth said. "And Harry Lupino ain't gonna happen, either."

"But Luanda told Harry—" I started, and then realized how crazy that sounded. Luanda told Harry? Luanda spoke to dead people. Luanda wore feathers. Luanda wasn't that reliable. Obviously I would have to focus solely on her to stop harassing Harry. Actually, I was relieved not to have to contend with Ruth and her matters of the heart.

"Kid, take us home," Ruth ordered Remington.

"Yes, ma'am," he said, and stood.

He had put his hand out to help me up when the door to the shop opened again, and this time Spencer walked through. He looked around and spotted me. His attention went down to my injured foot and then over to Remington.

"Are you kidding me?" he exclaimed to no one in particular.

"Hello, boss," Remington said. "Just taking these two ladies home."

Spencer approached and got in his face. The two men were big, but Remington was bigger, like a tank but muted in his simple clothes and dorky glasses. Besides, he was so calm and cool, he was almost asleep.

"And you stopped for tea?" Spencer asked. His face

was red, and his chest rose and fell like he had just run a mile.

I interrupted them. My foot was starting to hurt, and I wanted to go home to Grandma and eat mashed potatoes. "What are you doing here, Spencer?"

"Your grandmother called me to come pick you up. Something about a fake psychic and a chicken leg."

"If that lunatic got ahold of my chicken, she really will be talking to the dead," Ruth grumbled, standing up and going for the door.

# Chapter 5

✦ ♥ ✦

*We're in the matching business, but we are also in the love business. What does that mean? It means a whole lifetime of things. For starters, it means we direct people to their love matches, but it also means we dissuade people from their false love matches. This is what separates us from the average ordinary matchmakers. Those other fakakta matchmakers just want to make a match, any match. We are in the love business. We make only love matches. Focus your energy on that. Love and only love.*

**Lesson 51,**
**Matchmaking Advice from Your Grandma Zelda**

GRANDMA WOKE me at around eleven the next morning. "Are you awake?" she asked, nudging my shoulder.

"No."

"Are you sure?"

"Yes."

I opened one eye to see her face inches from mine. I put the pillow over my head.

Grandma sat down at the edge of the bed. "You need to be awake. It's going to be a long day and colder than the forecast said."

"Are you sure?"

"That Luanda woman's got my radar all wonky, but I've never been wrong about the weather, dolly. Here."

She tugged at me, and I sat up in bed. She handed me some clothes—a black velour tracksuit with BINGO CHAMP 1989 bedazzled on the back of the hoodie in purple neon.

"Are you sure?" I asked.

"That woman is matching my matches all wrong. Love hangs in the balance. It's chaos."

Her face hung, dejected. My grandmother was usually upbeat and in control. Now she was getting bested by a New Age pseudo-hippie, and my heart went out to her. I put the tracksuit on.

Grandma had spent the entire evening complaining about Luanda. "She's bad for this town, bad for what's decent in this world!" she shouted over dinner.

"You mean she's bad for business," Ruth said, with her mouth full of fried chicken. "Bad for *your* business."

"She's taken my clients, and she's going to match them with unsuitable matches," Grandma sputtered. "Unsuitable, do you understand?"

"What can we do?" I asked. I really wanted to know. It was unthinkable that Grandma's match-making business would tank. She was an institution in town.

"You have to spy on her, dolly," Grandma said. "Spy on her and bring me back proof that she's a fraud."

"Spy?"

"She doesn't need to do that," Ruth said. "I'll tell anybody who'll listen that she's a fraud, just like I tell everyone you're a fraud, Zelda."

"Ruth, if you're weren't so old and going to die soon, I would kick your butt," Grandma snapped.

Ruth swallowed, and her face drained of color. "How soon are you talking about, Zelda?"

Grandma had gone on about Luanda until after midnight, when she finally let us go to bed. My foot wasn't too bad, but I took a pain pill, anyway, and slept like the dead.

Grandma's velour tracksuit fit me perfectly. It sucked having spider clothes. No matter what—even if I got a nail in my other foot—I would get them de-spidered today.

"I've got bagels downstairs, dolly," she said. "Come down, and we can talk more about how you're going to catch the fake psychic."

Downstairs, Ruth was sitting at the kitchen table, reading the paper and eating a bagel, her hair in tight hot-pink curlers. I took a step back in shock.

"Ruth, is that what I think that is in front of you?" I asked her.

She self-consciously touched her mug. "No lip from you," she said.

"But it's coffee," I said, sitting next to her.

"What do you expect? I'm living with your grandmother in this lunatic asylum. It was either coffee or I was going to hang myself by the curtain rod. I'm not sure I made the right choice."

I smiled. "You once told me coffee was the downfall of civilization. You told me coffee drinkers were the reason America was going the way of Rome—

a decaying, rotting, failed society. Once when I asked you for a macchiato, you called me a storm trooper. Just last week you told a man who ordered an espresso that he was King Kong in khakis."

"Stay there while I get my bat," Ruth said.

I touched Ruth's shoulder. "Just playing with you, Ruth. No need to go Mark McGwire on me."

"Holy crap! I think I left my Slugger at the house across the street," she said.

I smeared some cream cheese on a bagel. "No problem. I'll get it for you when I go over there later."

"Why are you going over there?" Grandma asked. "I'm not sure that's a good idea."

I knew it wasn't a good idea. That house was cursed. "I'm sure it will be fine," I reassured her. "I'm taking a tour of the premises."

"Oh," Grandma said. She loved the idea of snooping in someone's house, but since she never left her property, she could get the report from me. Still, she appeared concerned. She stood up and looked out the window to the backyard. "The wind has shifted, dolly. Soon it's all going to hell in a handbasket. Nothing is as it seems. Love is going to split into what it's not. And it's all because of that woman."

Ruth harrumphed. "Where have you been, Zelda? The world's already gone to hell in a handbasket. Went there years ago. You're just smelling the brimstone."

We thought about hell and brimstone for a while as we ate our brunch. We had all the time in the world, it seemed. My only case was to unmatch Uncle Harry, which had to be the easiest task ever. Ruth's business was totaled, and the insurance people weren't coming until tomorrow. Grandma's business had been obliterated by Luanda, and the Tuesday morning Second Chancers meeting was canceled.

"That woman has my Second Chancers!" Grandma cried, with onion bagel in her mouth. "They're trusting that fake woman with their second chances." She washed down the bagel with coffee.

Grandma took her job seriously. It was more of a calling than a job to her. I wondered if it would ever become that to me or if I was doomed to get yet another temporary job to pay my bills. I had sort of gotten attached to Cannes and the matchmaking business. I realized right there at Grandma's table, eating an onion bagel with cream cheese, that I was thrilled I had made two real matches in town, and I was worried that Luanda really was a threat to the business and my future happiness. Maybe the job was growing on me.

"My radar is all wonky," Grandma said. "I keep getting the rebel yell in my head over and over. It's the Battle of Bull Run in there." She pointed to her bouffant hairdo.

But her radar wasn't as wonky as she thought. The rebel yell got louder until suddenly the front door burst open, and the sound of high heels on Grandma's wood floors *click-clack*ed toward us.

"Darlin', it's whup-ass time," Lucy announced, breathless, from the kitchen doorway. "I've been plotting all night, and I've got it all worked out. We are going to tan that woman's hide until the word 'Harry' makes her run screaming."

"Have some coffee," I said, gesturing to the seat next to me.

"I don't have time for coffee!" Lucy screeched. "We have business to do, Gladie. We have ass to whup."

Lucy was wild-eyed, but I noticed that her eyes were still perfectly lined, her mascara had lengthened and separated each lash beautifully, and she wore a gorgeous cashmere shirtdress that must have cost thousands.

"Her ass will still be there in an hour," I said. "Besides, there's Danish, too."

"Cherry?" Lucy asked, and sat next to me. "You!" Lucy yelled at Ruth, noticing her for the first time. "Listen, old woman, you'd better get back, or—"

I handed Lucy a Danish. "Already been there, Robert E. Lee. She knows nothing about it."

Lucy looked at me like she had forgotten I was there.

"It was Luanda going rogue," I assured her.

"You're a little het up there," Ruth noted. "Whose ass are you planning on whupping?"

"That Luanda woman's, of course."

"Take a number. Zelda wants her run out of town."

"She does?" Lucy asked. We caught her up on Grandma's beef with Luanda, and it incited Lucy even further. "You know, this sounds more and more like we should involve the cops. Where's your lovely police chief at?" she asked me.

"How should I know?"

Ruth snorted. "Her lovely police chief read her the riot act on our way home last night."

"You know he's not that lovely, and he's hardly mine," I said. "Besides, it wasn't the riot act, Ruth."

But it was pretty close to the riot act. He had warned me to stay out of trouble. He told me it was my fault that I stepped on a nail and had to go to the hospital. He said I got injured because I was nosy. I pointed out that I was just trying to save a man from being bludgeoned to death, but he didn't care, didn't listen.

"Besides," he had said to me, "stay away from Cumberbatch."

"The new detective?"

"The *probationary* detective. I'm just trying him out for a couple weeks."

"He seems fine," I said.

Spencer swerved the car. "He doesn't seem like anything to you, Pinkie. He's not what he seems. Stay away."

But that was last night, when I was coming off the influence of fabulous pain meds. I hadn't had the presence of mind to ask what he meant by Cumberbatch not being what he seemed.

"Every good-looking man who comes into this town buzzes around Gladie," Ruth said now; she sounded like she had discovered Bigfoot was real and he'd stopped into her shop for a cup of tea. She counted on her fingers. "That chief, the tall drink of water from next door, and now the new police nerdy fella. Hey, where is that tall drink of water? I haven't seen him lately. Maybe your magic is wearing off, Gladie."

The kitchen grew quiet except for chewing and sipping noises. Where was the tall drink of water from next door? Was my magic wearing off? Grandma knew the whole story, of course, without me ever having to say a word to her, but all Lucy knew was that Holden had to go away for a while. She was such a good friend, she didn't ask any more questions, choosing to respect my privacy.

"What new police nerdy fella?" Lucy asked.

"A Trekkie with a badge," I told her.

I poured myself another cup of coffee, and the front door opened and closed again. This time the sound of much-more-sensible shoes crossed the wood floors, and Bridget appeared at the kitchen doorway. Her cropped hair was uncombed, and her big hoot-owl glasses hung at an angle on her face. She went around the table and hugged every one of us.

"I didn't get a minute of sleep last night," she said. "My phone has gone bonkers."

To prove her point, her phone went off again, and she answered it. "Would I ride what all night? Why would I be wet? It's not raining outside." She hung up the phone and flopped down on a chair. "It's been like that all night. I don't want to lose any bookkeeping clients, but I can't make out what they're after."

Lucy took Bridget's phone. "Would you mind if I answered the next time for you, darlin'? In my line of work, I'm used to handling all sorts of people."

Bridget's face relaxed in a wash of relief. "Oh, would you, Lucy? I need a break."

It was only a few seconds later that her phone rang again. "How can I help you, honey?" Lucy asked into the phone. "Uh-huh. Uh-huh," she said. "May I ask how you got this phone number, darlin'? I see. Fine. Yes. Okay, bye for now." She clicked off the phone and took a sip of coffee.

"That explains it all nice and simple," Lucy said. "Bridget darlin', your number has been given out as a sex line."

"What do you mean?" Bridget asked, pushing her glasses up her nose.

"Men are calling your number to talk dirty, darlin'."

Bridget's whole body snapped back in a convulsive shock wave. "Talk dirty?" She sat, stupefied, staring into space. I could easily imagine her replaying the conversations she had had since last night, and it all clicked into place in the logic centers of her brain.

"I'm a prostitute," she said, deflated.

"No you're not," I told her. "It was an accident."

"They published the number wrong," Lucy explained. "We'll call the phone company and get it worked out."

"No, I'm a prostitute," Bridget said. "I've been hugging the whole town. They got the wrong impression."

"You're hardly a sexual warrior," Lucy countered. "You're the victim of bad data entry."

Bridget sniffed and slumped in her seat. "I'm a prostitute. What will I do the next time my phone rings?"

"Nothing," Lucy said. "Your battery is dead. Your whoring is on hiatus."

Bridget took a big gulp of air, as if she had forgotten to breathe. Her eyes refocused, and she cocked her head to the side. "Gladie—what are you wearing?"

GRANDMA DECLARED brunch over, insisting that I start spying on Luanda immediately to prove she was a fraud and get Grandma's business back on track. "And save all those people from bad matches," she stressed.

Grandma's mission suited Lucy just fine, because she wanted to get her hands on Luanda, as well. I was less than happy about going around town in my velour tracksuit and nylon boot.

As it turned out, we didn't have to go far. We opened the front door, and there was Luanda, wailing on the sidewalk across the street. Grandma, Ruth, and Bridget joined Lucy and me in the driveway to watch Luanda dance around and sing.

"Lord, it's like she's choking a cat," Ruth said. "That's reason enough to kill her."

"We're not going to kill her," I said, more to Grandma and Lucy than to Ruth. "We're just going to talk to her. Reason with her."

Luanda pawed the sidewalk with her foot and sang, "Woo, woo, woo." Her skirt was layers and layers of lace and tulle; she looked like a ballerina on acid. Reasoning with her would be challenging.

"How about we kill her a little bit?" Lucy asked.

"Let me find my Louisville Slugger," Ruth said. She took a step down the driveway, but Grandma pushed her out of the way and ran past her, down to the end of her property line.

"You're a fraud, a fake, a phony!" she yelled out. "You're anti-love. You're an ill wind!"

Luanda stopped shrieking and dancing and glanced around, trying to figure out who was yelling at her. I thought it was pretty obvious. It was the old lady crammed in a Donna Karan strapless knockoff and ballet slippers.

Luanda took a vial out of a pocket in her skirt, uncorked it, and sprayed some mysterious liquid across the street. "Heal, heal!" she shouted in Grandma's direction. "Allow balance to shine its light on you!"

"You're babbling nonsense!" Grandma said, and swayed in place. I hobbled toward her and held her up.

"Are you okay?"

"Go get her! Go get her!" she yelled, pointing toward Luanda.

"I'll get her," Lucy offered.

"Hold on, I'll come with you," Ruth said. "You'll want my Slugger."

I sighed. It was like running a day care for hyperactive toddlers.

"No!" I yelled. "I'll get her. Everyone stay here. Except for Grandma. Bridget, help Grandma inside." I wagged my fingers at all of them. The world is in bad shape when I'm the mature one in a group.

My foot throbbed. I had forgotten to take the antibiotics. My jaw clenched with anxiety. My neuroses clicked in. I was probably gangrenous, I thought. They would have to cut off my foot, maybe my leg, if I didn't get medication, quick. I looked down. I kind of liked my feet. I enjoyed having two.

But as big as my fear of dying from infection was, I couldn't let Lucy use Ruth's bat to kill Grandma's archenemy. At the very least, I would have too many people to visit in prison.

I limped halfway across the street. Luanda had lit a small branch on fire and was whirling it around her head. I wasn't the only one who needed medical care. Luanda was a few cards short of a deck. I didn't doubt Grandma's assertion that she was a phony, but I thought it was due more to psychosis than to malev-

olence. I stopped to allow a Prius to park in front of
the house across the street. Mrs. Arbuthnot stepped
out.

She wore a serious pantsuit and carried a handbag
that wouldn't have been out of place on the arm of
the queen of England. Luanda shook the flaming
branch at her, and, without preamble, Mrs. Arbuthnot took a can of Mace out of her purse and sprayed
Luanda for all she was worth.

"Son of a bitch! What the fuck!" Luanda screamed,
and threw the burning branch into the air.

"I think this is what's called karma," Ruth said
over my shoulder. "Never saw it in action before."

I was frozen to the spot. So was Mrs. Arbuthnot. I
wondered if she was shocked at what she had done.
Much to his credit, Michael Rellik, the flipper, ran
out of the house, turned on a hose, and doused first
Luanda's branch and then Luanda's face, which was
probably burning pretty badly from the Mace.

Mrs. Arbuthnot woke from her stupor and fum-
bled in her purse for her cellphone. Bridget came out
of the house, and she, Ruth, and Lucy joined me on
the street.

"Would you look at that," Lucy said. "The old
biddy took her out for us."

Bridget shook her head. "I hate woman-on-woman
violence. What would Gloria Steinem think?"

What *would* Gloria Steinem think? We probably
weren't what she had in mind as modern, liberated
women. She probably would have Maced all of us.

Luanda used the hem of her skirt to mop her face,
leaving a thick, winding swath of black and blue
under her eyes and over her cheeks—the remnants of

her mascara and eye shadow. She looked like she was going to do battle in medieval Scotland, and considering how the day was going, maybe she was.

"I could be safe in my tea shop right now if it weren't for you," Ruth said to me.

"I wasn't the one driving!"

"Holy hell." Bridget moaned the uncharacteristic biblical reference as she stared down the street.

Our heads snapped toward that direction. Running at a breakneck pace up the street was Remington Cumberbatch. I recognized him only through his nerdy glasses and Bruno Mars haircut. Otherwise, he could have been any random Hercules look-alike in shorts, running shoes, and no shirt, his face all hard edges, and the perfect cappuccino-colored skin of his torso, back, and arms decorated in intricate warrior tattoos.

"Jesus, Mary, and Joseph," Bridget moaned again. "I really am a whore."

"No, darlin'," Lucy said, clutching at her chest. "That man could make any woman think naughty thoughts. I'm thinking a whole slew of 'em."

So was I. I bit my lower lip. Remington had hid a lot under his polo shirt and cotton Dockers.

Bridget rubbed her eyes. "Nope, he still looks like The Rock."

"Like a Greek god," Lucy corrected her. "He's Hercules. He's Adonis. He's—"

"He's Remington Cumberbatch, the new police detective," Ruth said.

Lucy put one hand on her hip and leaned into me. "Oh, is that what folks are calling a 'new police nerdy fella' these days?"

Suddenly Remington Cumberbatch stopped running. I thought at first the sight of Luanda had made him stop in his tracks, but his attention was fixed on the middle of the road. I glanced around to see who he was looking at.

"Don't bother," Ruth said. "He's looking at *you*, kid."

# Chapter 6

*Makeup can make you a star. I know what you're thinking. You're thinking some ugly ducklings are gornisht helfn, beyond help. But everybody can do with a little upgrading. Everybody improves with a good buffing. I'm known as the town's makeover maven, and it's not because I like gilding the lily. It's just that sometimes a lily looks like a Buick. It's not good when a lily looks like a Buick, dolly, but it happens more often than you would imagine. So change those Buicks back into lilies and watch them bloom! Don't get me wrong—too much of a good thing will turn you into a clown, a hussy, or Joan Rivers. But get your clients some mascara, get their teeth cleaned, and watch them bloom.*

**Lesson 70,**
**Matchmaking Advice from Your Grandma Zelda**

OUR EYES locked. I couldn't figure out what he was thinking. He was the definition of cool, not because of the tattoos but because he was unflinching, unfathomable, unblinking.

And he was hot.

He stared at me, his chest heaving with the residual exertion from his run. He was wondering either why I was wearing an eighty-year-old woman's velour tracksuit or how quickly he could take it off me. The thought made me break out into a fit of giggles.

"Oh, Lord, here we go," Ruth said. "Don't worry, Bridget, you're not the whore. Gladie is."

The flipper turned off the hose and engaged Remington in conversation. I noticed that Rellik sucked in his stomach and sort of puffed out his chest while he spoke to the detective. After a moment he waved us over.

Ruth stayed in the middle of the street, looking from Rellik standing next to damp Luanda to Grandma's house and back again. "Frying pan or fire? Frying pan or fire?" I heard her mumble.

Our little group walked the rest of the way across the street and formed a circle on the lawn. I said hello to Mrs. Arbuthnot, even though we had never been introduced, and I was careful not to make eye contact with Remington.

Luanda pointed at Mrs. Arbuthnot. "She aggressed me! She violated my chi!"

Mrs. Arbuthnot rolled her eyes. "You tried to light me on fire," she said calmly.

"I did no such thing!" Luanda stammered and sputtered. She balled her hands into fists and stomped her foot.

"Since you're all here early, we can start the tour now," Rellik suggested. His smile was still plastered on his face, and he wasn't any more attractive in the light of day. Still, he was very hospitable and very proud of his house, and I had to hand it to him for trying to distract the women from doing any more damage. "The men have the day off, anyway. Permits," he said with a wink.

"Not everyone is here," Mrs. Arbuthnot said. "Mavis and Felicia are planning to come. Mavis has a good camera, and she's going to take pictures for our responsible-growth report."

As if on cue, a light-blue Volkswagen Beetle drove up and parked on the street in front of us. Mavis stepped out of the passenger side and Felicia from the driver's side. I wondered who was handling the cupcakes while they were away.

"We've brought cupcakes for everyone," Mavis announced, holding up a white bakery box.

Rellik clapped his hands together. "Perfect. We can enjoy them after the tour. I'm sure you ladies will see we've respected the historic nature of the area."

"How did you like the book?" Felicia asked me.

"Uh," I said.

Rellik was anxious to start the tour. "Remember to watch your step. We try to clean up as we go, but this is a construction site, and there are tools and nails everywhere."

He looked at me and winked. I thought I heard Remington snicker, but when I looked at him, he was deadpan.

And hot.

Lucy tried to maneuver around me to get closer to Luanda, but I hopped in front of her and slipped my hand through the crook of Luanda's arm.

"So, I've always wanted to know more about talking to dead people," I lied.

Luanda's face brightened. "They're talking to me right now," she said.

I jumped away from her. Yikes. I hoped she was

lying or at least off her rocker. I didn't need any more dead people around me.

First on the tour was the living room. Just two months ago it was crammed with furniture and knick-knacks. When the owners moved out, the house went from dilapidated to more or less ready for a bull-dozer. But in only a couple of days, Rellik and his crew had transformed it.

Walls had been knocked down, forming an enor-mous great room, and the kitchen that had been stuck in the sixties was now a gorgeous area of stain-less steel and granite. It was a lot of work done in a short period of time. It wasn't exactly a reflection of the historic nature of the area, and I wondered if Mrs. Arbuthnot was going to blow her lid.

The house looked different, but a creepy feeling of dread still wormed its way up my spine and niggled at my stomach.

Or maybe that was the two bagels, pot of coffee, and cherry Danish I had for breakfast.

"I'm picking up vibrations," Luanda announced, and pushed a lock of wet hair off her face.

"Why? Did she Taser you when she gassed you?" Ruth asked, and laughed at her own joke.

Outside, the pool had been drained, and the plaster was half blasted off. A large machine lay at the deep end, with a large hose attached to it. Bags of plaster peppered the pool deck.

"This is going to be some house," Bridget noted.

Two men joined us in the back. Both were middle-aged, one dressed like a lawyer, and the other in ca-sual clothes. The second man was very familiar to me, but I couldn't place him.

"Oh, good, you're here. The house is almost there. Get your checkbooks ready," Rellik said with an exaggerated wink. He smiled and shook their hands. Potential buyers. They talked numbers for a moment and then joined our tour.

I never knew house flipping was so fast. The house had been run-down for decades, but within a few days it was halfway to being on the market and ready for a feature in *House & Garden* magazine.

"I can't wait to show you this next part," Rellik said. "We've actually made a basement."

"Why would you do that?" Ruth asked. "No basements in Southern California."

"Rellik Construction aims to please." Rellik steered us down a hallway and through a door leading to stairs. "But this is no ordinary basement."

Downstairs were two metal doors, sitting side by side.

"A dungeon," Ruth said.

"A bomb shelter," Bridget guessed.

Rellik shook his head. "No, they're panic rooms. They're going to be the finest ones in America. Go ahead, get in."

There was a flurry of enthusiastic shuffling toward the two rooms. Something about the idea of a spot for the express purpose of hiding was irresistible. And it was the perfect setup for a married couple—his-and-hers panic rooms.

I had to admit I was envious. I would have loved a place to go when I panicked, which was pretty regularly.

I couldn't wait to get inside. I envisioned a wet bar and satellite TV. I pictured an endless supply of chips and a really comfortable recliner chair. Maybe the flipper would let me hang out and escape the menagerie I was saddled with. I could be safe in a panic room. Nobody could throw me off a balcony in a panic room.

We shuffled into the rooms, separated evenly into two groups.

"Don't think I forgot about you, woman," Lucy warned Luanda. Luanda had elbowed her way in first—there was a trail of water behind her—and Lucy was fast on her heels.

"I'm not sure I like this," Ruth muttered, but either her curiosity got the best of her or she thought her bat was inside, because she didn't hesitate to follow Lucy.

Bridget's attention was fixed on Remington. Her head was tilted up, and her mouth hung open. Her eyes darted from tattoo to muscle and back again. There was a lot of both. I figured she was battling her internal feminist voice, and she was probably coming out on the side that ogling men purely for their physical beauty was only fair play.

Remington, however, was distracted by other things. By the room. By me. He turned to me and opened his mouth, as if to say something, but as soon as I entered the room, the flipper interrupted.

"There you go," he announced. "All in. What do you think?"

But he didn't give us a chance to answer. The door closed behind me with a click that was a little on this side of ominous. The room filled with a red light, and the only sound was an annoying buzzing, like mosquitoes. We collectively held our breath, but the door didn't open again.

The room was plenty big for the six of us, but it was bare, like the inside of a soup can. The floor was cement, the walls metal, and the door looked like it could protect Fort Knox.

Remington stepped around me and jimmied the door, but it was locked down tight. He banged on it with his fists, but it didn't budge. After a moment Ruth ran at it, shoved Remington aside, and started to scream for everything she was worth.

"Open the goddamned door!" she yelled, her claustrophobia obviously kicking in. A couple of rollers flew out of her hair and beaned Luanda in the head. "Very funny, Rellik," Ruth hollered. "Open the door!"

If Rellik was playing a practical joke, he was taking his own sweet time with the punch line. Ruth calmed down long enough to put her ear against the door. But the only sound was the low-level buzzing.

"This is not happening," I said. Denial has always been my first line of defense. Unfortunately, my second line is chocolate, and there was none in the panic room. My third line is a lime margarita with extra salt, but I wasn't seeing any of them around, either.

Ruth threw her arms up, making her housedress rise to reveal her knobby knees. "Trapped!" she yelled. "Trapped like a rat on a ship!"

"I'm sensing negative energy," Luanda singsonged, stating the obvious.

"I'll show you negative energy, you man stealer," Lucy threatened.

"Really?" I asked Lucy. "You're going there now? When we're locked in a tin can?"

"Why are we locked in the panic room?" Bridget asked.

"Isn't it obvious, darlin'?" Lucy responded. "There's no way to get out."

"No, I mean, why would he do that? Why would he lock us up?"

Bridget had a point. Why would Rellik the flipper lock six people in a panic room in the basement of his remodel? What was the point? Even serial killers killed one at a time, didn't they?

"Maybe it's a mistake," Bridget said. "Maybe the door closed by accident, and he can't get it open. It's a panic room, after all. Maybe he can't get in. Maybe he's yelling on the other side, telling us he's getting help."

"Oh," Ruth said. Her body visibly relaxed, and our communal freak-out went down a few notches. Bridget made a lot of sense. Maybe it took a diehard atheist not to jump to conclusions. I sat down on the cold cement floor with my back up against the wall.

"I guess we'll be here awhile," I said.

"Call for help on your phone," Ruth told me. But I didn't have my phone. My phone was at the bottom of a canyon. Bridget's phone was dead in Grandma's kitchen, next to Lucy's phone, which she had left in her Birkin bag. Ruth was still in her housedress, and I doubted she even owned a cellphone. Our eyes shifted to Remington.

"Off duty," he said, and patted his naked, hard six-pack to show he was pocketless.

"How about you, witch lady?" Lucy asked Luanda. "You got a phone hiding in that getup?"

"I don't need phones," Luanda said. "I commune on a deeper level."

"We're at a pretty deep level now," Ruth said.

"I guess we'll have to be patient," said Bridget. She took a seat next to me, sitting cross-legged on the hard floor. She wore wool slacks and a cotton sweater with a stain on her chest. Coffee, by the looks of it. Big circles under her eyes were outlined in the red light.

My legs lay stretched out in front of me, a slip-on sneaker on one foot and the nylon boot on the other poking out of the bottom of Grandma's tracksuit. We weren't the most fashionable group. Except for Lucy, we looked like a group of homeless people or perhaps a circus troupe. It occurred to me that the other panic room was the well-dressed room.

"Do you think the other room has recliners and cable TV?" I asked Bridget.

"I don't know. My panic-room experience is limited."

"It would be typical to get trapped in the *Silence of the Lambs* room while the other group is lounging in the lap of luxury, free to come and go as they please," Ruth grumbled.

We let that thought hang in the air for a minute. "Trapped in the *Silence of the Lambs* room" didn't sound all that appealing, and, again, the mystery of just what was happening outside and why we were locked in weighed heavily on us. The mounting anxiety was palpable. It wasn't easy to be patient and even less easy to remain calm.

I caught Ruth eyeing the door. I hoped she wasn't going to charge it again. I didn't think her old bones could handle the impact another time. Remington took a step toward her, probably getting ready to contain her if she freaked out. I couldn't figure him out. He was as cool as a cucumber and barely uttered a word. Was he some James Bond type, ready with a plan to protect us all, or was he an overgrown dumb stud muffin who was too stupid to talk?

As if to answer, Bridget's stomach growled. "I didn't eat breakfast," she explained. "And I was up all night."

"Mavis has cupcakes," Lucy said.

"And cable TV," I added stupidly.

"Are you sure you don't have a phone?" Lucy asked Luanda.

"At least send out your psychic vibes and get some help," Ruth told her.

"That's not how psychic vibes work," Luanda said, and bit her nails. Ruth snorted and adjusted her housedress. "I sense a lot of negativity in this room," Luanda whined, working hard on chewing through the nail of her ring finger.

"Really? You sense negativity?" Lucy shrieked. "Because, darlin', I think it's time I told you a thing or two about negativity."

"Lucy, please," I said. "We need to save oxygen." The room had gotten distinctly warmer, and I began to pant ever so slightly. What if we died there in the basement, suffocating in the airtight room? Suffocation was a lousy way to die—better probably than Ebola, but still really, really lousy.

The panic room was working. I was panicking real well now.

"I want to be old," I told Bridget. "Like really old. Like *Guinness World Records* old."

"You say that now, but when it takes you an hour and a half to take a crap and you need a handful of pills to bend down and tie your shoes, you'll think different," Ruth said.

Lucy crossed her arms, like she was holding herself back, and she probably was. Luanda took up all her attention. The fact that we were locked in a panic room didn't faze her at all.

"They probably called the fire department already. It shouldn't be much longer," Remington said, towering over us. His voice was deep, rich, and silky and floated through the room, touching us all. Maybe he was closer to James Bond than to a dumb stud muffin, I thought optimistically.

Despite his calm demeanor, Remington felt along the edges of the door, as if looking for a weakness in the structure, any way to get free.

"I'm sure the air is running out," I said.

"Maybe we can get more air to come out of that vent," Luanda said.

We followed Luanda's line of sight to a spot on the wall just under the high ceiling. Sure enough, there was a vent about a foot wide.

"Air!" I yelled, and jumped up, sending pain shooting from my foot through my body.

"I can't reach it," Remington said, stretching his hands toward the vent. "Would you climb up on my shoulders?" he asked me.

My eyes flashed to his shoulders: massive, muscly, and the color of hazelnut creamer. Yum. I broke out into a fit of giggles, which rose to a fever pitch and finally settled down to loud snorting.

"For the love of Pete," Ruth grumbled. "Get a grip on yourself, girl." She wagged her finger at Remington and demanded, "Hey, genius, why on earth did you pick danger-prone Daphne?"

Ruth had a point. I probably shouldn't have been his first choice, not with the nylon boot, but it delighted me to think of climbing all over Detective Cumberbatch, and for the moment I forgot that I was probably going to suffocate to death. Besides, there might be some real air through that vent, and I wanted to get my mouth as close to it as possible.

Remington crouched down in front of me. "All aboard," he said. I swallowed another fit of giggles and hitched myself onto his shoulders, wrapping my legs around his neck. He secured me, gripping my thighs, and stood up straight like he was carrying a small child, not a full-grown, corn-fed woman.

"What do you see?" he asked as I peered through the vent.

"Nothing. Dark." But there was definitely air. I gulped it greedily. At least we wouldn't die like that, but then my imagination went to all the other ways we could die. How long could we go without water? I wondered if Ruth would eat me.

"Can you hear anything?" he asked.

"No." But then I heard a distinct murmuring. I shushed our group and pressed my ear to the grate. Yep, there were voices on the other side.

"Hello!" I hollered into the vent. "Hello! Hello! We're trapped!"

The murmuring got louder, followed by a scraping sound, like something large was being moved across the floor.

"I knew they had furniture," I said.

"Ask when they're going to open the door," Ruth commanded.

"Tell them to call the fire department," Bridget told me.

"Tell them I'm getting calls from the other side," Luanda said, then rolled her eyes back and started to hum.

"Hello! You all right?" A voice came through the vent. It sounded just like Katharine Hepburn.

"I think Mrs. Arbuthnot is speaking," I told our group. "Get help! We're stuck in here!" I yelled into the vent.

"We're stuck, too!" Mrs. Arbuthnot yelled back. "No way out!"

"The flipper locked us in," a male voice shouted from the other side. I assumed he was one of the two buyers. "Rellik is crazy!"

"Call for help! Call for help!" Ruth cried. "What's wrong with people? Usually they're all over their cell-phones, can't live without them. It's beep this and beep that. I can't get people to stop with their goddamned cellphones in my shop, and now suddenly nobody has a phone? Nowadays you can do every-thing with a phone. You can go to college with a phone, you can give birth with a phone. Where the hell's all the phones?"

I was about to remind the group in the other room about their phones, when a loud noise came through the vent, followed by screams.

"Are you okay?" I asked, and was answered by more screaming. It went on like that for a good cou-ple of minutes. They screamed and screamed until finally they were silent again.

"I don't like the sound of that," Lucy said.

"Mrs. Arbuthnot?" I asked, but the voices were gone and in their place was a machine-like noise, as if they were driving a Volkswagen around in the other room.

"Can you see anything at all?" Remington asked.

I pressed my face up to the vent and squinted. I could make out a light on the other side, which seemed to dance and buckle.

"I think the light is getting brighter," I said, pressing my face harder against the grate. The mechanical, motor-like sound was getting louder, too. "I think I see something. I think it's a duck beak."

"A what?" Ruth asked.

I smashed my face as much I could against the vent. "Yeah, a duck beak," I said. The light kept getting brighter and the sound louder, until suddenly the light went out and it became completely dark in the vent.

"What the—" I said, and flinched backward, but it was too late. The duck's beak opened and threw up all over me, its heavy vomit spitting through the vent with remarkable force, covering my face and blinding me.

I screamed, gagging on the duck vomit and throwing myself off-balance. To his credit, Remington caught me before I fell. He grabbed my thighs in a viselike grip, but my butt slipped off his shoulders, leaving me to hang halfway down his back. I squirmed and shimmied until finally I got a firm hold on Remington. But now I was facing the other way, upside down, his face planted deep in my crotch.

"This would be embarrassing if I didn't have duck vomit on my face," I said.

"It's still embarrassing," Ruth noted.

"I don't think it's duck vomit," Bridget said.

I wiped my eyes as best I could with Grandma's jacket, and Remington let me down gently, cupping my buttocks with his hands and lifting me away from his face. The duck vomit—or whatever it was—was squirting out of the vent, spitting at regular intervals. Remington scooped some off my face and rolled it between his fingers.

"Plaster," he said.

"That crazy bastard is filling the panic room with plaster?" Ruth asked no one in particular.

"Are you sure it's not duck vomit?" I asked.

"I'm ready to leave now!" Luanda announced, and threw herself at the door with amazing force. The impact knocked her out, and she fell to the floor unconscious. I envied her. I would have loved to be unconscious.

Dots of plaster had settled on Luanda's face, making her look like she had a cheek full of white moles. I probably looked a lot worse. I was covered in the stuff, and it was starting to set.

"I'm thinking this isn't good," I said.

# Chapter 7

◆ ♥ ◆

*Communication is a funny thing, dolly. Sometimes somebody talks to you in English, but you can't understand a word. That's because not everybody is such a hot communicator. What am I saying? Most people are not such hot communicators. For matches, this can work to their advantage. Sometimes, communication is overrated and love grows better when people are off-balance and a little lost. Other times, though, bubeleh, it's a nightmare. A tragedy. Without good communication, a match can feel lost, trapped even. They might be stuck saying, "Why is this happening to me? How can I ever get out of this?" Here's the honest-to-God truth, dolly: Sometimes there is no answer. Sometimes they really are trapped. So it's up to you to get them untrapped. Get them out. Communicate.*

**Lesson 89,**
**Matchmaking Advice from Your Grandma Zelda**

THERE WAS a lot of panicking. Everyone was making noise at the same time, except for Luanda, who was either still knocked out or had just decided it was better to feign sleep. Remington was also silent, which wasn't new for him. Still, I would have liked him to snap into action. I mean, what would Captain Kirk do?

Without any idea how to extricate us from what looked like a really horrible death, we concentrated on our fate and the crazy psycho killer Michael Rellik: How evil and crazy must he be to lock us up and plaster us to death? What had we ever done to him? From the sound of it, he had already finished off the group in the other room. What kind of monster murders cupcake bakers?

What kind of monster murders a matchmaker?

I grabbed one of Remington's large arms. "Did you hear that?" I asked him.

"What?"

"Somebody shrieked."

"I'm pretty sure that was you," he said.

"No it wasn't."

"I'm pretty sure it was."

Without comment, he raised his hands to my chest and grazed his knuckles over my breasts. Despite my fear of dying, my body reacted to his touch. I gasped, and my insides melted like chocolate left out in the sun.

"Is this the moment for that?" I asked him, but my body was telling me it was. It didn't mind at all that I was getting felt up minutes before I was going to die, stuck in a dungeon with my two best friends, a loony psychic woman, and Ruth.

Remington arched an eyebrow and moved his hands to the center of my chest. He pinched the metal tag of my jacket's zipper and pulled it slowly down.

What was he thinking? Did he honestly believe I would get naked right there in the panic room? Inside my mind, I was protesting heartily, but outside, I allowed him to unzip me and remove my jacket, leaving me in my T-shirt.

"Hop back on," he told me, holding my jacket in his hand.

"Excuse me?"

"On my shoulders. Here we go." He knelt down and maneuvered me onto him. "Stick it in the grate," he instructed, handing back the jacket.

"Oh," I said, trying not to sound disappointed.

I weaved Grandma's velour tracksuit jacket in and out of the slats in the grate, jamming up the plaster perfectly. In fact, the plaster helped to seal the vent shut.

Remington put me down, and Bridget, Lucy, Ruth, and I embraced in a jumping-up-and-down group hug.

"You're a genius, nerdy fella," Ruth told Remington, but he was busy inspecting the door again. In a flash of realization, I understood why he wasn't celebrating. We had effectively shut off our only supply of oxygen.

I approached him, making a show of taking lint off my shirt. "On a horror-movie scale, are we leaning toward *Saw III* or are we merely at a *Scanners* level?" I whispered.

He stopped studying the door and faced me. His dreamy, big dark eyes oozed into my reproductive system and started it up like a crank on an old-timey car. He was beautiful in the most traditional he-man definition of the word. But he was serious. Deadly serious, with an emphasis on the deadly. I gulped.

"So I should start sawing?" I asked him. My throat

had gotten thick, and there was a distinct burning in the back of my eyes.

"I was a goner, anyway," I continued. "Gangrene. I forgot to take my antibiotics this morning. Gangrene is a bad way to go." My voice hitched. I didn't want to go. I had just arrived. I wanted years more. I wanted to grow old and decrepit and have others take care of me.

"You don't say much," I noted. "Kind of the strong, silent type. Me, too." Remington arched an eyebrow. "Talking is overrated," I said. "I mean, unless you have something to say, like how we're going to get out of here." He looked deep into my eyes—like, Mariana Trench deep—and the meaning was clear. "There is no way out of here, is there?" I asked. A tear rolled down my cheek, and my nose filled. He wiped the tear off with his thumb and let it rest on my face a moment.

"My skin is usually softer," I said. "The plaster has hardened." His hand dropped to his side. "You have a lot of muscles."

Remington's mouth turned up in a smile. "I fight."

"Excuse me?"

"UFC," he said.

"Huh?"

"Mixed martial arts," he explained. "Cage fighting. I used to do it full-time, but now I do it on the side. Being a cop is safer."

"We're kind of in a cage now," I noted.

As if on cue, we looked around at our panic room. Dark, with a red tinge. The air was fetid, and the temperature was rising. Sweat rolled down my back.

I was tired. Sleepy. Luanda was snoring loudly, curled up in the fetal position on the floor.

"This is crazy," I said. "Grandma should know I'm in trouble. It's that woman's fault." I pointed at the sleeping Luanda. "She's jamming her signals!"

Luanda snorted. "What the fuck happened!" she shrieked, and sat up.

"The detective saved us from being entombed in plaster, but now we're going to suffocate to death," Lucy explained to her.

"Unless Rellik decides to kill us himself, like he did to the people in the other room," Bridget pointed out.

Luanda stood and straightened out her skirts. The feathers in her hair had fallen forward, making her look like a bird. A bird from the sixties. She was either brewing a major freak-out or she was on the verge of a stroke. Her right eye drooped, and there was a distinct spasm in her nostril.

She chest-bumped Remington. "What the hell are you going to do, copper?" She growled, "What kind of crap luck do we have, getting the only incompetent loser cop stuck in this tin can with us?"

I thought Luanda was being unfair. The Cannes police force was made up almost exclusively of incompetent loser cops, and none of them looked nearly as good without a shirt as Detective Remington Cumberbatch.

"Professor McGonagall has a point," Ruth said. "You're supposed to protect and serve. Not a lot of protecting and serving going on."

Remington remained stoic in the face of so much criticism and inevitable death. He exuded quiet strength, and despite the attacks on his competency,

I was glad he was there. I felt safer. He had already saved us from a plaster-induced death, and I was holding out hope he could get us out of there alive.

"Is this a bad time to say I have to pee?" I asked. I shouldn't have gone for that third cup of coffee this morning. I was pretty close to having an accident. I was squeezing my knees together, but it wasn't helping.

"What kind of cop goes out without a gun?" Luanda asked him. "Or a phone? Any cop would be better than you. I wish any other cop in the universe were locked up in here with us."

The red light went out, plunging us into darkness. We froze, waiting for the light to come back on, but it stayed pitch-black.

"Do you hear that?" Bridget asked.

"Like a rattlesnake is at the door," Lucy said.

"No," Ruth said. "It sounds like a teakettle, an angry one. Like it's going to blow."

"Flash bomb," Remington said, and pushed us to the other side of the room, gathering us in his long arms. Just as we reached the wall, bright light flooded the room, forcing me to shield my eyes. A loud boom went off at the door, and it creaked open.

Remington charged the door but was taken down when a man was hurled into the room. Remington stumbled backward under the weight of the body but quickly caught his balance, tossing the man aside like he was a rag doll.

But he wasn't quick enough. The door clicked closed, and despite Remington's furious attempts to open it, we were once again locked in, the lights turned off, leaving only the dim, buzzing red glow.

The man lay facedown on the floor near a puddle of wet plaster. He wasn't moving, and I hoped he wasn't dead. Not only because I would need a whole lot of Xanax if I were trapped in a small room with a corpse, but also because I recognized the cut of his suit.

Remington rolled the man over with his foot. He stared for a moment. Then he exhaled slowly and ran his fingers through his Bruno Mars hair. "Hello, boss," he said.


FOR THE first time in what seemed like forever, our attention was shifted beyond our imprisonment. Police chief Spencer Bolton lay unconscious on the panic room floor.

I held my breath, willing him to show a sign of life. My lower lip threatened to wobble, and my eyes got watery. It was unthinkable that Spencer could be dead. He was way too obnoxious to die. I had just gotten used to him—almost—and if he didn't wake up soon and say something offensive, I was going to lose it.

"Goddamned crazy Rellik is working his way through town," Ruth said. "He's dragged in half of Cannes already. At this rate I could open Tea Time in here."

"I wish he'd thought to kidnap Bird Gonzalez," Lucy added. "At least then I could get a shampoo and set while we're stuck here."

"I wonder if his psychosis was triggered by being raised in a sexist, misogynistic society," Bridget said.

Spencer moaned.

"I think he needs mouth-to-mouth," Luanda said. "I'll do it." She dropped to her knees and leaned down.

"I think he's breathing," I told her.

"The cosmos is telling me he needs the kiss of life," Luanda said.

"Is that what they're calling it these days? The cosmos?" Ruth asked. "Lady, your cosmos is way too old and loony for that boy."

"I think we need to give him some air," Remington said, gently lifting Luanda off Spencer and moving her to the side.

Spencer stirred, opened one eye, took stock of his condition, and jumped up into his best Rocky stance.

"Chill, boss," Remington said. "You're among friends."

Spencer's eyes darted from person to person until they landed on me. "Are you kidding me?" he asked in my direction.

I put my hands on my hips and scowled at him. "What are *you* doing here?" I asked, as if he were crashing our party.

"What am I doing *where*? What are *you* doing here?"

"She's trapped in this panic room with the rest of us, darlin'," Lucy said.

"Panic room?" He directed the question to Remington.

Remington caught Spencer up on our situation, his demeanor never changing from his usual calm and cool. His voice was all business, unemotional, and yummy smooth jazz.

Spencer rubbed his head. "Rellik got me, too. I was

searching the house, and suddenly I was hit from be-hind. Never saw him."

"Why were you searching the house?" I asked.

"Your grandmother, Pinkie. She said a phony matchmaker was jamming her signals, but I should take a look at the flipper's house. He must have seen me coming. He took me by surprise." He wiped his cheek with the back of his hand. "What's this white stuff on my face?"

"What do you mean, 'phony matchmaker'?" Lu-anda asked.

"You got knocked out by the bad guy again?" I asked him.

"What's your point?" He had crossed his arms in front of him.

"It's just that . . . Never mind," I said.

"No, Pinkie, what were you going to say?"

"It's just that, well, what good are you? Every time there's a psycho killer about to kill me, you get your head bashed in."

Spencer's face turned bright red, almost disappearing in the red light. "That's only happened twice!" he shouted, holding up two fingers to illustrate his point.

"The two times you were there when a psycho killer was about to kill me!"

Lucy grabbed my arm and tugged me back toward her. "Darlin', he's about to explode," she said. "You better take cover."

"Did you at least keep your gun?" I asked from behind Lucy.

Spencer patted his body. His eyes grew enormous, like high beams on a country road.

"All right!" Spencer announced after a minute. "Let's get out of here."

"The door is sealed shut, boss," Remington told him.

"I figured as much, Tiny," Spencer said.

The two men huddled in talk of escape. Meanwhile, Luanda began to moan and speak in tongues.

"Just what we were missing," Ruth complained. "Stop sucking up the oxygen, Barbra Streisand."

"I'm communing," Luanda said.

"You're sucking air, you mean," Ruth said.

"I think we should remain calm," Bridget said. "We are all sisters in the cause and should support one another."

"I see cancer in your future," Luanda told Bridget.

Lucy gasped. "Don't talk to my friend that way. Take that back, you crazy fraud."

"I am not a crazy fraud. I am Luanda Laughing-Eagle."

"See, that's very interesting," Bridget said, trying to calm the situation. "What tribe are you from?"

Luanda blinked. "What tribe? I am my own tribe."

"First lucid thing you've said," Ruth muttered.

"I see gum disease in your future, old hag," Luanda told Ruth.

"Ha!" Ruth shouted, and wagged her finger in Luanda's face. "Shows what you know. I already have it! I bet you didn't see that coming, psycho lady."

Things went pretty fast after that. Luanda and Ruth charged each other like rhinos. There was a lot of shuffling and a few lady grunts as they locked in combat, which looked remarkably like an episode of *Dancing with the Stars*.

"Locked up by a crazy killer in a dark panic room, with no oxygen or means of escape, and an octogenarian and a phony witch lady decide to rumble," Lucy said. "I never want to leave this town. Cannes is a village on happy juice. LSD. It's *The Wizard of Oz* on shrooms."

"I'm not a proponent of woman-on-woman violence, but I'm secretly hoping Luanda gets owned and Ruth beats her ass," Bridget said to me.

I was, too, but I was also worried that they were using up the last of our air. I was also worried that Ruth was going to have a cataclysmic stroke and I was going to get an elbow in the eye from Luanda, who was swinging her arms with wild abandon. She hadn't made contact with Ruth yet, but, with my luck, she was going to find my skull sooner or later.

"Are you kidding me?" Spencer pulled them apart and held them at arm's length from each other. Somehow a feather had come out of Luanda's hair and landed in Ruth's mouth. Ruth spit it out as she huffed and puffed from the exertion of her fight. Luanda was breathing easier, but she was sweating so much that her hair was dripping, and her clothes stuck to her in thick, wet layers.

"We're getting the hell out of here," Spencer said. "Everybody in the center of the room."

We moved together into a tight circle.

"The door is locked, handsome," Lucy told Spencer.

"I think outside the box." Spencer removed his jacket and gave it to me to hold. "Just for a minute, Pinkie. Don't burn it or sneeze on it. You think you can handle that?"

"So funny I forgot to laugh," I said.

Spencer rolled up his shirtsleeves and proceeded to throw his body at the walls. The racket was earsplitting as he pounded the metal with his shoulder. Who did he think he was, Superman? I was about to laugh at him for trying to break through the walls of a super-high-tech modern panic room, when the wall buckled and dented under the pressure of his battering-ram strength.

He took a step back and surveyed the damage. "That's what I thought. They focus the security on the obvious, on the door. They never think outside of the box."

Then it was just a matter of time. Spencer and Remington put everything they had into mangling the wall. With the possibility of escape becoming a reality, I breathed easier and even had to pee less.

"If they weren't saving us, I would be pretty PO'd that they were having the females stand back while they saved us," Bridget said.

"It is rather sexist in a hot, stimulating way," Lucy commented.

Watching Remington and Spencer literally rip apart the wall with their bare hands was indeed stimulating. They grunted and their muscles rippled as they worked. Shirtless Remington was a sight to see. Spencer wasn't half bad, either. I couldn't look away. I bit my lower lip and caught myself panting.

"This is the most foreplay I've gotten in thirty-five years," Ruth said.

The noise was deafening. Each manipulation of the metal wall sounded like a car crash. After about twenty minutes, a sliver of bright light broke through the gap in the wall, along with a rush of fresh air.

Spencer ordered us to get out of the way. Remington peeled back a section of the wall, and Spencer climbed through. I held my breath.

The sound of voices floated through the opening. Remington motioned us to stay back, but we moved forward as a group, trying to see or hear what was going on.

I could make out Spencer's voice. He was using his authoritarian cop voice, but I couldn't hear the words. Was he negotiating with Rellik? Had he found the bodies of the poor people next door? I thought of Mavis and Felicia and their lovely shop, of how kind they were to me, even though Felicia wanted me to read.

I sniffed and wiped my eyes. With my fear of dying melting away, my focus turned to the murder of the innocent people next door. The cruelty and injustice was too much to bear. How could one man feel that he had the power to extinguish lives on a whim? How could he be so evil?

My nose ran, and I wiped it with the back of my hand. Bridget put her arm around my waist and leaned her head against my shoulder. I heard her hiccup and swallow back tears. Our grief was contagious. Soon Lucy was sniffling and wiping her eyes, too.

"I hope the cop tears him to pieces," Ruth said.

But there was no evidence of Spencer tearing anyone to pieces. In fact, there was no evidence of him at all. His voice had receded and then grown quiet.

"Detective Cumberbatch," I said. My voice came out like a little girl's, meek and small, but it spurred him on. With all his strength, Remington pulled at the metal wall. It gave way by inches, making a horrible sound.

That's how it turned out that the only one who could save us was busy on the other side of the room when the door finally opened.

# Chapter 8

◆ ♥ ◆

*People keep looking up my sleeves, dolly, like I'm Penn & Teller or something. They want to know what magic I'm weaving, what tricks I'm plotting. But with me, what you see is what you get. The only thing up my sleeve is a used Kleenex. But that's not how it is with other people. Nope. With other people, there's a whole hell of a lot up their sleeves. You get what I'm saying? Here's a clue: Nothing is as it seems. No, I don't mean all the time. Ninety-nine percent of the time, everything is exactly as it seems. He's what he seems; she's what she seems; the match is exactly what it seems. But that pesky one percent, dolly—you should keep the door open for the possibility that nothing is as it seems. Remember, keep the door open.*

**Lesson 95,
Matchmaking Advice from Your Grandma Zelda**

WHILE REMINGTON focused on his task, the door opened with a bump and a clang. We screamed in unison—all except for Remington, who was up to his shoulders in mangled wall.

"Throw something at him!" Bridget shouted.

"What? We don't have anything," I said.

Ruth pushed Luanda toward the door. "Give me a

hand," Ruth told me. "Let's toss Luanda. There's a good heft to her. She'll knock him out, for sure."

Luanda struggled against her, but it wasn't necessary. Luckily, we didn't have to javelin-toss Luanda at whoever was coming through the door.

"All right, folks. The cavalry has arrived. Rellik skedaddled. Everybody out."

Spencer stood at the door, his shirt torn, his hair mussed, his pants smeared with plaster, and a big self-important grin on his face.

Ruth was the first one out, and we followed quickly behind her. I breathed in big, greedy gulps of air when I stepped out of the panic room and then gasped in shock when I saw who else was in the basement with us.

Mavis, Felicia, Mrs. Arbuthnot, and the two men from the other panic room were alive and well and staring at us like we, not they, were the ghosts.

"Holy hell, they've risen from the dead," Ruth said.

"We were never dead," Mrs. Arbuthnot announced.

"I was beaten up," the man in the suit said. His face was bruised, his nose bloody, and he was working on a big shiner.

"And we were tied up," Felicia added.

They were dirty but not nearly as much of a mess as we were.

"Did you have furniture?" I asked.

"Two recliners and a few folding chairs," the man in the suit replied. "Why do you ask?"

"I knew they had recliners," I told Remington. "We picked the wrong room."

I wasn't totally correct about choosing the wrong room. Sure, we were locked in without furniture, almost plastered and suffocated to death, and we looked horrible—sweaty, plastery, and badly dressed—but the folks in the other panic room went through real terror.

"He told us we were going to die," Mrs. Arbuthnot told us. "He kept coming in and out; each time was worse."

"He beat me up," the man in the suit repeated.

"He had a gun," the other man added.

"You look familiar," I said to him.

"Yes, you do," Lucy agreed. "Where have we met before?"

"I broke into her car for her," he said, pointing at me.

"Uncle Harry's security guard!" Lucy said, remembering. "Hi, I'm Lucy Smythe." She put her hand out, and he shook it with his left hand. Lefty. I flashed back to the couple of days I had worked at Lefty's Five and Dime in Fresno. They had every gadget and gizmo for left-handers. I couldn't use a thing in the store.

"Kirk Shields," he introduced himself.

"And I'm Frank Richmond, and I need medical care. I was beaten," the man in the suit informed us yet again.

As if Frank Richmond had magical powers to summon medical care, the sound of sirens reached us.

"Oh, good, an ambulance," he said.

"Actually, an ambulance, fire truck, three police cars, and a police cruiser," I clarified. I had a lot of experience with emergency services.

"I want to hug everyone, but my hugs are too

powerful. They can have a negative impact," Bridget said.

"You can risk it with me," I said. She hugged me, and Lucy joined in. I felt a wave of gratitude for my friends. We stood, supporting one another, as we trembled with the relief of being alive.

Spencer had cleared the house, finding no sign of Rellik. He escorted us upstairs, where the paramedics checked us out. Spencer had his police investigate the panic rooms, which were now the scene of the crime.

There were murmurings of sending us all to the hospital to get checked, but I refused to go. Besides anxiety, a bursting bladder, and plaster on my face, chest, arms, and in my hair, I was fine.

Once I refused to go, the rest of the group followed me like revolutionaries from a scene in *Les Misérables*. Even Frank Richmond refused to go to the hospital, accepting only the paramedics' care.

Our group of eleven filed into the paddy wagon to go to the police station. I was last in line, behind Bridget, who had decided to brave disaster and hug everyone, after all.

"How about you, Spencer?" I asked, before I climbed into the van. "He cracked your head pretty good. You don't want another episode like last time."

"Why? Are you planning on giving me another visit?"

"I'm covered in plaster," I said.

"Is that what this is?" he asked, flecking a bit of dried plaster off my cheek.

"What did you think it was?" I asked.

"Pinkie, with you the list is so long."

He was right. In the past few months I had fallen into just about every gross substance known to man. I was a walking disaster. "The list isn't long," I told him. "Take that back."

Spencer smirked his annoying smirk. "Get in the van, Pinkie." He put his hand out. I slipped my hand into his, and he guided me into the van. There was the usual electric current I felt when I was in close contact with Spencer, but this time there was something extra. I caught his eyes, and I knew he felt it, too.

"Uh," I said.

"The van," he croaked, tugging me up into the back.

"Oh, I forgot, I have to pee," I announced, but it was too late. Spencer had slammed the doors shut, and the van started toward the police station.

THEY TOOK our statements in batches. Spencer, Remington, and Officer James started with Mavis, Felicia, and Mrs. Arbuthnot, questioning them in separate rooms. Bridget, Lucy, and I made ourselves comfortable in the waiting room.

Cannes police headquarters was a new, modern building of glass and marble, with comfy armchairs in the waiting room. The desk sergeant, Fred Lytton, got us some water and made sure we were as comfortable as we could be in our sweaty, plastery clothes. I had suffered the worst of it. Grandma's velour tracksuit was torn and covered in dried white sludge. Her jacket, of course, was still wedged in the vent in the panic room. I was left in the pants and a white T-shirt.

"You sure look pretty today, Underwear Girl," Fred told me. "I mean, Ms. Burger," he added. My underpants were pretty famous among Cannes law enforcement, after an unfortunate accident back in August, but Fred had been warned against referring to it. "I like your hair like that."

"It's plaster, Fred," I said.

"It's pretty, like an angel."

My hair hung down in long, hard white strips. "Do you think Bird will have to cut the plaster out of my hair?" I asked Bridget. Last month Bird had chopped Bridget's hair into a short bob after most of it caught fire. It suited Bridget, but with my curly hair, I would look like Tinker Bell on acid.

"I think if you soak it long enough, it should come clean," she said.

Lucy adjusted her cashmere dress. She didn't have a hair out of place. It dawned on me I should aspire to be her. She was pretty, well dressed, rich, and had a bitchin' car. *Had* a bitchin' car.

Meanwhile, I had a car that was tied together with twine, I was wearing my grandmother's clothes, and my only paying job was to unmatch Uncle Harry, which in my line of work was the definition of epic fail.

"How's Julie, Fred?" Bridget asked. "Last time I saw her, she was coming out of the clinic with a bandage on her face." Fred and Julie were my first match, and they were perfect for each other in a mousy, scared-of-their-own-shadows kind of way. Julie was

Ruth's grandniece and a sometimes employee at Tea Time.

"Oh, that," he said. "She had a run-in with a seagull."

"Not a lot of seagulls up in these mountains," Bridget noted.

"Julie seems to attract them," Fred replied, as if he were listing just one of her marvelous attributes. "And bears," he added.

"Bears?" I asked.

"California brown bears, mostly," he said. "Although there was that one grizzly. That was a hairy pickle, I can tell you."

Ruth made her way toward us, yelling at various cops as she walked. Impatient. Her curlers hung at weird angles. We were a motley crew, and it was time to go home.

She took a seat next to Lucy. "Are there bears in Cannes?" I asked Ruth.

"Only around my niece. She's the pied piper of wildlife and broken teacups."

Luanda floated around the precinct, moaning and singing something that sounded like "Moo, moo, moo."

"She's communing with cows," Lucy said.

"She's in some kind of trance," Bridget said.

"She's bat-shit crazy," Ruth said.

"Stop tickling me under the chin with your feathers, lady!" one of the officers yelled, and swatted her away.

"I never did get my Slugger from that house," Ruth complained. "It sure would come in handy."

"It sure would," Lucy agreed.

Luanda did a couple of pirouettes and arrived at the front desk. "I see love in your future," she told Fred.

"You do?" he asked.

Warning bells went off in my head. "What are you doing?" I asked her.

"I know the perfect woman for you," Luanda continued, ignoring me. "She's been married a few times before, so she has a lot of practice."

"Hold on a second," I said, rushing the front desk.

"Ms. Burger matched me with Julie. She's my girlfriend, but she's never been married," Fred said, as if he was rethinking Julie's suitability.

"She's not the one for you," Luanda assured him.

"What?" I screeched.

"Just because a person says she's a matchmaker doesn't make her a matchmaker," she told Fred. Ouch. I checked to see if I was bleeding. Luanda had hit pretty close to the target with that comment.

Luanda riffled through her layers of clothing and took out a soggy business card. "Take this," she told Fred. "I'm having a meeting tomorrow night at seven. I'm doing a group matchmaking session. I'm a believer in bulk."

Fred took the card and studied it. My mouth had dropped open, and I couldn't get it closed. Luanda floated away to "moo, moo, moo" in the processing room.

"Gladie looks like Marie Antoinette just before the blade came down," Ruth said. "Quick, say, 'Let them eat cake.'"

Bridget wrapped her arm around my shoulder. "Are you okay?" she asked me. "Don't listen to her. You made a great match for Fred—I mean, if I believed in the archaic, misogynistic, trade-your-daughter-for-a-goat tradition of courtship and marriage."

"I'll hit Luanda, if you want," Lucy offered. "I'm stronger than I look."

"Damn that missing bat," Ruth complained.

I'm not a violent woman, but I wouldn't have minded having Ruth's bat at that moment. I understood exactly how Grandma felt about Luanda. It wasn't only that she had moved into my territory and was messing with my matches and hard work, but I worried that she would screw up Fred and Julie and rob them of a lifetime of love, which in my heart of hearts I was sure they would live with each other.

The air changed suddenly, like the atoms had rearranged themselves and transformed the normal police-station air into a cloud of liquid heat.

"You ready?" Remington had appeared at my side, his voice deep and soft, like a really light and fluffy molten lava cake. I licked my lips and breathed in his musk. He had changed into a tight Cannes police T-shirt, which stretched over his muscles.

"Ready?" I breathed.

"I'm going to take your statement."

"Oh," I said. I took a step toward him and tripped over my feet, falling forward into his arms. He held me close a little longer than necessary.

"Are you kidding me?" Spencer had popped his head between us. "You don't waste any time, Pinkie. Making the rounds?"

I pushed away from Remington. "Look who's talking."

Spencer tugged at my arm. "Let's go. I'm taking your statement."

"I've got this, boss," Remington said, putting his hand on Spencer's.

I could hear Spencer's blood pressure rise. I wanted to take a step out of the blast zone, but I was wedged between them. I held my breath. Remington was bigger and stronger than Spencer, but Spencer was pretty big and strong. And he was angry. Spencer was good at angry. Remington nodded and took a step back.

"You can take *my* statement, Hercules," Ruth told Remington. "Not that anybody asked or anybody cares. I mean, what could an old lady in rollers know, huh? Am I right? Are you even listening to me, or is the voice of a woman without viable eggs out of your range of hearing?"

WE WERE there for hours. Spencer wanted to know how I knew Rellik and how I had managed to get locked in the panic room. I asked him the same thing. It was unclear why a house flipper would entrap eleven innocent people—twelve, if you counted Spencer.

Had he flipped more than a house—like, his lid? Had he been planning on killing us in terrible ways, only to be thwarted by my grandmother's jacket, Spencer's appearance, and our escape? Was he now wandering the town, drooling from the mouth and searching for new victims?

We took the paddy wagon back to Grandma's house. Ruth got dibs on the shower first, which gave me time to strategize with Lucy. We had decided to raid Luanda's the next night. I wanted to get Luanda off Uncle Harry's back and stick around to make sure she didn't mess with Fred.

I wasn't exactly sure how I was going to get Luanda to unmatch Uncle Harry, but she had put a burr under my saddle, and I was ready to buck or kick her in the head or something else horsey. She made me mad.

"And prove that she's a fraud," Grandma reminded me. "Expose her for what she really is before she does permanent damage."

Grandma had only Luanda on her brain. The fact that we had all been kidnapped and almost killed didn't seem to faze her.

"I'm gifted in matters of love, not death, dolly. And that fake woman has got my love vibes all screwy."

I sighed. My love vibes had already been screwy, and it was doubtful I would ever get them straight, despite Grandma's assertions that I had "the gift." Love vibes aside, I was getting a reputation for my death vibes. Thank goodness nobody had died in the panic rooms, or my reputation would have been sealed.

Bridget and Lucy picked up their purses and, after Bridget hugged us, I saw them out. I made sure to double-bolt the door and turned in time to see Ruth descending the stairs with a gun in her hand.

"Really?" I asked.

"I refuse to be a sitting duck," she said.

"Is that loaded?"

"No. When the psycho killer comes to finish off what he started, I plan on throwing this at him. Of course it's loaded, genius!"

I threw my hands up. Ruth was eighty-five years

old, with slow reflexes and limited vision, not to mention arthritis, and I'd heard at least three of her joints had serial numbers. Still, she was in better shape than me and she probably had learned sharpshooting from Patton himself.

"Great, Ruth, just please keep it away from Grandma. I don't want her shooting herself by accident."

Ruth snorted. "If she's all-seeing, she shouldn't have any accidents."

"You win."

I was filthy. Beyond filthy. Besides my plastered hair, I could only partially open my right eye, and I was picking up a distinct odor, which had to be coming from me, since the Cannes dump had been closed three years ago.

Even though there was a 50 percent chance that Ruth would shoot me in the back, I climbed the stairs to my bathroom. From the look of my filthy nylon boot and the fact that I hadn't taken my antibiotics or changed the bandage on my foot, I had an 80 percent chance of gangrene, and I needed to get clean on the double.

I SOAKED in the shower, as Bridget had suggested, but it took half a bottle of conditioner to get the last of the plaster out of my hair. Finally clean and dressed in a cotton nightgown, I hobbled out of the bathroom and into my bedroom.

I was only half surprised to see Spencer sitting on my bed.

"Don't you like your house?" I asked. Spencer had

turned up in my bedroom on more than one occasion in the past couple of months, each time uninvited.

"There's a lunatic out there, Pinkie. I'm just checking up on you."

"I'm not worried about Rellik," I said, and was surprised that I was telling the truth. For some reason, I didn't think I had anything more to fear from the flipper. Perhaps he had run off to some other town. In any case, I figured I had been a hapless victim and not a specific target.

"Your foot's not looking that great," Spencer noted.

"I was afraid to change the bandage. I was afraid to look underneath it."

Spencer patted the bed next to him. "Give it here."

I sat on the bed and lifted my foot onto his lap. "Don't hurt me," I said.

"You mean, be gentle with you?" He smirked.

"You never change. How's your head?"

"The paramedics said I would live. Bandages?"

I handed him the package the hospital had given me.

"I never noticed how big your feet are, Pinkie." He caressed my toes, making them curl. I tried not to squirm, but my body wouldn't comply.

"They're normal, woman-sized feet."

"Hmm . . ." he said, like I had told him I'd flown into town on an ostrich.

Spencer gently unwrapped my foot. He placed the soggy bandages on my nightstand and inspected my injury. "Holy shit."

"What? What? Is it gangrene? Is it black and lifeless? Are there worms growing out of it?" I fell backward on the bed and covered my eyes with my hands. "I knew it. I knew it. I didn't take the antibiotics, and now I'm going to die. Rellik killed me!"

"Nowadays they just cut off your leg for gangrene. It doesn't kill you," Spencer said.

"Oh, my God! They're going to cut off my leg? But that's going to hurt."

"They're not going to cut off your leg. You're fine, no gangrene."

I bolted upright. My foot was gross, with crusty blood on my sole. "Are you sure? Then why did you say 'holy shit'?"

Spencer sprayed my foot with a solution and began to dress it in clean bandages. "It was just that without the bandages your foot looked really big. What are you, a size twelve?"

I punched him in the arm. He was solid as a moose. "I'm a nine and a half," I lied. I'm a size ten, but Spencer was so annoying.

"There you go, Cinderella." Spencer finished wrapping my foot and tucked me into bed. He ran downstairs and came back a few minutes later with my medicine, a salami sandwich, and a root beer.

I took a bite of the sandwich, and Spencer popped open the root beer. He took a swig and put the can down on my nightstand.

"You're a lot quieter than usual," I said. "Why are you here?"

"What are your intentions with Cumberbatch?"

"Excuse me?"

"The new detective, the probie, Cumberbatch."

"I understood that part. It's the intentions part I'm fuzzy on."

Spencer scooted closer to me. "So you're not going with him to the Apple Days Swingathon tomorrow night?"

"The what?"

Spencer exhaled. "That lying sack of shit."

It thrilled me to no end that Remington was lying to Spencer about taking me to the Apple Days Swingathon, whatever that was. With Holden gone and Spencer off women, I could use a little flirtation. But I was tired and injured and probably forever traumatized by my kidnapping.

I yawned. "I think I'm ready to go to sleep now. Good night, Spencer." I nudged him with my leg, and he got off the bed. "Thank you for saving me, by the way."

"Cumberbatch couldn't save you," he reminded me.

"Yeah, but he has a killer body."

"I have a killer body, Pinkie." It was true. Spencer had a body that men would kill to have and women would kill to be under.

"Not as killer as Remington's," I said, and buried myself deeper in the covers, my eyes shut, halfway to REM sleep. I thought I heard Spencer grind his teeth. "Be careful when you leave. Ruth is armed," I told him.

"She's what?"

But I was too far gone to answer. And I would need my rest. My life was about to get interesting.

# Chapter 9

✦ ♥ ✦

*"He's not my type." Have you heard this before? These days, every nebbish from here to Albuquerque has got a type. And the types are always wackadoodle. Blondes, brunettes, noses, hips, boobies, lips. Dolly, types read like a shopping list at the plastic surgeon's office. When I hear "type," I shut down and shut them up. Tell your matches enough already with the types. Types change. Lists change. Go with the flow; open yourself up; love is forever. Hair color is for four to six weeks.*

**Lesson 42,**
**Matchmaking Advice from Your Grandma Zelda**

**THE NEXT** morning, Grandma's kitchen was packed with people. The Single No More class was canceled because Grandma's clients had jumped ship to Luanda, but life still had to go on. For my grandmother, that meant a permanent.

Hairdresser Bird Gonzalez made a house call to Grandma every Monday, but today was Wednesday.

"Sorry about the wait, Zelda," Bird told her as she rolled her hair into tight curls. "All the Apple Days events have got me backlogged. It's a relief being away from the salon, I can tell you. It's been nonstop. I've got carpal tunnel in my scissors hand."

Bird had brought the pedicurist, who was going at Grandma's feet with a cheese grater. Meryl, the blue-haired librarian, who usually delivered books to Grandma, was sipping a cup of coffee, and Grandma's friend Sister Cyril was sitting next to her, slicing off a piece of cake.

"Hi, Gladie," Sister Cyril greeted me. "You want a piece of apple crumb coffee cake? It's heavenly."

"I got it at Cup O'Cake," Meryl said. "The shop was standing room only. Half the town was pretending to buy pastries, but they were really there to get the four-one-one on the whole kidnapping thing. It was like a Who concert. I couldn't get near Mavis or Felicia, but I figured I could get the lowdown from Zelda."

"The fake psychic has got my radar all wonky," Grandma told her.

I took a seat and poured myself a cup of coffee. "I was kidnapped, too, Meryl."

"I heard you stepped on a nail." She glanced down at my nylon boot.

"That was before I got kidnapped," I mumbled into my coffee cup.

"There you go, Zelda." Bird stepped back from Grandma's head. "That needs to sit awhile." She put a machine on the counter and opened the refrigerator.

"I thought it was just Mavis, Felicia, Catherine Arbuthnot, and two gentlemen," Meryl said. I caught her throwing a look to Sister Cyril, like *There goes crazy Gladie again.*

"I was in the other room," I sputtered. It was bad enough that I had been kidnapped and almost killed by a psycho maniac, but not being believed about it really got my hackles up.

Bird flipped a switch, and her machine roared to life. The noise was deafening. She shoved some green leaves down a hole in the top of the machine, and it got even noisier.

"Bird is juicing," Grandma yelled to me.

Bird turned around while continuing to cram vegetables and fruit into the grinder. "I've lost eight pounds in three days, and I feel great!" she announced, her voice rising above the din.

She turned off the machine and held up a glass of green liquid. "The best diet I've ever been on. Take a swig, Gladie. So much better than your coffee."

I doubted it was better than my coffee, and, besides, every diet Bird had put me on ended in failure. But eight pounds in three days was hard to resist. The juice smelled like vomit and looked worse.

"Your skin will thank me," Bird said. I had no idea what my skin had to do with it, but I felt that I had to taste the juice or hurt Bird's feelings. She held it out, a smile plastered on her face.

All eyes were on me. Even the pedicurist took a break from Grandma's heels to look my way. I accepted the glass from Bird and sipped at it. It tasted like pond scum with a touch of tree sap. I had a flashback to my month as a technician at a wastewater-treatment plant in Nevada.

I swallowed and tried to suppress my gag reflex. I gave Bird the thumbs-up and returned the glass to her.

"Isn't it fabulous?" She beamed. "So clean. Makes you feel like you can run a marathon." It made me feel like I had the stomach flu. "You take that one," she said, handing me back the glass. "I'll whip up another for myself."

I stared at the juice. How would I get it down? How could I pour it down the sink without Bird noticing?

"What other room?" Meryl asked me. "Did he try to kill you, too? Did he beat you up?"

"No, I was in the plaster room. He tried to plaster us." But death by plaster didn't impress Meryl.

"I heard he terrorized Mavis and the others," Meryl said. "He had a gun and a knife."

Once again, I was reminded that I had been in the wrong panic room. I was in the boring, unscary panic room, while the others saw all the action and were now getting all the respect.

Ruth entered the kitchen and took a seat. "And what else did he have, Meryl? A nuclear weapon? A tank? Rhythm?"

"Ruth, how nice to see you," Sister Cyril said. "It's a surprise to see you here."

Ruth snorted. "That's because I haven't been here since 1995."

My grandmother and I locked eyes. My father died in 1995. I didn't know that Ruth had gone to the funeral or come to the house for shivah, the traditional Jewish week of mourning where the house is open to all visitors. My father's death was the wound that wouldn't heal in our family. My grandmother hadn't left her house since then, and my mother . . . well, my mother had gone in the other direction.

"I wouldn't be here if Gladie hadn't demolished my shop."

"I wasn't driving the car!" I yelled, but nobody heard, because Bird was juicing again.

Ruth cut herself a slice of cake and took a bite. Bird turned off the machine and held up another glass of juice. I didn't know how she could get it down. I looked at mine. It was still there. I hadn't figured out how to dump it without Bird noticing.

"What the hell are you doing, Bird?" Ruth demanded.

"She's juicing," I said.

"Like Barry Bonds?" Ruth asked.

"Like a woman who wants to be healthy," Bird corrected, taking a long gulp.

"Blech," Ruth said. "How can you be healthy with half the Amazon jungle down your gullet?"

"What do you know about healthy living, you mean old lady?" Bird snapped. Since Ruth was old enough to have seen dinosaurs roam the earth and was obsessive about healthy teas and whole foods, I didn't think Bird had a valid argument. Still, she had gotten under Ruth's skin.

"You look ridiculous, like a rabbit on acid," Ruth shot back. "You're packing enough vegetation to grow a park in your stomach. You're going to have to hire a landscaping service for your colon. Your butt will need a lawn mower. You might as well hang a sign around your neck saying 'Turf for Sale.' Ridiculous people follow ridiculous fads."

"Now, now, let's not fight over puréed vegetables," Sister Cyril said.

Bird grabbed her scissors and waved it in Ruth's

direction. "It's not a fad. It's a movement. Ask Gladie. She's doing it."

"Uh," I said, with a mouthful of cake.

Ruth shook her head. "Zelda, your granddaughter doesn't have a lick of sense. How can you let her do this foolishness?"

Grandma seemed unconcerned with my foolishness. She had a foot up in the lap of the pedicurist, her hair in rollers and stinky solution, and her hand wrapped around a cup of coffee, all the while dressed in a fetching hot-pink crushed-velvet housecoat.

"I was kidnapped," I said.

"So was I," Ruth noted. "Half the town was kidnapped. What's your point?"

"Which room were you in, Ruth?" Meryl asked.

"She was in the room with the fraud," Grandma said. "That phony matchmaker woman, the enemy of love, who's now got her hooks into Harold Chow."

"That name sounds familiar," Meryl said.

"Harold Chow needs a special kind of woman. That phony baloney is playing with fire, and if something isn't done fast, there will be hell to pay tonight," Grandma continued. I understood she was talking to me, and I felt a rush of guilt.

"Lucy and I are going over there for the evening meeting," I told her.

"Take your car," Grandma said. "Don't let Lucy drive you."

Ruth snorted. "Now you tell her."

"Is it wise for her to be going out when her kidnapper is on the loose, Zelda?" Sister Cyril asked.

"I don't know about kidnappers. I know about love,

and that woman is reckless with my love matches," Grandma said.

"Besides," Meryl added, "he's long gone. I heard there were Michael Rellik sightings in San Diego. He's probably in Mexico by now."

Ruth took the last slice of cake and stood up. "I have to get back to Tea Time. I've got the insurance inspector coming, and I have to find out just how bad he's going to screw me in the ass."

"Well, that's descriptive," Sister Cyril said.

I stood up, as well. "I have to go, too. I have spider clothes."

"You sure do, dolly," Grandma agreed. "There's some nasty ones in there."

I walked out with Ruth, pretending I had forgotten about the juice. At the front door, Ruth stopped me. "Hey, little girl," she said, "I don't appreciate you ratting me out to the cop."

"What do you mean?"

"He reamed me a new one last night, said I shouldn't have a gun, especially around you. Something about you and Jonah. I don't know. Anyway, I've got it hid good so he'll never find it."

"He might be right about the gun, Ruth."

"My Slugger is gone forever. I went over there this morning, and there was no sign of it. I'm not going to be defenseless if that lunatic tries to kill me again."

"Fine," I said. "Just keep it away from Grandma. I don't want any accidents."

Ruth snorted. "If she's so all-seeing, she already knows where it's hidden, and she couldn't have any accidents." It occurred to me that if Ruth's gun was hidden away, it would be of little use to her if Michael

Rellik showed up to finish off what he had started. But I didn't want to draw her attention to the flaw in her plan, because I wasn't a big fan of guns. Ever since someone had tried to shoot me a couple of months ago, guns scared the bejeezus out of me.

"What do you mean, you went over there this morning? To the house across the street?" I shuddered. I never wanted to set foot in that house again. Besides, it was a crime scene now, covered in police tape. "What did it look like?"

"Beautiful," Ruth said. "If it had a bed, I would move in and get the hell out of this nuthouse. No sign of a crazed kidnapper except for the panic rooms, which were torn up pretty good, and the police traipsed dirt and broken glass around, but I could live with that." She squinted and leaned forward. "You okay, kid?"

"Yeah."

She tapped my chest. "Inside okay? You've gone through a lot lately. So have I, but I have a flask," she said, patting her pants pocket. "You want a swig?"

I wanted a swig more than I wanted to dance naked with Holden, more than I wanted to eat a waffle taco.

"No, I have to drive," I said.

"Bad things happen to good people all the time," Ruth continued. "Look at my tea shop."

"I'm okay, Ruth. Really."

But I wasn't sure I was okay. I had had enough of being kidnapped and almost killed. Matchmaking was dangerous work. I took a screwdriver from the utility drawer in the entranceway so I could start my car.

"See you later," I said. We left the house, and I

closed the front door behind us. Ruth jogged down the driveway and took a right toward her shop. At eighty-five, she was in better shape than I was. Perhaps I should have drunk the juice, I thought. But the thought was quickly followed by another one: My breakfast had been cut short, and Dave's Dry Cleaner's and Tackle Shop just happened to be close to Cup O'Cake.

I PROMISED Dave he could keep all the creepy crawlies he found in my suitcase, just as long as he didn't open it in front of me. He was delighted by the unexpected windfall. He assured me he would get my clothes back to me, spider free, tomorrow. Since I was in my Cleveland Browns sweatshirt again, I practically drooled at the thought of having something decent to wear. Overnight, the weather had turned from chilly to cold, and I couldn't wait to get into my shearling coat and turtlenecks.

That's why, despite my nylon boot, my rusted-out DIY car, and my trauma from being kidnapped and locked in a small room, I drove the short distance to Cup O'Cake in a great mood. I would have even sung to the radio, if it still worked.

I almost changed my mind, however, when I saw the crowds at Cup O'Cake. Meryl was right. It was packed to the rafters. Inside, folks surrounded Mavis and Felicia like looky-loos passing a car accident.

Mavis and Felicia were more than happy to regale their customers with the details of their incarceration. I heard "terror" and "beaten" as I walked through the door.

Felicia spotted me and waved me over. I pushed my way to the front of the group with little effort, since the other customers already had their food.

"So nice of you to come see how we're getting on," Mavis told me with a big smile.

"I was kidnapped, too," I reminded her. Sheesh, why couldn't anyone remember that?

"Of course you were," Mavis said. "And I have just the thing for you. It's in honor of Apple Days and our freedom from being kidnapped."

She handed me a pastry. "We're calling it the Attica apple explosion. Try it."

I took a bite. It was better than sex, although my memory was a little hazy where sex was concerned. The name said it all. The Attica apple explosion exploded in my mouth with an apple sweetness that would have made me riot if I had slightly more energy.

"Good, right?" Felicia asked me. I nodded, my mouth full of the explosion.

I ordered a latte and another explosion and sat at the table next to the fireplace. The armchair was comfortable, and I stretched my legs out in front of me.

"May we join you?" Mavis asked me, waking me from my stupor. I had been staring into the fire, finally allowing my mind and body to relax after a couple of horrible days. I don't know how long I had been sitting there like that, but when I took a sip of my latte, it had cooled.

Mavis and Felicia sat down next to me with plates of gourmet sandwiches and fruit salad. They clinked glasses of what looked like orange juice and took long sips. The crowd had thinned out, and Mavis and Felicia were taking a deserved lunch break.

I liked them. They exuded a vibe of positivity. Even after being kidnapped and almost murdered, they were happy and smiling.

"There's really nothing better than a ham-and-cornichon sandwich," Mavis said, taking a bite.

"How's your foot, Gladie?" Felicia asked.

"Better. I thought maybe you would be closed today."

"Nothing's better than normal to get back to normal," Mavis said.

I wondered if that were true. I didn't have a lot of normal in my life. My mother wasn't all that nurturing, unless you consider passing out at a parent–teacher conference in a cloud of booze fumes nurturing. And since I quit school when I was a teenager, I had been moving from one temporary job to another. Even my so-called job as matchmaker wasn't all that normal.

"It must be nice working here," I said. I had worked in a bakery for a week, but I got fired for eating the profits.

"Yes, much nicer than—" Mavis started, but she was interrupted by the tinkling sound of the door opening. Mrs. Arbuthnot entered, and their attention turned to her and getting her order.

I tried to focus on my coffee, but my thoughts went to my job and Luanda and how to get her to unmatch Uncle Harry and to back off Fred before she screwed up his match. Other than pounding her face with a frying pan, I had no idea how to get my point across. Besides, I didn't think Grandma owned a frying pan. She was a take-out queen, not Betty Crocker.

I took my screwdriver and headed for the door, but Felicia stopped me. "Gladie, your grandmother called. She said you need to head over to Lucy's. She said she found something."

With Grandma's ability to find me wherever I was, maybe I didn't need to replace my cellphone, I thought. I thanked Felicia, and she ran back to talk to Mrs. Arbuthnot. The old lady seemed less lemon-headed than usual. Maybe the kidnapping had mellowed her, or maybe she was traumatized, or maybe I was growing used to her. In any case, I was glad Felicia was distracted by her and hadn't remembered about the book she had given me. I snuck out before she could bring it up.


LUCY LIVED just outside the historic district, in a gorgeous white and glass house. Inside, it was the epitome of modern, with sparse, uncomfortable-looking furniture. I always felt underdressed when I visited.

Lucy opened her front door and was surprised to see me. "My grandmother said I needed to come over, that you found something," I explained.

"How did she—Never mind," Lucy said. "Come on in. Bridget is here."

I heard Bridget's phone ring as I climbed the stairs. "I know what you're doing!" she yelled. "No, that's not my *Fifty Shades* voice! No, I won't ride you until—Hey! Do you even realize you are objectifying women?"

I made it to the second floor to see Bridget sitting on a white couch, her cellphone against her ear, her fingers running through her bob haircut, and her big round glasses hanging off the end of her nose. Lucy ran over to her.

"Hang up, Bridget," Lucy urged her. Bridget stuck her finger up in the international "just a moment" gesture.

"I'm almost done," Bridget mouthed. "No, I will not do that to you," she continued on the phone. "Why? Because it's disgusting and most likely against the law. No, I won't do that, either. Let me tell you about Bella Abzug."

Lucy took the phone from her and clicked the OFF button.

"I thought you told the phone company about the wrong number," Lucy said.

Bridget pushed her glasses up on the bridge of her nose. "I was going to, but then I had an epiphany. I can reform these men."

"Oh, darlin'," Lucy told her. "Those men don't want to be reformed."

"That's what they think now," Bridget said. "But I can't pass up this chance. Think about it, Lucy. I get to go directly to the source. I don't know why I didn't think of this before. Think of the changes I can make in our sexist society."

Lucy snapped her fingers. "Speaking of our sexist society, I almost forgot." She picked up a remote control, pushed a button, and a large television rose up from what I thought was a white cabinet. She clicked another button, and the television came to life.

"I've been snooping," she said, proud as punch. "You know, on the police nerdy fella."

You could have knocked me over with a feather.

There were so many people Lucy could have snooped on. The list was practically endless, and it started with Luanda, Michael Rellik, and Uncle Harry. I couldn't imagine why she was snooping on detective Remington Cumberbatch, except for the obvious facts that he was slightly better-looking than most any man on the planet and he was built like a testosterone-packed truck.

"Oh, good," Bridget said. "You got any peanuts, Lucy?"

Lucy put out a spread of chips, dip, and nuts. I scooped up some guacamole with a tortilla chip.

"Check this out." Lucy clicked a button. "Who does that look like?"

A half-naked man, muscled and covered in tattoos, shook a fist at the screen. "That's Detective Cumberbatch," I said.

"Bald," Bridget added. "I like him better without hair."

"You're both wrong," Lucy said. "That's not Remington Cumberbatch. That's Junior Clay."

Bridget scooted closer to the television. "He looks just like him—a twin."

"That's because Junior Clay is Remington Cumberbatch, darlin'," Lucy said, smiling. "I looked him up after he told Gladie he was a cage fighter. Junior Clay is his fighting name."

I'd forgotten that Remington had been a cage fighter. What had he called it? UFC. He certainly looked the part. On the television he bounced in place, shaking out his arms as if to relax them. Another man—scarier than Remington, with a flat nose, a scar down one cheek, and just as muscly—slapped his fists together. The two men were focused on each other with what looked like murder on their minds.

I caught myself biting my fingernails and grabbed the bowl of chips.

"I'm not much for violence," I said, munching on the chips.

"Me, either," Bridget said. "Although it is an interesting look at the evolutionary process."

"This is violence *plus*. Keep watching," Lucy ordered.

The two men went after each other, punching and kicking. Then, in a blur, Remington got the other guy down on the floor and wrapped his legs around his torso. They ground into each other, sweating and grunting.

"What is this? What are we watching?" Bridget asked. She fanned herself with a magazine. I was feeling overheated, too. Remington and the other man writhed on the floor in a compromising situation.

"Why didn't I know about this before?" I asked.

"Don't turn it off," Bridget ordered.

"Oh, honey," Lucy said, "I've got three hours recorded. Sit back and enjoy the afternoon."

"Sounds good," I said, but I wasn't listening. I was transfixed by the action on the television. "What are they doing now?"

"I looked it up," Lucy told me. "It's called the bare-naked choke hold. Isn't that perfect?"

I nodded.

Lucy sat next to me and put her feet up on the coffee table. "I bought us tickets for Junior Clay's next bout, tomorrow night," she said. "You know, so we can study it closer up."

\* \* \*

IT WAS a good way to spend the day after a kidnapping. I was thoroughly rested by the evening and thoroughly filled with empty calories. Lucy insisted on dressing me for Luanda's meeting.

Bridget decided to field calls from perverts instead of going to the fake psychic's singles' group.

"Tea-bagging? I'm more a coffee drinker myself," Bridget said. She lowered the phone. "I can't make out what these men are talking about most of the time," she told Lucy and me, and put the phone back up to her ear. "Can we get back to our talk about three-ways after I tell you about the Equal Rights Amendment?" she asked into the phone.

I walked up to the third floor with Lucy. "Do you think she'll be all right?" I asked her.

"If she converts even one man, darlin', she'll be over the moon. I think it's good therapy for her."

Bridget was at her best when she was crusading, but I had my doubts she could convert any of her callers to her feminist beliefs.

Lucy's closet was bigger than my bedroom and looked like the inside of Saks Fifth Avenue. It almost brought tears to my eyes, especially when I caught a glimpse of my sweatshirt-wearing self in one of the mirrors.

"This," Lucy said, handing me an ice-blue strapless dress.

"Isn't it a little dressy for the occasion?"

"This," she insisted. I put on the dress and one of a pair of sling-backs. I didn't look half bad, even with the nylon boot on my other foot. "Lord, Gladie," Lucy said. "No wonder all the lookers want you."

"They don't want me," I countered. I got a lot of flirting but not a lot more than that.

"They will if you wear this." She put a diamond necklace around my neck and pinned up my hair.

"Isn't this a bit much for a chat with Luanda?" I asked.

"Oh, that reminds me."

Lucy opened a drawer and took out a Taser.

"What's that for?" I asked, but I had a sneaking suspicion.

"That's plan B, in case that woman refuses to get her hooks out of Uncle Harry."

"How about we leave that at home? I have a good plan A," I said, taking a step out of range. Actually, I had no plan at all. I had no idea what to say to Luanda to get her to back off, and I had even less of a plan to prove she was a fraud.

Lucy didn't care about the existence or inexistence of my plan. She put the Taser in her purse, dabbed on some lipstick, and turned off the closet light.

Tonight it seemed like the whole town was armed and I couldn't convince anyone to put down their weapons. I hoped Luanda wasn't packing heat.

# Chapter 10

✦ ♥ ✦

*Dolly, in this business we get all kinds of people. Some are easier to match than others. You'd be surprised to know that introverted, shy, don't-talk-much clients are some of the easiest to match. One of the hardest kind to match is the showman (or showwoman). Sure, they have charisma and they're pleasing to the eye. Sure, they attract all sorts of romantic partners, but sooner or later their partner realizes it's just a show. And, without the show, a showman is only half a man (or woman).*

**Lesson 24,**
**Matchmaking Advice from Your Grandma Zelda**

LUCY BROUGHT me down to her garage. Inside was a brand-new Mercedes, an even newer and fancier model than the one she had crashed into Tea Time.

"Lambskin-leather seats, Gladie," Lucy told me, her eyes gleaming. "Cherrywood dashboard. It was supposed to go to Justin Timberlake, but I pulled strings."

I sat in the passenger seat, settling into the ultrasoft leather. "I might have had an orgasm just now," I said.

"It's nice, right? I swear, I'm glad I crashed my old car. Justin Timberlake sure has good taste."

She started up the car, and the gorgeous Southern twang of Garth Brooks oozed out of the stereo speakers.

"Hold on," I said, remembering. "Grandma said I have to drive."

"My new Mercedes?"

"No, I think she meant I had to drive my car."

Lucy turned off the engine, and Garth Brooks went quiet. "Did she say why?" Lucy asked.

I shrugged. Grandma never said why, but it was usually wiser to take her advice.

"Damn, I left my screwdriver upstairs," I said. "Do you have one?"

Lucy gave me a screwdriver from her garage wall. It was shiny, pink, and new. Even Lucy's tools were nicer than mine, I thought, as I started up my old rusted-out Cutlass Supreme. No lambskin, cherrywood, or Garth Brooks, but I couldn't complain. It still got us where we were going.

Luanda had set up shop in an abandoned warehouse near the old gold mine in the northwest corner of the historic district. The parking lot attached to the building was almost filled with cars, but we found a place in the back.

We were fifteen minutes late for the meeting, and everyone was inside. The warehouse was lit with candles and Christmas tree lights. Men and women stood around in uncomfortable silence.

"Lord, she sure knows how to bring them in," Lucy noted.

"Where are the snacks?" I asked. Grandma had stressed the importance of keeping potential matches fed. She always said that love couldn't bloom on an empty stomach. Munching would have helped ease the tension in this room. Nobody mingled—not a peep from anyone. You could hear teeth grinding and stomachs growling.

"No wonder Grandma is apoplectic," I told Lucy. "Luanda is breaking all the matchmaking rules."

Lucy scanned the room. "Where is the Amazing Kreskin? Let's get up front."

We pushed our way to the front of the room, where a raised platform was draped in a batik cloth. As if we had summoned her by our presence, Luanda floated up onto the makeshift stage. She was wearing layer over layer of flouncy black material. Her teased hair hung down to her waist and was topped with a whole selection of multicolored feathers. She had rings on every finger and strings of beads around her neck.

She stuck one hand out straight in front of her, as if she were going to sing opera, and covered her eyes with her other hand.

"I see! I see!" she cried—ironically, since her eyes were covered. "I see love! I see happiness for each and every one of you."

The room erupted in applause.

"Well, kiss my go-to-hell," Lucy muttered.

Luanda raised her hands above her head. "What's that? What's that?" she asked the air. "I hear you, but I can't make you out. What is that you are trying to convey to your servant from the cosmos?"

"I'm going to Tase her," Lucy said.

I put my hand on Lucy's arm. "Can you wait until I'm nowhere around? With my luck, you'll get me instead of her."

"Destruction!" Luanda screeched. "Despair! Depression! Detritus!"

"A lot of 'D's," I said to Lucy.

Luanda dropped her arms and gave me a pointed look. "Shh!" she hissed.

All eyes turned to me. I slouched down behind Lucy.

"Your love matches have eluded you," Luanda told the crowd, her voice booming in a singsong. "You have paired with the wrong person, but all that is going to change tonight. After tonight you will search no further, because tonight you find your soul mate. Your other half is in this very room."

I looked around, and everyone else was doing the same thing, trying to make out who could possibly be their other half. I caught a sixtysomething man with a paunch and comb-over giving me an appreciative smile.

"Harold Chow's got you in his line of sight," Lucy said.

"That's Harold Chow? My grandmother is worried about him."

"I'm worried about him, too," said Lucy. "His shoelaces are untied, and his fly is open. He looks like ten miles of bad road and open for all kinds of unfortunate happenings."

Luanda sat cross-legged on her stage and motioned for the crowd to sit, as well. There wasn't a chair to be had, just cold hard floor.

"Darlin', if that witch thinks I'm going to sit my Chanel ass down on the filthy industrial linoleum, she's been talking to the wrong dead people."

I pulled Lucy to the side, close to the wall, away

from the crowd. They all dutifully sat down, although few could make it into the cross-legged position. It was more of a middle-aged, metabolically challenged group than a youthful, vegan yoga set.

"Talk to me," Luanda commanded her audience. "Tell me your needs."

"I need love fast," one man shouted back. "I've got blue balls something awful. You can't imagine the suffering. It's like someone is driving a truck through my gonads. I'd like to cut the damned things off, but if you got someone in mind for me"—he paused and scanned the crowd—"then I'll keep them a while longer and hopefully my soul mate can fix the problem."

Luanda looked a little shaken, and there was snickering throughout the room.

"Your other half is here, Blue-Ball Man!" she announced after a moment. The women squirmed in unison, probably hoping she wasn't talking about them and that they weren't Blue-Ball Man's other half.

"Tell me your fears, oh, lovelorn among us," Luanda continued to the rest of the group. I thought it was pretty obvious what their fears were after the whole blue-balls conversation, but a little voice piped up out of the quiet.

"I have a fear, Luanda," a tiny woman in gabardine and gloves squeaked from the center of the room.

Luanda put her hand up, palm forward. "Hold on, little bird, I'm getting a message from the other side." Luanda's eyes rolled around in their sockets.

"I really wish there were snacks," I whispered to Lucy.

"Luanda calling spirits. Luanda calling spirits," Luanda said to the air above her head. She nodded like she agreed with whatever the spirits were telling her. "Okay, continue on, little bird," she said after a minute. "The spirits have told me about your fears, but you need to tell me yourself, to purify the toxicity in your heart."

"Okay," the little woman squeaked. "When I feel an erect penis, I lose all rational thought."

Again, Luanda looked a little shaken. I wondered how the spirits would deal with the erect-penis problem.

"Oh, little bird," Luanda said finally, after regaining her composure, "it's like those wise words from the philosopher—I don't know his name: 'We don't swim in your toilet. Please don't pee in our pool.'"

I didn't think Grandma had to worry about Luanda. Her advice was pretty lackluster compared to Grandma's. Still, the heads in the crowd nodded as if Luanda had said something really wise and on topic.

"And now comes the moment you have all been waiting for," Luanda announced. "You've paid the nominal fee through your PayPal account with the iPad that was passed around, haven't you? Good. Then here it is. Your conjugal happiness is a matter of seconds away."

Luanda closed her eyes and pointed her index finger at the audience. She made a big circle, as if her finger were a divining rod.

"I have a bad feeling about this," I muttered.

Luanda made quick work with her finger, pairing up the entire group of about fifty in a matter of minutes, like a giant game of eeny-meeny-miney-mo. The crowd stood and greeted their so-called soul mates. The room was filled with chatter.

Lucy tugged at my arm. "Now's our chance," she told me. "Get your plan A ready." Yikes, I had forgotten I was supposed to come up with a plan A. I was running on empty in the ideas department.

We climbed up on the stage, and I tapped Luanda on the shoulder. She turned and looked at us, puzzled.

"Hi, Luanda," I said. "Do you remember us? I'm Gladie. This is Lucy. You were kidnapped with us."

"And you have your hooks in Uncle Harry. He wants you to leave him alone, pronto," Lucy added.

"Yes, that, too," I agreed.

"Harry Lupino and Ruth Fletcher are my finest match," Luanda said. "They are the great love not seen since the love between my ancestors, a beautiful Indian princess and a glorious shaman man."

"I think they say 'beautiful Native American princess' now," I pointed out. The noise in the room was growing louder.

Lucy poked Luanda in the chest. "Harry wants you to back off. You got me, woman?"

"Ruth isn't happy with the match, either," I added. "And she has a bat. And a gun."

"The spirits guide me. I am Luanda!"

Luanda's shouts seemed to be echoed by other shouts in the room. The people in the crowd were moving like a wave, pushing against one another.

"Listen, snake," Lucy growled at Luanda. "You are not making love matches. You are *blocking* love matches."

I gasped. I had been hit with a lightning bolt of insight that knocked me off-balance. "Oh, Lucy," I breathed.

The crowd erupted in more shouts. "She pointed at me," one of the men yelled at another.

"No, she pointed at *me*!"

The two pointed at each other, punctuating each "pointed at me."

"Luanda," I said with sudden realization. "There are more men than women here. You mis-coupled."

She bit her lower lip. "The spirits are calling me. I'll see you later." She lifted up her skirts, stepped off the stage, and hit the ground running.

Lucy was quick on her heels. I was rooted to the spot. For some reason, I felt I should try to calm the situation. Maybe I felt some responsibility as another so-called matchmaker.

"Now, now," I said, trying to get the men's attention. But my voice didn't carry, at least not above their shouts.

"If you point at me again, you'll be sorry!" shouted one of the men, pointing all the while.

"Oh, yeah?" the other shouted back, and pointed at the other man's eyeball. "What are you going to do about it?"

And then the words were done, because the one man grabbed the other's finger, stuck it in his mouth, and clamped down like it was a steak at an all-you-can-eat buffet. The other man was indeed sorry. He screamed and tried to pull his finger away, but the first man had a good set of choppers. He held on like a pit bull.

The screams were earsplitting and made the hair stand up on the back of my neck. The tussle in the middle of the room expanded out like ripples from the finger-biter to the middle-aged love-seekers in the four corners of the room. Something inside me—maybe Luanda's spirits—told me to get the hell out of there, but the only way out was through the crowd.

"I really wish there were snacks," I said to myself. I bit my lip to stop it from trembling. As Fred would say, I was in a hairy pickle.

Below me, it was complete mayhem. Punches were being thrown, and a few of the smarter people were making a run for the door. The man with the finger in his mouth was still holding on, and the other man had stopped screaming. His body had drained of color, and he'd collapsed to his knees.

I was alternately plotting safe routes to the exit and trying to figure out a way to save the man before he was one finger short of a hand, when I heard sirens. Paramedics and four police sirens, according to my experienced ears.

I was unusually happy to see Spencer. He arrived first through the door and spotted me instantly, as if he had Gladie radar.

I read his lips: "Are you kidding me?" he said. He barked orders, and his men fanned out and quickly got the crowd under control. All except for the man with the finger in his mouth.

"Let go!" Spencer ordered.

Finally, the victim fell back, free from his attacker. But unfortunately he fell back with one less finger. Bitten clean off. Blood poured out of his hand, and the other man stood triumphant, the finger still in his mouth.

"Okay," I said, and all went black.

* * *

I CAME to in the back of Spencer's car, with an oxygen mask on my face and my head in his lap.

"Pinkie, you are a hot mess," he said, stroking my head.

I took the mask off my face. "I don't even rate an ambulance?" I asked him.

"The finger's in there," he explained. To his credit, he knew I would want to be far away from the disembodied finger.

"You look nice," he said. "Dressed up. What's the occasion?"

"Lucy's closet."

He nodded. "Why is it that everywhere there's trouble, Gladys Burger is there?"

"Don't call me Gladys."

"I'm a cop, and I don't see as much trouble as you do. Can't you be more like me?"

"No," I said. "I'm carbon-based."

"You breathing all right? Do I need to call over the medics?"

I sat up. "I'm fine."

"Good. Let's go. My men are handling this party."

I scooted over to the passenger seat and peered out the window, but Lucy was nowhere to be seen.

"They tell me that apple season is the most tranquil time of the year in Cannes," Spencer remarked. "Not a lot of chewing off digits, usually."

"It wasn't my fault," I said.

"Uh-huh."

Spencer promised me food and something serious to drink, far away from Luanda and dismembered fingers. That turned out to be at the Swingathon.

He parked in the loading zone in front of the building. I could hear music through the closed doors. "Is this a date?" I asked him.

"Come on, Pinkie, I'll feed you," he said, ignoring the question. He opened my car door and helped me out. His hand was warm, dry, and just rough enough to be comforting in a manly way. As usual, his touch made my feet tingle, and the tingle went all the way up.

My light-headedness had disappeared with the promise of food. "Perhaps I should reflect on the fact that I'm hungry after what I just witnessed," I noted.

"Pinkie, I would advise in your case that you should probably reflect as little as possible on your life."

A live band was playing Benny Goodman music. Couples were swinging each other around the dance floor, which was lit by a disco ball. Spencer ushered me to the buffet table and started a plate for me without asking what I wanted to eat. Then he steered me toward the bar and ordered me a rum and root beer.

"Sit," he ordered, pointing at a nearby table.

I dug into the food. The egg rolls were delicious. I ate three and took a swig of my drink. "One thing is good," I said. "At least I don't have to prove Luanda is a fraud. I think she proved that point herself tonight."

"Always sticking your nose in where it doesn't belong," Spencer said.

"It is my business. It's matchmaker business."

"Touché. Here, have another." He passed me another rum and root beer, and I took a sip. I was feeling good, even after it dawned on me that I had forgotten to take my afternoon dose of antibiotics and could be working on gangrene as I sat there in Lucy's fancy dress.

There were a lot of familiar faces at the Swinga-thon. I had met them all because, sooner or later, every Cannes citizen walked through Grandma's house. That is, until her business was squelched by Luanda the interloper.

The room was pretty. Dark, with strobe lights and period decorations. I moved in my seat to the music and took another drink.

"Be careful, girl," Ruth said, approaching me. She was dressed in a gray tentlike long dress, and pearl strands hung from her neck in a sweep down to her waist. "Drinking like that—you don't want to end up like your mother."

"Shows what you know, Ruth," I said. "My mother was a binge drinker, and she drank alone. The only thing she did socially was—well, you know."

"Shows what *you* know," Ruth countered. "Once, I witnessed your mother down a bottle of peach schnapps while enjoying the company of half of the Cannes Shriners' chapter. And I'd tell you what she did on Halloween in '96, but I don't want to upset you."

I already knew what my mother had done on Halloween in '96. It was famous in town and was the catalyst to us moving out of Cannes in a Volkswagen bus my mom had bought on trade.

I spotted Lucy entering the room and waved her over. "Where were you?" I asked.

"The witch lost me, but I saw her come in this direction."

"Want a drink?" I asked, and handed her my cup, but it was empty. "How did that happen?"

Spencer went to get me another drink, and we were visited by Remington Cumberbatch. "You're dressed," Lucy noted, disappointed. He was wearing fitted slacks, a white button-down shirt, and a tight vest. He looked like a very large English stockbroker.

"May I have this dance?" he asked me.

I jumped up, and the room spun around me. Remington caught me easily. "You all right?" he asked.

"Perfect."

I couldn't really dance with my nylon boot, but Remington held me up and swayed me to the center of the dance floor.

"You look lovely, Gladie," he said.

"A man bit off someone's finger tonight," I said.

"I heard. But they sewed it back on."

"Oh. That's a relief."

"It's been a tough few days for you," he noted.

I shrugged and hiccupped. "I'm used to it. Not a lot of downtime for matchmakers, you know."

"It's a tough job."

"But at least I think tonight proved that Luanda is a fraud. So that's one job done. Check!" I made a check mark in the air with my finger.

"Congratulations on proving she's a fraud," Remington said.

"And congratulations on your face," I said. Remington Cumberbatch was really hot, like lava hot. His hand never slipped from high on my back, and he never made an inappropriate comment, but his pupils were dilated, and I knew he would be on top of me if I gave him the slightest encouragement.

"I have a very comfortable bed," I said.

Remington raised an eyebrow. "Is that—" he started, but he was interrupted by Spencer, who was holding another rum and root beer for me.

"Vamoose, probie," Spencer growled. Remington tipped his head in my direction, removed his hands from my body, and walked away without looking back once. Spencer took his place, pulling me close with one hand.

"He's not that good-looking," Spencer said without preamble.

"He's not?"

"No, he's not your type at all."

I snorted. "You mean the polite, charming, intelligent, and hotter-than-hell type? What do you care, anyway? You're taking a break from women, remember?"

"Why *don't* you care? Are you and Holden kaput?"

I didn't know what Holden and I were. He was away, and I didn't know when he would be back. If he would be back. And I didn't know what role I would play in his life if he did come back.

"No, Holden and I are doing just fine," I said. "Thanks for asking."

"Juggling a lot of romantic interests can get dicey, Pinkie. Learn from my mistakes."

He had a point. I now had three potential flirtations in my life, and that was at least two too many.

"At least Luanda is taken care of," I said. "What a shambles tonight. She won't be long for this town, at least not as a psychic matchmaker."

•

But once again I was wrong, wrong, wrong. Lu-anda raced into the ballroom and raised her arms to get everyone's attention.

"I am Luanda," she shouted. "And I know where the kidnapper Michael Rellik is hiding!"

# Chapter 11

✦ ❤ ✦

*Happy accidents are really happy, bubeleh. In this business, we need all the help we can get, and the most-welcome help comes out of thin air without any effort on our part. Years ago I was trying to match Joyce Temkin. In the modern parlance, Joyce was a "hard bitch." There's not a lot of men who are interested in a hard bitch, and no matter what I tried, I couldn't match her. Then, one sunny day, I invited Joyce over for an alfresco lunch in the backyard. In the middle of our meal, I went inside to get more lemonade. At that very moment, dolly, high over our heads, a man jumped out of a plane, and his parachute didn't open. You could call that an unhappy incident, but it worked out really well. Wouldn't you know it, that meshuggener landed right on Joyce. They shared a room in the trauma unit over in San Diego and fell in love. It turned out that Joyce wasn't nearly as hard as we thought. If she had been, the parachutist would have been a goner.*

**Lesson 2,**
**Matchmaking Advice from Your Grandma Zelda**

THE MUSIC screeched to a halt, and the guests stopped dancing. Spencer walked over to Luanda, and Remington joined them. Lucy made a beeline in their direction, and I headed her off before she could Tase Luanda.

"You're a wily one," Lucy said to Luanda.

"Don't start, Pinkie," Spencer warned.

"I didn't say anything!"

"Come quick," Luanda said. "My spirit guide has instructed me."

"Do you know where he is or not?" Spencer demanded. "I'm not much for listening to spirit guides."

Luanda leaned forward and got in Spencer's face.

"Follow me, handsome, and I'll take you right to him."

I WAS pissed off. I'm not normally an angry person. Panic, fear, and hunger are my go-to emotions. But Spencer was pissing me off. I limped after him as he escorted Luanda to his car.

"Are you serious?" I demanded. "But she's a fraud!"

"Hands off Uncle Harry!" Lucy yelled from behind me. I glanced back and caught her riffling through her purse.

Ruth had walked out, too. "Girl, you only have about a minute before Dixie Tesla electrocutes the witch and sends us all to jail."

I turned Spencer around with all the force I could muster. "Didn't I just finish telling you that I had to prove Luanda's a fraud?" I asked him. "Why are you placating her?"

I shivered, and Spencer took off his jacket and draped it around my shoulders.

"As the chief of police, I am required to run down any reasonable leads concerning the whereabouts of an escaped kidnapper, especially a kidnapper who kidnapped the chief of police."

I sucked air. "But if *I* were to tell you about the whereabouts of anybody, you would order me to stop meddling."

Spencer wagged his finger at me. "That's right, Pinkie. Stay out of it. Let the professionals do their job. Believe it or not, the cops know what they're doing."

"Boogidee, boogidee, bezow bee bop," Luanda sing-songed. "I hear you!" she yelled into the air.

Spencer smirked his annoying little smirk. "Looking good tonight, Pinkie," he told me, his voice low and smooth like an after-sex cigarette. He traced his finger along the top of my dress. "What could one night hurt? One night to rock your world."

"That's the problem with you, Spencer," I said. "You're not good with math. You've never been able to count higher than one."

I let them go without saying another word. Spencer helped Luanda into the backseat. Remington took shotgun, and Spencer started up the car. Lucy tapped me on the shoulder.

"Give me the screwdriver," she urged. "Hand it over."

"I don't have it. Besides, my car is back at Luanda's old factory."

"Oh, hell," Lucy said. She pulled at the front of Ruth's dress. "Hand over your keys, old woman. I need your car."

"I'm not giving you my car!" Ruth clutched her purse to her chest. "Let me go or I'll head-butt you."

Some people think small towns are boring.

Lucy made an inhuman noise, like something out of a horror movie. Like *The Wolfman* or *Glitter*. Ruth dropped her purse in Lucy's hands.

"Fine," she said. "But if you so much as scratch the paint, I'll tear the drawl out of you."

Ruth drove an Oldsmobile that was older than mine, but hers was in pristine condition. I snuck a peek at the odometer from my place in the backseat. Thirty thousand miles. I wondered if Ruth had ever left Cannes in the last fifty years.

"Where are we going?" I asked.

"We're following the coppers. I'm going to give Luanda a talking-to, once and for all," Lucy said.

She started the car and followed Spencer at a safe distance. I remembered Grandma's warning about not letting Lucy drive, but the car was moving too fast for me to jump out, and there was no chance she would stop and risk losing Luanda.

"This is not so bad," Ruth said, stretching her legs out in front of her. "A beautiful ride up into the mountains."

We were south of town, climbing up toward the apple and pear orchards. It was a clear night, full of stars, and I took a lesson from Ruth and let myself relax. I hadn't had much chance to take a breath during the past few days.

I had been thrown over a balcony, impaled, kidnapped, locked up, and almost plastered to death. In addition, I had witnessed a man chew off a finger. But I had survived the past few days virtually unscathed, considering, and could still enjoy a starlit evening.

Meanwhile, I had two relatively simple tasks to

complete—unmatch Uncle Harry and prove that Luanda was a fraud. I also realized I had another task to handle, something closer to home and more important, but I would have to figure out how to deal with that and when was the best moment.

"Yeah, this is kind of nice," Ruth said. "Wish I had a cup of my tea, though." It was sort of unthinkable for Ruth to be without her shop. Tea Time and Ruth were synonymous. She had owned and run it for my entire life and far longer than that. It was more than a job for her. It was a calling. She was like a nun but with uglier clothes.

"Did you have a good time at the Swingathon?" I asked her.

"Nah, Hank had to leave early. His bunions were acting up." Hank Frazier was Ruth's escort for most social events; he ran the fruit stand on Main Street.

"That's a shame," I said.

"And Meryl was doing her *Girls Gone Wild* impression," Ruth continued about the town's blue-haired librarian. "I never want to see her do tequila shooters again. I want to rip that image from my brain. To her credit, it wasn't her idea. Frank Richmond was the one getting blitzed. She just tagged along 'cause she's sweet on him."

"Frank Richmond," I repeated. "That name sounds familiar."

"Keep up, Gladie," Ruth snarled. "He was the one in the other panic room, the one who was beaten up. I guess I can't blame him for getting blotto, but he kept going on about his successful business in Irvine and how he gave it all up to live in our idyllic town. I wanted to slap him."

We climbed up higher into the mountains, and the road turned from asphalt to dirt. Spencer's car was far in the distance, and Lucy turned the bright lights on.

"Where is that crazy woman dragging those coppers to?" Ruth asked.

"Maybe this isn't such a good idea. How about we circle back to Luanda tomorrow?" I asked.

"We can't turn back now," Ruth said. "Besides, I found my Slugger in the bushes across the street, and I put it in the trunk."

"And I have my Taser," Lucy reminded me.

The car skidded, but Lucy righted it quickly. "Mud," she explained. "The roads are slick up here."

I checked my seat belt and closed my eyes.

"They're stopping," Lucy said. I opened my eyes and, sure enough, Spencer was pulling over to the side. We drove up behind him, and Lucy parked the car, careful to keep the lights on. "Let's go."

"I'll get my Slugger," Ruth said, hopping out of the car. Lucy grabbed her purse and got out. I opened my door, but Spencer blocked my exit.

"Are you kidding me?" he asked. He held a flashlight and shined it on my face.

"It wasn't my idea," I said. "They made me." I tried to push my way past him, but he stood firm. "I swear, Spencer. I have no desire to see Michael Rellik. I mean it. I have no wish to meet my kidnapper ever again. Girl Scouts' honor, I'm not meddling." I stuck three fingers up in the air.

"Were you ever a Girl Scout?" Spencer asked me.

"No, but I've eaten their cookies. Honestly, I don't care about Rellik. I'm leaving it up to you to catch him."

Surprisingly, it was the truth. Sure, I was curious to know why Rellik had terrorized us, but the answer was most likely that he was crazy. So there really wasn't any mystery, and I would have preferred to be at home, watching a *Big Bang Theory* marathon.

"Stay out of trouble," Spencer warned me, and stood aside.

"Don't worry." Ruth was brandishing her bat. "I'll protect her. I wouldn't mind getting a whack at the bastard."

"Nobody is doing any whacking," Spencer said, but I noticed he didn't take her bat away.

"I'll watch over her, boss," Remington offered, and stood behind me. He was putting out a lot of heat, like one of those portable Amish fireplaces, but with an animal magnetism that drew me toward him until my back leaned against his front.

Remington Cumberbatch was solid as a rock, hard everywhere. My breath hitched. He represented possibilities—not the possibilities I thought I wanted and demanded from Holden and Spencer, but possibilities nonetheless.

"I don't need you to watch over her, probie," Spencer said. "I need you to stick to the witch. If Rellik was out here, we've probably already scared him off."

"He's still out here," Luanda announced, her voice rising into the night, sending shivers down my spine. "We will find him, and then all of Cannes will know of my powers. And I'm not a witch," she added. "Although some of my best friends are witches. All dead, of course."

I sighed. It was exactly the opposite of what Grandma had assigned me to do. If we really did find

Rellik, it would mean the end of Grandma's match-making business, which was unthinkable. Like Ruth's Tea Time, Grandma's Matchmaking Services was an institution in town, and her whole life. I didn't think she could be happy without her vocation.

Spencer ran his fingers through his hair and walked over to Luanda. With Spencer's back turned, Remington let his hand travel up the side of my body from my hip to under my arm, his fingertips grazing my breast. My core melted like a chocolate lava cake. I moaned.

"You okay, Gladie?" Ruth asked.

"Yes," I croaked. "Just tired."

I was happy for the darkness. I took a step back and allowed him to press his body against me. His hand slipped around to my belly and then lower. It occurred to me that Luanda might not be the only crazy person out here. Letting myself get fondled by a hot Trekkie not ten yards away from Spencer was pretty wackadoodle.

"Probie!" Spencer called, as he walked into the grove of trees with Luanda.

Remington leaned over and surreptitiously kissed the side of my neck. His face was rough with an end-of-the-day beard, but his lips were baby soft. I looked down to make sure my body hadn't burst into flames. Good news: I was still intact.

But one thing was certain. I was playing with fire.

Remington did as he was commanded and jogged over to Spencer and Luanda. She was back to speaking in tongues, and I heard her gibberish recede into the trees.

"You know, this is a weird town," Ruth said, resting her bat on her shoulder. "Are we ready, ladies?"

Lucy was a few steps in front of us. Spencer and Remington had flashlights, and we walked toward their light.

It wasn't easy to walk that way at night over rocks and twigs on an uneven, muddy ground in the dress shoe and my nylon boot, even with the stars lighting up the sky. We made slow progress, stumbling here and there.

"Why are we doing this?" I asked.

Ruth shushed me. She was as into our field trip as Lucy was. They both had revenge on their minds, and it was spurring them on, giving them courage and a certain don't-care attitude about ruining their shoes in the mud.

I squinted against the darkness as we walked into the grove. The starlight created shadows in the trees, making them look alive, like a scene out of *The Wizard of Oz*. Ruth and Lucy pulled ahead of me, hell-bent on catching up to the other group. The lights came and went as Spencer and Remington walked between the trees.

I was forced to walk slower than my friends, not because of my injured foot, which made me hobble, but because of Lucy's high-heeled sling-back, which got stuck in the mud with each step.

I pulled Spencer's coat tight around me against the cold. Tomorrow, Dave would be done with my dry cleaning, and then I could finally wear my own clothes. Not that I had anything spectacular to wear, but at least I would be warm, and I wouldn't have to keep borrowing from others.

"He's close! He's close!" Luanda shouted from up ahead.

"Holy crap!" Spencer exclaimed.

Lucy and Ruth ran up to the other group, and I limped behind them, catching up finally to see them all surrounding a freshly dug mound with an indistinguishable body part sticking out of the dirt. Remington and Spencer shined their flashlights on it.

"Who did the bastard kill now?" Ruth asked.

"I think I'm going to be sick," I said.

"The witch actually found something." Lucy sounded like she had discovered that Bigfoot exists.

"Yep, I'm going to be sick," I said.

"Don't contaminate the crime scene," Spencer told me.

"Okay," I said, taking a step backward.

"And don't hurl on my new jacket," he added. "Shit, I paid full price for that."

"Okay," I repeated, taking another step back and to the side. I slipped behind a tree, but I could still see Spencer and Remington, now on their knees, digging up the mound with their bare hands. So I moved farther to the side, deeper in the trees, until the mound and whatever was under it were far out of my sight.

"Boss, take a look at this," I heard Remington say.

"What are you playing at, Miss Laughing-Eagle?" Spencer demanded after a moment.

"Rellik is here!" Luanda insisted. "He's hiding among these trees. Do you hear that?"

I heard a jingling. "It's a dog collar, Miss," Remington said.

"Somebody buried their pet Rover out here." I knew that voice. It was the sound of Spencer ready to tear someone's head off. I took another couple of steps away and leaned up against a tree.

"No," I heard Luanda say. "It's the sound of the spirits calling me. Woo, woo, woo!" A creepy feeling of dread crawled up and down my body. The more Luanda continued to woo-woo and talk to her invisible people, the more I began to believe that Rellik really was out here, hiding. Maybe he was lying in wait for me. Maybe he was close by. Maybe I was too far away from the others.

I took a step away from the tree and went down hard, tripping over a root. I stayed on my hands and knees and took stock of my damage. I seemed to be okay, but, once again, I had done a number on borrowed clothes.

Lucy's dress was torn up the back, and I had ground Spencer's coat into the mud when I took my tumble. But that wasn't the worst of it. As I went down, tangled in branches and roots, the chain of Lucy's diamond necklace was ripped from my neck and flew into the thousands of acres of Cannes's fruit-tree groves.

I crawled around in a panic, trying to find the necklace. Lucy would never forgive me for losing it. It had to have cost a fortune.

"Maybe something else is buried with the dog," I heard Ruth say with a hopeful edge to her voice.

"Keep digging," Spencer commanded.

I was thankful to hear them shoveling dirt, because it gave me needed time to find the necklace. I continued to search the ground in wider and wider circles from where I went down. It was a hopeless endeavor.

"I'll never find it," I muttered. "I'm stupid, stupid,

stupid." I couldn't believe I was out in the dark, crawling around among the wildlife, with a possible kidnapper and dog murderer watching me.

Worse than that, instead of finding Lucy's necklace, I was touching more than my share of squishy gross things in the mud. "Yuck," I mumbled. "Blech."

But I couldn't quit. I had already ruined her shoe and ripped her dress. I tried to focus on the task at hand and not on the possibility of stumbling on a rattlesnake or having a spider crawl up my dress.

But I worried for nothing. I didn't come in contact with any snakes or spiders, and, against all odds, I did find the necklace. I breathed a sigh of relief.

Lucy's necklace was right in front of me, right under my nose, as I crawled on all fours in the thick line of trees overgrown with brush. There it was, the diamond picking up the starlight, shining through the night, resting comfortably on the corpse of Michael Rellik, who lay in stunned silence, his eyes open and unblinking, his body riddled with bloody holes.

"Yep, I'm going to be sick," I said.

# Chapter 12

*❤*

*Relationships can take unexpected turns, dolly. It's one of those nasty secrets that nobody tells you. That intoxicating, obsessive, glorious, in-love feeling at the start of a relationship that we think will last forever? Well, guess what. No, I'm not saying it has to go away entirely. I'm saying it can turn into something else, go to unexpected places. I'm talking about twists and turns, dolly. Expect the unexpected. Or don't and just accept being surprised.*

**Lesson 81,**
**Matchmaking Advice from Your Grandma Zelda**

I THINK it was the sound of my retching that got their attention, or maybe I screamed, but it was a matter of seconds before Rellik's body was illuminated by Spencer's and Remington's flashlights.

"Gladie, you found Rellik," Lucy said.

"Well, how about that? Zelda was right. You do have the gift," Ruth said.

"Did you hurl on my coat?" Spencer asked.

SPENCER GOT on his phone, and in a short while we were invaded by half of the Cannes police force and fire department.

The area was roped off, and Remington, who was supposedly a forensics expert, got to work on the scene while we waited for the regional coroner.

Fred and Sergeant Brody escorted me to the fire truck and wrapped a blanket around me. "Mostly we wanted to see you," Fred explained.

Sergeant Brody nodded. "We heard you were naked."

"No, I just ripped my dress up the back," I said.

"That's still good," Fred said.

"Not quite as good," Sergeant Brody said, obviously disappointed.

"I also sort of upchucked on Spencer's coat," I added.

"Where? Can I get a picture?" Brody asked.

THE CORONER arrived about an hour later. By that time, Remington had finished with his investigation into the crime scene, and we all stood around at the fire truck, talking about low-carb diets, football, and apple pie recipes.

Luanda was taking credit for finding Rellik and was on her cellphone, pretty much telling everyone in town that her psychic abilities were proven and that her matchmaking fees would, unfortunately, have to go up.

I had failed Grandma. She could never compete with that kind of PR. If I hadn't found Rellik, Luanda's business would have suffocated under the weight of her dog discovery and everything would have gone back to normal for Grandma. But no. Once again, I had to trip over a dead person. Once again, death was my calling card.

I was despondent, Lucy was steamed, but it was Ruth who was truly pissed at Luanda. "*Now* you have a cellphone? You couldn't have had one when we were locked away in the dungeon?" she demanded.

Luanda waved her away, busy telling someone on the line that, yes, she could pick the winning lottery numbers but for a price. She clicked off her phone.

"My work here is done," she announced in her usual loud singsong voice. "The spirits must rest, and I must be away." She lifted her arms like she was planning to fly home. "Well, Chief?" she asked Spencer after a moment. He looked up, as if he wanted to fly home, too.

"I'm in the middle of a murder investigation, ma'am, and I have to meet with the coroner just now. As soon as I can, I'll have one of my men drive you home," he said in his cop voice.

"I'll drive you," Lucy offered, clutching her Taser-laden purse to her chest.

"But no funny business, or I'll grand-slam your ass," Ruth said, waving her bat.

I decided to leave well enough alone, heed my grandmother's warnings, and wait for a cop to drive me home. Lucy took off with Ruth and Luanda. I watched as she slowly turned the car around and made her way down the dirt road.

The coroner approached me, wearing paper booties and a jumpsuit. "Are you the young lady who corrupted my crime scene?" he asked. He smelled like my mother. Like the inside of a bourbon bottle.

"Uh," I said.

"What did you eat today, the entire junk-food aisle at Walmart? What a holy mess over there."

He wasn't half wrong. I had eaten a full bag of chips, at least, two Attica apple explosions, and all the appetizers at the Swingathon. A heat enveloped me, and I knew I was bright red. I probably glowed in the dark.

Spencer shot me one of his annoying smirks, and Remington had the decency to look away. I tried to think of a quick retort to the drunk coroner, but I came up empty.

"Come on, boys," the coroner ordered, and Spencer and Remington followed him, but not before Spencer pulled me aside and warned me to stay with Fred at the fire truck.

"I know that look, Pinkie," he told me. "You're positively giddy."

"I don't know what you're talking about," I lied. I did feel a certain giddiness, like elves were dancing in my stomach. It didn't feel all that bad.

"It's the meddling-murder thing you've got. You can't help yourself."

"That's not true," I insisted. "Were those bullet holes or was he stabbed?"

"Stop the giddiness, Pinkie. I order you."

"You what me?"

"You heard me."

I did as he said and waited at the fire truck with Fred. "You want a Milk Dud, Underwear Girl? I got some in my pocket."

"Sure, Fred." I took one from him. It was warm and melty and helped cover up the vomit taste in my mouth.

"Would you excuse me a minute?" I asked.

"The chief wants you to stay here."

"I have girl things to do in the trees, Fred."

He took a step backward. "Oh. Okay, sure. Go ahead."

I limped toward the crime scene, careful to hide behind a nearby tree. I didn't actually want to see Rellik's dead body again. But there had been something odd about it, and I needed my questions answered.

I peeked around the tree. The coroner was kneeling over poor, unfortunate Rellik. "Dead eight to twelve hours," he said. "These entry wounds to be determined at autopsy. Are you outsourcing to San Diego?"

"Um, no. Doc Stevenson is going to perform it," Spencer said.

"With me attending," Remington added. His voice was still smooth jazz but with a hard edge I hadn't heard before. Authoritarian.

The coroner stood and inspected Remington. "The chief told me about you. CSU?"

"Trained."

"Uh-huh." The coroner nodded and took off his gloves. "Well, it's a simple case of murder. Stabbed to death with something small. Repeatedly, obviously. Who was he?"

"A kidnapper," Spencer said.

"We reap what we sow," the coroner remarked wisely, and then hiccupped. "Probably his partner did it, or maybe it was revenge."

I thought about that for a moment. There was no evidence that Rellik had a partner, but I bet Grandma would know for sure. What was going to happen to the house now that Rellik was dead? Would it stay in some kind of real estate probate limbo, half remodeled? Did Rellik have family who would inherit? Did kidnappers generally have family? Or even friends?

The revenge theory was more interesting. Could one of his victims from the panic rooms have found Rellik and given him a taste of his own medicine? That would mean twelve suspects. I thought I could rule out Spencer, Lucy, Bridget, and me, which left eight. A lot of suspects.

It dawned on me that Luanda had taken us right to the corpse, and I didn't think it was because she was a psychic.

"Suspect number one," I muttered, drawing Spencer's attention. The three heads turned my way, with three different looks of surprise on their faces.

"Are you kidding me?" Spencer asked.

"She's a nosy one," commented the coroner.

WE DROVE into town behind the meat wagon, as Spencer called it.

"I don't know why you wouldn't let me look at the body," I said. I sat in the backseat with my arms crossed in front of me. Spencer was being his usual ass self, ordering me to stay out of his investigation.

"Why do you want to look at it?" he asked. "You want to throw up on him again?"

"No, smart-ass. I—" I started, but then changed my mind about telling him why I wanted to look at the body. If I told him there was something about it that set off warning bells in my head, he would make a crack about what was in my head and tell me to stay out of his investigation. Somehow, I would have to work around Spencer.

"Are we going to talk about the TOD?" Remington asked Spencer.

"What about it?"

"Well, it's been cold lately."

"Oh, crap," Spencer said.

"What? What?" I asked, pulling at my seat belt. "Why is that bad?"

"It's not bad if you're dead," Remington explained. "It means Rellik wasn't killed eight hours ago. The coroner was wrong. Rellik was murdered more than twenty-four hours ago."

"When we were in the panic rooms?" I asked.

Nobody said a word, but I could hear the brains kicking into gear. There went my suspects. We were all locked up at the time of his murder. That meant Luanda was innocent.

"What caused the holes in his body?" I asked.

"I don't know," Remington said. "Something small. We couldn't find the murder weapon."

"Shut up, probie," Spencer demanded. "First rule in Cannes police work is don't tell Gladie Burger anything."

"Hey!" I shouted.

Spencer drove me to pick up my car at Luanda's abandoned factory, after I lost a fifteen-minute argument about why he should take me with him to the morgue to see Rellik's body. Actually, two minutes into the argument, I realized there was no way I would make it into the morgue without fainting, but on principle I wouldn't give in to his dictatorial attitude.

I saw my car immediately. The building was dark, but there was a light on in the almost-empty parking lot. Spencer drove up beside my Cutlass Supreme and let me out.

He pulled me close to him by the lapels of my borrowed coat. "Remember what I said, Pinkie. Stay out of it. There's a murderer out there."

"There's always a murderer out there," I said.

"Only since you got to town," he pointed out. "I gotta run. They're doing a rush on the autopsy."

"Oh, good. Let me know what they find."

"Funny," Spencer said, and hopped back into his car. I was relieved to see him drive away. I didn't appreciate him ordering me around. After all, if it hadn't been for me, Spencer never would have known Rellik was murdered in the first place.

Then I realized I didn't have a screwdriver. I couldn't start my car, and I was stranded in a parking lot in the middle of the night. And that wouldn't have been so bad if Harold Chow wasn't running toward me at a breakneck pace, completely naked, yelling, "Woman! Woman!" repeatedly like he was counting females in the country one by one.

"Help," I squeaked. "Help. Naked. Help."

"Woman!" Harold continued, running full out like a circumcised Olympian with a potbelly and receding hairline. "Woman! Woman! Woman!"

"Naked. Help. Naked," I squeaked. It had been a hell of a week. It was probably fitting that I died like this, run over by a streaker with a one-track mind.

"Harold," I managed. "It's me, Zelda's granddaughter. Gladie."

It was like he didn't hear me. Unblinking, he maintained his trajectory. Just before he got to me, I jiggled open my car's door handle and closed myself in. Harold seemed confused for a moment and then banged on the hood.

If he had half a brain, he would have tried any of the doors, which would have opened pretty easily. But Harold only banged on the hood and mumbled incoherently, like his brain had been sucked out by aliens.

"The zombie apocalypse," I breathed. There was no other explanation. Something had turned Harold Chow into a zombie, and it was only a matter of time before he caught me and changed me into a zombie, too.

It wasn't the way I wanted to die. I wanted to die of old age while on tour with the Rolling Stones, staying at the Crillon hotel in Paris and eating boeuf bourguignon.

"I'm not in Paris," I whined, but Harold didn't appear to hear me.

Before Harold Chow could eat my brain, however, another car drove into the lot, blaring a siren and shining a light on him. Detective Remington Cumberbatch had come back for me.

Harold took off, running toward town. Remington parked next to my car, stepped out, and knocked on my window.

"You all right?"

I opened the door. "Harold turned into a zombie," I informed him. "He was going to eat my brain. My grandmother warned me this would happen. It's the phony witch's fault. She's an enemy to love, and she's jamming Grandma's signals."

"I'm going to take you home," Remington said, helping me out of my car.

"Do you think Harold is going to eat anyone's brains?"

Remington guided me toward his car and opened the passenger door for me. "It's doubtful."

"He looked hungry. And naked." I shuddered. I didn't want to see Harold Chow naked.

Remington clicked my seat belt into place and closed my door. He sat in the driver's seat and started up his car. I put my hand on his arm.

"I'm a little tired," I said.

"I'm going to drive you home."

"Grandma warned me about Harold Chow. She said horrible things would happen. I let her down."

We drove the couple of minutes home, and Remington walked me up the driveway. Grandma opened the front door before we got to it.

"Grandma, Harold Chow is a zombie," I said. "He almost sucked out my brain."

"Oh, she's got it bad," Grandma said, and stepped aside for us to enter the house. "Take her upstairs to her room. She needs rest."

"Thanks for calling me," Remington told Grandma. "He was on her car when I got there."

"I knew this would happen," Grandma said.

Remington walked me up the stairs with his hand around my waist.

"This is my room."

He closed the door behind us. Without a word, he slipped Spencer's coat off my shoulders and tossed it on the chair next to my bed.

"Aren't you supposed to be doing an autopsy?" I asked.

"The doc had an emergency. The autopsy's been moved to tomorrow morning." He slipped his fingers under the hem of my dress, lifted it slowly over my head, and dropped it on top of the coat.

"Oh," I breathed.

Remington gave off a lot of heat and took up a lot of space in my room. He never said much, but his presence could not be ignored. He didn't make eye contact; his attention was elsewhere on my body.

"How did you get to me so fast?" I asked.

"Your grandmother called me on our way to the station. The chief dropped me off at my car. Don't worry, he doesn't know about Harold. Or this."

He unhooked my bra with one hand and let it drop to the floor. We stood like that for a moment, as if it was the most normal thing in the world for me to be standing half naked in front of him.

"I don't know what I'm prepared to give you," I said.

"I'm not asking anything from you."

He tugged at my panties until they fell to my ankles, and I stepped out of them. Remington threw back my covers and pulled me toward the bed.

"In," he said.

I lay down, and he tucked me in. It was his turn, and I watched as he stripped naked, folded his clothes, and laid them out on the chair. He was breathtaking. Perfect. Every muscle defined.

Remington lifted the covers off the other side of the bed and lay down. Unbelievably, I fell asleep before his head hit his pillow.

*  *  *

WHEN I woke late the next morning, Remington was long gone. I lay in bed for a while, staring up at the ceiling. The house was quiet. No visitors and no zombies. There was a knock at the door, and Grandma came in with two cups of coffee.

"Sexsomnia," Grandma said.

"What?"

"Harold Chow's syndrome. It's call sexsomnia. He walks in his sleep and goes for it."

"Oh."

"You crapped out with Luanda, huh?"

"Yeah."

She handed me a cup of coffee and sat down on the bed. Grandma rarely asked anything of me, and when she finally had, I'd let her down. Not only had I failed to prove Luanda was a fraud, but I helped seal her reputation as a psychic.

"I'm not giving up," I declared. It was an odd thing for me to say, considering that giving up was my specialty. I was a gold medalist giver-upper. I had given up on everything from high school to clarinet lessons to 356 jobs since I was sixteen.

Grandma patted my leg. "Of course you're not giving up."

"I'm still convinced she killed Rellik," I said. "I just don't know how to prove it."

Grandma sighed. It was unusual for her to sit around without anything to do. "The house is stuck in probate while they search for his next of kin," she told me. "Supposedly he has a sister in Oklahoma, but they're wrong."

"What about a partner?"

"A lone wolf. My signals are still jammed. But I see him working on a lot of houses. And I see him lit up, surrounded by fire."

"That makes sense," I said. "Kidnappers probably go to hell."

Grandma nodded. "That could be it."

"What about a buyer for the house?"

"I've been trying to convince Frances Farian to buy it. She has a litter of cousins that come in every year, and she could use the extra space."

"But he didn't have any buyers before that?" I asked. "Because he said something that day. He said his company aims to please. That's why he built the basement and the panic rooms. Who was he trying to please?"

Grandma shrugged. "That woman's got my radar all wonky."

"I can't figure out a way to get into the morgue, but after I get my clothes from Dave, I'm going to go back up the mountain with Lucy. I have a feeling there's more to find up there."

"Good idea, dolly, but Lucy won't get out until this evening."

"Get out?"

"The hospital. Ruth's there, too. In for observation in case of internal bleeding, but they're fine."

I drank the last of my coffee and put the cup down on the nightstand. "Help me out here, Grandma. I lost a step. Why are Lucy and Ruth in the hospital?"

"The car accident. Swerved in order not to hit Harold Chow when he was running down Main Street in his birthday suit. Luckily, the Apple Days hay-bale display blocked most of the impact, and when they hit Tea Time, there was already a hole in the wall. So it wasn't nearly as bad as it could have been."

"Wait a minute," I said. "Press the rewind button, Grandma. Lucy drove a car into Tea Time? Again?"

"Like a puzzle piece fitting in a puzzle. Like a key through a keyhole. They went right through the gap in the wall. Ruth's car would have been just fine if they hadn't hit the bar."

"No way."

Grandma nodded. "Pure oak, built just after the Civil War. Wyatt Earp stood at that bar and drank a whiskey over a hundred years ago. And, wouldn't you know it, not even a dent. Can't say the same for Ruth's car."

"Yikes."

Grandma got up and took the coffee cups. "By the way, you don't need the boot anymore," she said. "Your foot is fine now. You can stop the antibiotics, too."

I hugged her. "Now, that's how it's supposed to be done. No 'woo woo woo,' no talking to invisible people."


MY CAR was waiting for me in the driveway, with Lucy's pink screwdriver on the driver's seat. There was a fifty-fifty chance that either Spencer, Remington, or Fred had brought it over, but I was hoping for one in particular.

It was a beautiful day but definitely cold. True to his word, Dave had all my clothes ready for me—cleaned, pressed, and hung on wire hangers, wrapped in plastic. He advised me to forget about the red suit-case.

"I can't guarantee there aren't eggs," he said, which was enough to convince me to leave the suitcase.

I changed in his back room. Finally, I was warm and in my own clothes: wool slacks, a turtleneck, a sweater, and my shearling coat.

"Thanks for the job, Gladie," Dave said. "I got some great specimens. I put them in a jar, if you want to see."

I didn't want to see. He helped me put the rest of my clothes in my car.

"Cup O'Cake is running a special on apple–fig mini-tarts," Dave told me. "They make my worms grow great, but they're also really good with coffee."

"Good idea." Taking a few apple–fig tarts with me when I visited Lucy and Ruth in the hospital might smooth over the fact that I had abandoned them right before their accident, I thought.


THE DOOR to Cup O'Cake opened with a tin-kling of the bell, and inside there was a roaring fire and the usual heavenly smells. A small group of fa-miliar faces congregated by the cappuccino maker.

Mavis, Felicia, Mrs. Arbuthnot, Frank Richmond, and Kirk Shields stopped talking when I entered. I waved to cut the awkward moment.

I sauntered over to the table of apple–fig mini-tarts and studied them. I could feel eyes on me. It was a common reaction after I'd had a run-in with a dead person, which wasn't uncommon since I'd moved to Cannes. I was getting a reputation as a murder magnet. They were probably studying me to make sure I didn't have corpse cooties, before they got too close.

Kirk Shields came up behind me. He was dressed in his security uniform, with a heavy utility belt. "Good choice," he said. "I ate five of them. They go great with coffee."

"How about a latte?" Mavis asked me.

"Sure, Mavis, thanks." I ordered two tarts with my coffee and a box to take to the hospital.

"You off to Uncle Harry's?" I asked Kirk.

"Yeah, I have the second shift. No rest for the weary!" He guffawed and slapped my back. I guess he wasn't worried about corpse cooties. "I heard you found our kidnapper. How on earth did you do that in the middle of thousands of acres of trees?"

"Luck."

Mavis handed me a plate of tarts and a latte in a large china cup. Kirk passed her his credit card to pay his bill, and she rang it up at the cash register. He followed me to my usual chair next to the fire.

"So, nobody tipped you off about Rellik?" Kirk asked me.

"Excuse me?"

"I heard about you. You've solved some murders," he continued, leaning down. Kirk smelled of soap on a rope, the cheap kind you get at a drugstore. "Maybe you have a source. Somebody called you, told you where to look for Rellik."

"No," I said. A creepy feeling traveled up my back, like that moment right before Alien shoves its bizarre, battering-ram second mouth into your head.

"Let the poor girl enjoy her coffee and tarts," Mavis told him as she approached the table. "Here—I brought you a box of doughnuts on the house, to remind you of old times."

He took the box in his left hand and signed his credit-card statement.

"I'll tell Mr. Lupino that I saw you," he said, and left with his doughnuts.

I sat back and took a bite of one of the tarts. It was phenomenal. I was becoming addicted to Cup O'Cake, and it would be a hard transition back to Tea Time when Ruth finally reopened.

The only other customers, Frank Richmond and Mrs. Arbuthnot, also exited the shop, leaving me alone. The quiet was heavenly. Felicia busied herself dusting off books.

"Hey, Felicia," I said. "I'm going to get right on that book you loaned me, I promise."

"Don't bother," she said, her voice cold and distant. "Just return it when you can."

"I really want to read it, Felicia. Honestly," I lied.

"Don't lie to me, Gladie. I was a teacher for years. I've been fed a load of bull by more than my share of students."

"No, I mean it—" I started.

She put her hand out, palm forward. "Save it." She threw down her rag and went into the back room. It wasn't the first time I had been yelled at for not completing a homework assignment, but I hated letting down Felicia. She was so earnest in her love of literature, and I had spit in the face of that love.

The tide had turned against me at Cup O'Cake. I wasn't feeling the same warm wave of welcome I had felt before. I put money down on the table, took my box of tarts and screwdriver, and left.

\* \* \*

SOME GREAT genius at the hospital had decided to room Lucy and Ruth together. As I walked down the hall toward their room, I heard them before I saw them. Ruth was in the middle of throwing a fit.

Luckily for Lucy, most of Ruth's ire was directed at the hospital staff, but she had just enough left in reserve to throw a bunch of abuse Lucy's way.

"For the love of God, they cut my gallbladder out while I laid on my kitchen table, and I was working the next day," I heard her complain. "Why on earth do I have to stick around in this death trap? This is where Ebola and flesh-eating bacteria were created. We didn't have all those kinds of diseases before hospitals were invented."

I turned the corner into their room, plastered a smile on my face, and held the box of tarts up high. "Hello, hello," I said. "I'm so glad you're all right."

"All right? All right?" Ruth paced the floor and counted on her fingers. "My car? Destroyed. My shop and livelihood? Ruined. And now my freedom has been forcibly removed. What is this, a hospital or a gulag?" She clanged her bedpan against the wall.

Lucy crooked her finger at me. "They took away my Taser, darlin', and I could really use it right about now," she whispered.

Even in her hospital gown, Lucy was done up to perfection. A Georgia peach, even though she was from Alabama.

"What are you whispering about?" Ruth demanded. "You want another car to drive through my shop?"

"I think I'll be going now," I said.

Lucy grabbed my arm. "Wait. Any word on Luanda? She ran out of Tea Time before the paramedics arrived."

"I haven't heard a peep out of her," I said.

"I couldn't get her to budge on Harry," Lucy said. "I tried everything. I hope she burns in hell."

"You just rest, and I'll see what I can do," I told her. "Don't go anywhere."

I didn't tell Lucy, but I was reasonably certain I knew how to handle Luanda and Uncle Harry. First things first, however: I needed to get back up on the mountain and inspect where Rellik's body had been dumped.

I called Bridget from the hospital-lobby pay phone, and she answered after the first ring.

"No, I will not sit on your face. No, I will not bark like a dog. No, I will not call you Mommy. But let me tell you about Susan B. Anthony," she said.

"Bridget, it's me, Gladie."

"Oh, Gladie, thank goodness it's you. It's been so long since I got a non-sex call. This is a non-sex call, isn't it?"

"Yes. I was just wondering if you'd like to go on a field trip with me."

# Chapter 13

✦ ♥ ✦

*Energy is important, bubeleh. Nowadays, people talk a lot about energy, but they're talking about good energy and bad energy. All kinds of fakakta energy. Ignore that energy. I'm not talking about that. I'm talking about plain old-fashioned everyday energy. I'm talking about high energy and low energy. I'm talking about energy and no energy. I'm talking about the fire in your belly that makes you move forward. Or backward. Or around in circles. Because movement of any kind requires energy. So sometimes your matches go nowhere and you're thinking it's because there's no love, but actually it's because there's no energy. Nothing you can do about it. You have to have fire in your belly to make things happen.*

**Lesson 78,**
**Matchmaking Advice from Your Grandma Zelda**

I MET Bridget at her place, and we drove up the mountain in her Volkswagen Beetle. The phone didn't stop ringing, but she was very good about not using it while she was driving.

"I can't figure these men out," she said. "Why do they keep calling? What pleasure could I be giving them? I've been trying to analyze it, but I don't think I'm any closer to the truth."

"I think it's a pretty base pleasure they receive."

"Amazing that this idiotic, animalistic gender has subjugated females for millennia."

Poor Bridget, she was having no luck turning around the perverts to her cause.

"Maybe you should have the number changed," I suggested, "so you don't have to talk to these guys."

"I'm not giving up yet, Gladie. I still have hope."

I filled Bridget in on the murder. She thought the logical answer was a partner in crime, but, since no money was involved, I had my doubts about that idea.

"Let's see what we find," I said.

The drive seemed shorter in the light of day, but the dirt road was still as muddy as it had been last night. Emergency services had torn up the area where they parked, providing us with a clear sign where to stop. Long tracks cut through the road and into the grove.

"What a mess," Bridget said.

My body tingled, and I felt the rush of blood in my ears. I hopped out of the car and walked into the grove, careful to look down for clues.

"What are we looking for?" Bridget asked.

"Something. Anything. I just have a feeling. Why are you looking at me like that?"

"You sound like Zelda," she said.

"No I don't."

"But with her it's love; with you it's murder."

"That's so not true," I said.

We reached the dog a few minutes later. The police

hadn't even bothered to rebury it. "First we found the dog," I explained.

"I know that dog," Bridget said. "I recognize the collar." There were no tags on the collar, but it was decorated with little Batman symbols. "It's Jim Farrow's dog. What's he doing way up here?"

"Who's Jim Farrow?"

"He's a plumber. Lives on Gold Digger Avenue. He fixed my toilet once and brought his dog with him. What was her name? Oh, yeah. Paws. Poor Paws. I guess Jim wanted her buried up in the grove. Nice place for a dog."

I leaned down. I couldn't tell if Paws had died of natural causes, but her death was recent. There wasn't a lot of decomposition.

"It's a big coincidence, two corpses up here, even if one is a dog," I said.

"Gladie, maybe folks are buried up here all the time, and we just didn't know about it."

It was an interesting hypothesis, but it didn't ring true. The grove was a busy place: The trees were big business, and a lot of people were employed to handle them. The bodies would have been discovered sooner or later.

"Where are the workers?" I asked, looking around. "Shouldn't they be pruning or something?"

"The big harvest is done. It's seasonal work up here. They have a few weeks off now, at least."

"Let's keep looking around," I said.

The area where Rellik had been dumped was framed in police tape. Little flags dotted the ground, which I suspected marked where the body was found.

I froze in place and scanned the area. Last night, the body was hiding amid a lot of brush, and the trees were intact. Today, branches were broken and the brush was trampled on and dispersed in piles around the area.

Emergency services had done a number on it. I was sure the police had taken photos before they started removing brush, but the chances that Spencer would show me those photos were slim to none.

I closed my eyes and tried to remember the scene. It was hard, since it had been dark, I had been on my hands and knees, and then I had upchucked and run away.

"It was like he had been thrown over there," I said, pointing to a place under a tree. "Dumped."

"The murderer must have been strong," Bridget noted.

"Good point. He must have been very strong. Rellik wasn't a small man."

"So he was killed somewhere else and dumped here," Bridget said.

"Another good point, Bridget."

I lifted the police tape and ducked under it. I studied the ground where Rellik was found but didn't find any blood.

"I think you're right, Bridget. He had a lot of holes in him. It would mean a lot of blood."

We searched the area, turning up leaves and twigs. We found an old newspaper, a rusty spoon, and a ChapStick. Nothing to bring us any closer to unraveling the mystery of Michael Rellik's death.

"We're missing something," I said. "I know we are. Something's up here."

I dropped to my hands and knees and combed through the underbrush with my fingers. Bridget searched the branches.

"I'm thirsty," she said after about an hour. "I've got snacks in the car. How about we take a break?"

I was disappointed. I had been sure there was something here for us to find, something that would give us important information. Without it, I was no closer to getting answers, and I really, really wanted answers. But these days, since I'd moved in with my junk-food-loving grandmother, I never said no to snacks.

I stood up and dusted myself off. My clean clothes were now dirty but still intact, and I was loving my shearling coat. So much better than a threadbare Cleveland Browns sweatshirt. Bridget took a step away from the tree and yelped.

"Oh, wow, I almost did a Gladie," she said.

"What do you mean?" Almost doing a Gladie could mean a lot of different things.

"I almost stepped on this." She bent down and picked up a nail from the ground.

"Is that blood on it?" I asked.

The nail was straight and new—clean, except for the blood. Bridget wrapped it in a tissue and put it in her purse. "Was that what you were looking for?" she asked.

Something told me it was. We'd have to get it to Spencer to make sure, but my tingly feeling was telling me the nail in Bridget's purse had made the holes in Rellik's chest.

I was thirsty now, too, and couldn't wait to open a

celebratory bottle of water. We stopped a few yards away from where we'd left Bridget's car by the side of the road and stared at it.

"Are we moving, or is my car moving?" Bridget asked.

"I think it's your car." It was rocking in place with a lot of gusto but going nowhere.

"What could make it move like that?"

"An earthquake?" I guessed.

"An earthquake that only affects the ground under my car?"

She was probably asking the wrong person, since I thought I was living through the zombie apocalypse just last night.

"Maybe a sinkhole," I said.

"Do you hear that?"

There was a low rumbling noise that came and went, and it seemed to be coming from inside Bridget's car.

"A volcano?" I guessed again. None of my theories were very reassuring. We walked closer to the car, watching our step in case there really was an earthquake, sinkhole, or volcano.

"Gladie," Bridget asked, "are you seeing what I'm seeing?"

"I doubt it."

"That's good, because I'm seeing a bear in my car."

"Oh, well, then, yeah, I'm seeing what you're seeing," I said.

"Gladie, there's a bear in my Volkswagen Beetle."

"It's got a lot more headroom than you'd expect for such a small car." The bear was sitting in the driver's seat, happily eating our snacks, but after a moment it looked up, noticed us, and growled a ferocious sound. It clawed at the seat, doing enormous damage.

"I wonder if I'm covered for bear," Bridget said.

"Bridget, let's get the hell out of here."

Bridget grabbed my arm and stood firmly rooted to her spot. "No. We're supposed to freeze. Go ahead, Gladie, play dead like me."

"Isn't that what you do for possums? Play dead?" I asked, never looking away from the bear.

"I don't know. I've never had a possum in my car. I've only had a bear in my car."

I didn't want to die like that, eaten by a bear. It was way down on my list. Below malaria but a notch above being burned alive.

"I vote for running," I said.

"I don't think I can, Gladie. I can't feel my legs."

"I'll feel them for you. Let's get the hell out of here."

"I can't move."

Our debate came to a crashing halt when the bear finished the snacks and grew tired of ripping apart the car's interior. It slid out of the car, dropping huge, clawed paws onto the muddy ground.

"I'm closing my eyes now," I said.

"It's looking right at us," Bridget whispered. "Keep playing dead."

"In a minute we won't have to play," I said.

"It's turning around and walking the other way."

"Maybe it's going to get mustard."

I opened one eye to see the bear's butt recede into the grove. I exhaled loudly, and my body slumped.

"Let's get the hell out of here," Bridget said. Obviously Bridget could feel her legs again: She was running full out to her car. I wasn't far behind.

We had to tag-team the drive back into town, because the bear had eaten the driver's seat. I crouched down and did the pedals while Bridget handled the steering wheel, and we drove that way until we got to the police station.

We bypassed the front desk and marched straight to Spencer's office. He jumped up from his desk and put his hand over his face.

"What is that smell?" he asked.

"Bear," Bridget said.

"Excuse me?"

"We found something," I announced. "For our case."

Spencer's eyes got big. "*Our* case? What case is that, Miss Marple?"

"Rellik, of course." I heard him grind his teeth together. "Are you crying?" I asked.

"You stink," he explained. "You're making my eyes water."

"Show him what we got, Bridget."

"I don't want to see," said Spencer. "Pinkie, you're giddy again. It's written all over you."

"No I'm not."

"Not only are you giddy, but you're more giddy. You're giddy up."

Bridget dug the tissue-wrapped nail out of her purse. "Here," she said, handing it to him.

He took it and unwrapped it. "Probie!" he yelled.

Bridget's phone rang, and she took the call out in the hall. "Finger you?" I heard her ask.

Remington ran into the room. "Yes, boss?" he said, barely glancing my way. He was wearing brown

Dockers and a blue button-down shirt. Spencer showed him the nail.

"What did you find in autopsy?" I asked.

"None of your business," Spencer said.

I turned to Remington. "What did you find in autopsy?"

"Pinkie," Spencer said in his I'm-warning-you voice.

"May I see the report? May I see the body?" I asked, but Spencer was giving me the cold shoulder.

I sighed and took two steps toward Spencer. He choked and pinched his nose. "Why do we have to dance this dance again?" I asked. "You know how it's going to end. You're going to block me and warn me and threaten me, and I'm going to go around you and do what I want."

Spencer seemed to think about my argument for a moment.

"Is the nail the murder weapon?" I asked.

"Well—" Remington started. He glanced at Spencer, and Spencer nodded. "It may be one of the murder weapons. Rellik was shot multiple times with what we think was a nail gun."

"Oh," I said. It made sense. The contractor was killed with one of his tools. "Thank you. Now, was that so hard, Spencer?"

Bridget returned with her phone against her ear. "Yes, I love dogs," she was saying. "No, I don't have doggie style, whatever that is."

"Hey, Remington," I said. "I think I'm watching you fight tonight."

Spencer's eyebrow shot up. "You're what? He's what?"

"I can't go," Bridget said. She had ended her phone call. "I'm hanging out with Lucy after she's released from the hospital."

"Then it will just be me," I said.

My eyes locked with Remington's, and my uterus fluttered.

"I'll take your ticket, Bridget," Spencer said. "And I'll take you, Pinkie, so you don't have to go alone."

"I don't mind going alone."

"I'm taking you," Spencer said. "If you take a shower."

"Can you give us a ride home?" Bridget asked. "The bear ate my front seat."

SPENCER INSISTED we sit in the backseat of his car with the windows open. It wasn't until he saw Bridget's car that he realized that when she said "bear," she really meant bear. He dropped her at her townhouse, where I picked up my car, and then he followed me home, insisting on staying until we went to the fight in the evening.

Grandma was delighted to see him, especially since the house was so unusually quiet lately. "You're lucky the bear was in a good mood," she said, taking one look at me. "Take a shower, and I'll get dinner ready."

Grandma getting dinner ready meant a call for delivery. Even though I didn't smell a thing, I stuffed my clothes in a plastic bag and jumped into the shower.

Downstairs, Spencer was deep in conversation with Grandma at the kitchen table.

"She's a fraud," Grandma was saying as I walked in. "A phony. That Harold Chow business was her fault. Harold needs sensitivity and the right woman."

"Don't we all," Spencer said, swigging a can of root beer.

"You? You don't know what to do with the right woman, tateleh. You have fear, like my granddaughter. The scaredy-cat twins, you two."

I took a seat at the table, and Spencer popped the top of a can of root beer for me. "I'm not a scaredy cat. I took on a bear."

"You mean the one who ate Bridget's car or the one with the tattoos you brought home last night?" Grandma asked.

Spencer choked on his root beer, and I slapped him on the back.

"Has Luanda shown up?" I asked, while Spencer continued to choke, turning the conversation from my night with Remington.

"Last I heard, she was telling the world how she found Rellik and how invisible people were telling her interesting things," Grandma said.

Spencer gasped for air and wiped his mouth. "You know," he said when he recovered, "it might not be safe for her to publicize the fact she's psychic when there's a murderer around. He might see her as a threat."

"She *is* a threat," Grandma insisted. "A threat to love."

THE FIGHT venue was an hour outside Cannes. Spencer was strangely quiet during the ride. I wanted to ask him more about Rellik, about how he died and about his past and the possibility that he had a partner, but I didn't want to be the first to break the silence in the car. I didn't want to be the first to need to talk.

I turned down the visor and applied lipstick in the mirror. I carefully outlined my lips and colored them in with a glossy bright red. I caught Spencer watching me, but he still said nothing.

The outside of the arena was a hive of activity. All sorts of people came and went, excited by the night's show. A large neon sign in front advertised a series of fights. Remington, aka Junior Clay, was just one of the many fighters set to enter the cage tonight.

The parking lot was filled with fighters, too, but the amateur kind, already drunk and fighting over parking spaces, girlfriends, and whatever else caught their fancy. Spencer parked in the loading zone again, right in front of the entrance. Sometimes it was good being a cop, I supposed, if only for the parking.

Spencer escorted me inside with his hand on the small of my back. It was nice to walk in like that with a handsome man who gave me attention, not to mention made my toes curl when he said my name.

The noise was off the charts inside the arena. Rock music blasted through speakers, building the rowdy atmosphere to violence and whetting the appetite for blood.

I was about to ask Spencer to take me home. Despite my recent experiences with dead people, violence and blood made me sick at best, but more often it made me pass out. I changed my mind, however, when I saw the banners with photos of fighters posing in their shorts. There in all his muscular glory, in a fighter's stance with a scowl on his face, was Remington Cumberbatch, the silent naked guy from my bedroom only the night before.

I giggled like a schoolgirl, my voice at least two octaves higher than normal. My giggles were totally involuntary and came out of nowhere, and I tried to push them back to wherever they had begun in my body.

Spencer was horrified. He still wasn't talking, but he was wringing the program and looking from my hysterical self to Remington's picture and back again, as if he was going to kill one of us. The wise money was on me.

"You want a hot dog?" I asked. I took out a ten-dollar bill and waved it at him. He grimaced and grabbed my arm.

Spencer yanked me down the hall, flashed his badge to security, and walked me through a door and down a floor. He flashed his badge again.

"Junior Clay," he said, and was directed through another door.

The room was small, with cinder-block walls, a table in the center, and two folding chairs. Remington was in there warming up, punching at a flat-nosed man, who held up a cushion to protect himself.

"Boss," he said, surprised when he saw us. "What are you doing here?"

Spencer waved the program at him and read out loud. "'Junior Clay will fight a guest contender chosen from the audience in his second bout of the evening.' I'm the guest contender."

"What?" Remington asked.

"What does that mean?" I asked.

Spencer smirked his annoying smirk. "It means I'm going to fight Probie."

# Chapter 14

♦ ❤ ♦

*You know me, dolly. I don't like violence. I'm a love person. Love is my trade, and there is no room for violence with love, no matter what that Shades woman says about it. Violence . . . feh. Love makes the world go 'round. Love is all-powerful. But, in our business, we deal with matches that we don't altogether love. I mean they're a pain in the ass. They don't listen. They don't understand. We can't get anywhere with them. It's like talking to a wall. A really dumb wall, bubeleh. So, believe it or not, sometimes you can't get through to a match with words. Sometimes you need to slap them around a little. Or a lot.*

**Lesson 63,**
**Matchmaking Advice from Your Grandma Zelda**

"YOU SHOULDN'T go in the ring, boss," Remington said.

"Why not?"

"Because I'll kill you."

Spencer puffed up his chest. "Maybe not."

"Oh, I'm pretty sure, boss. You're going to die, and it's going to hurt before you stop breathing."

Remington wasn't threatening Spencer. He was speaking as if he was stating a fact. What's more, he was showing concern for Spencer. Concern tinged with something else: impatience.

Spencer was big, about six foot two, with wide shoulders, six-pack abs, and arms like tree trunks. But Remington was massive and moved like a professional athlete, light on his feet and completely in command of his body.

"Spencer," I said. "Are you sure you want to do this?"

"I can hold my own," Spencer said to Remington, ignoring me.

"Are you really going to kill him?" I asked Remington.

"If he doesn't die, he'll wish he had."

IT TURNED out it wasn't that easy to get "chosen" to be a guest contender. Spencer had to go up the ladder to senior management, flashing his badge as he climbed the rungs. We met with the president of the fight organization and his managers in a suite, which had a bird's-eye view of the arena.

They were busy eating steak and smoking cigars, stereotypical characters from every fight movie come to life in front of me. In the end, it wasn't Spencer's credentials that got him in but their attraction to the idea of a boss taking on his subordinate and, by all odds, getting killed or permanently maimed.

"You got balls," the president of the organization told Spencer. "Elephant balls. Kiss those balls goodbye, by the way."

"Saw a man get his balls punched up into his pelvis once," said one of the managers. "Seven-hour surgery, and he still was never the same. Never interested in you-know-what again."

"You sure you want your boyfriend to do this?" the president asked me.

"Well—" I started, but he wasn't interested in my answer. They were busy with the start of their event, and we were quickly ushered downstairs into a small room, where Spencer was supposed to warm up and get changed. A small monitor hung from the ceiling in the corner, with a view of the cage.

Another flat-nosed man handed me a pile of clothes and gloves. "Here you go. You're on in ninety minutes. You need anything else? A medical bag?"

"Excuse me?" I asked.

"You're his corner man, right?"

"She's just a spectator," Spencer explained.

"You need a corner man or you can't fight," he said.

That's how I became a corner man in a UFC mixed-martial-arts cage fight, which was a first for me. The closest I had ever come to working a fight before that was as a clerk at the biyearly women's shoe sale at Bloomingdale's in Jersey City.

"Spencer, I have a tendency to pass out at the sight of blood or someone . . . you know, someone being beaten to death," I said, after the flat-nosed man left the room.

"You'll do fine," he assured me. I handed him the clothes, and he stripped down. He was a beautiful man. It would be a pity to see him permanently maimed.

"Stop ogling me and tape up my hands."

We sat facing each other, with his hands in my lap.

It took me six tries before I got the tape right. On the monitor, girls in bikinis were holding up signs and jiggling their lady parts.

"This isn't bad," Spencer said. "I could get into this."

The blaring rock music reached us in our closed room. So did the cheers of the crowds.

"It's like *Thunderdome*. It's *Gladiator*. What if they have lions?"

"I'm the lion, baby," Spencer said with a smirk.

The first bout started, and our attention was glued to the monitor. The two men went at it, beating each other across the head. Blood squirted out of one of the men's noses, and he went down to the ground, where the other man squeezed the life out of him with his legs, all the while punching him in the stomach.

My eyes locked with Spencer's, and I felt a tingling in the back of my throat, as if I was going to cry or vomit or something equally embarrassing.

"What if you die?" I breathed.

"Die? I don't care if I die, Pinkie. I never thought I'd live this long, anyway."

His eyes never left mine, as if he was searching for something but unable to find it.

"I care if you die."

"Do you?"

"Yes. One dead person this week is enough for me," I said, sniffling.

The music got louder again, and we watched as the man with the bloody nose was carried out of the cage, unconscious. The jiggly girls returned, danced around, and then it was time for another bout.

This time Remington entered the ring. He hopped in place and focused on his opponent, a man who looked like he had escaped from prison by chewing through the fence. Again, the two men went after each other. Remington punched him twice and quickly got him down on the ground.

"He's not that good," Spencer said.

"Are you kidding? He's a machine. A killing machine, Spencer."

"I think I can take him."

"Take him where?" I asked. "To the movies? To task? To town?"

"He's strong, but so am I," he said. "Pinkie, are you worried about me?"

I was worried, worried that he would die, worried he wouldn't be as pretty anymore, worried that Remington would break his leg in some horrible way where the bone pokes out of the skin, like the poor Louisville college basketball player. I shuddered.

"Of course I'm not worried," I said. "You're a grown man. What do I care if you make a fool out of yourself?"

Spencer flinched. "I won't make a fool out of myself," he insisted.

I took a breath. "Why are you doing this?"

Spencer shrugged. "Everybody needs a hobby."

Remington made quick work of his opponent, winning in only a few minutes. Our door opened, and the flat-nosed man reappeared.

"All right," he said. "You're in the holding bay. Let's go."

The holding bay was two benches in a tunnel that

led out to the floor of the arena. The noise was so loud, it pounded in my chest.

"Can they turn the music down?" I asked the flat-nosed man. "Just a little? I have some inner-ear damage from an infection when I was twelve."

Spencer grabbed me by the front of my shirt and sat me down on one of the benches, next to a man with a FUCK YOU tattoo on his forehead.

"Hi," I told the FUCK YOU man. "I'm Gladie. Nice to meet you. Don't you think the music is too loud?"

"Pinkie, shut up," Spencer said.

"I don't understand why it needs to be quite so loud," I whined. "How about you all?" I asked the row of fighters, who sat facing us on the other bench.

"It gives me a migraine," one of the fighters agreed. He had only one eye, and the top of his left ear was missing.

"That's not right," I said. "Don't they understand about liability issues?"

"Are you a lawyer?" asked another fighter. "Because I got a beef that needs settling." The fingers of his left hand were gnarled, and his nose was bent at a right angle. It was like they had all gone through a communal meat grinder.

"Come here, babe, and sit with us," one of the fighters shouted.

"Yeah, let me take you for a ride on my Eiffel Tower," came an offer from the other side of our bench.

Spencer leaned in close to my ear. "Gladys, you are going to get me killed. I don't want to have to protect you from getting gang-raped by ten cage fighters."

"Don't call me Gladys," I said.

The flat-nosed man took two of the fighters into the

arena. Cheers and a few boos erupted from the spectators.

"You're going to have to hold this." Spencer handed me a little package. It was heavier than I expected and wrapped in his shirt. "It's my gun," he said into my ear. "Don't shoot anybody."

I gave it back to him. "I don't like guns. They make me nervous."

"They make me nervous, too, when you're holding them, but I have no choice. Bringing a gun to a cage fight would be considered an unfair advantage." He smirked and handed it to me again. I slipped it into my purse.

"You're next," the flat-nosed man told us. My stomach rose into my throat, and the room spun around. I gripped Spencer's arm for support, even though I was sitting down.

"Don't pass out yet," Spencer said. "They won't let me in the ring without my corner man."

"Corner-man babe," the flat-nosed man called, and handed me a tote bag, bucket, and stool. "Try to have him toss his cookies in the bucket and not the ring. We just had it resurfaced."

I nodded, and he pushed us out. A spotlight shined on Spencer as he jogged through the crowd toward the cage. I struggled to keep up while lugging the corner-man supplies.

I followed him to the stage and hopped up a few stairs into the cage. Spencer slipped off his shoes. I plopped the supplies down and wiped my forehead and took my shoes off, too. Spencer was dancing around with his arms raised.

"The things I have to do," I muttered under my breath, and danced around behind him, too. "Yay, violence. Yay, blood," I sang, as I hopped up and down and shook my head from side to side.

There was a shift of noise in the arena. The audience grew louder than the rock music. Something had gotten their attention, but I didn't know what. It sounded almost like they were laughing. I looked around to see what had changed, but it was all the same to me.

Spencer stopped dancing, and I ran into him. "What the hell do you think you're doing!" he yelled. He grabbed me by the scruff of my shirt and dragged me to our corner.

"I'm doing what you're doing!"

"Well, don't!" he shouted. "You're the corner man. The *corner* man! Got that? So stay in the corner!"

"Joke's on you, Spencer! The cage is round." I made a circle in the air with my finger, and the audience grew even louder.

Spencer wiped at his face with his gloved hands. "Where are your shoes?"

"I thought I was supposed to take them off. You did."

"Just give me some water and shut up," he said.

"I don't think I like your tone." I wagged my finger at him, but I riffled through the tote, searching for a bottle, because he looked a little worse for wear, and I didn't want him to get dehydrated.

"Come on, come on, the fight's about to start," Spencer complained.

"I don't think there's water in here," I said.

"Of course there's water. Look harder."

I took out a towel and a jar of Vaseline. "What's this for?" I asked, holding up the jar.

"The water! The water!"

"Fine! You don't have to have a cow!"

I laid the towel and the Vaseline out on the floor. I kept searching the tote and found a roll of gauze, tape, and Q-tips, and laid them out next to the other supplies. "Q-tips? That's a funny thing to have at a fight."

"Are you kidding me?" Spencer barked, and knelt down on the ground. He shoved his gloved hand into the tote and found the water bottle. He squeezed it and shot water into his mouth.

"What a cool straw," I said.

He handed me the bottle, and I took a sip. "What are you doing!" he yelled, grabbing the bottle back.

"I'm thirsty, too!"

The referee approached. "You're going to have to get your supplies out of the ring, or I'm going to disqualify you before the fight begins," he told Spencer.

"That might be a good idea, Spencer!" I said, thrilled to find a way out of the fight. "He's not really a fighter," I told the referee.

"Just get your shit off my mat," he said.

"They packed the bag very badly," I explained to the referee.

"Clean it up. Clean it up," Spencer ordered between clenched teeth.

"It's not my fault!"

I repacked the tote, and the music changed to an even louder, acid-rock song. I put my hands over my ears, but it didn't help to drown out the noise. The spotlight moved to an area on the floor, and in danced Remington Cumberbatch, now Junior Clay. He quickly got into the cage.

"Hey, Remington, look who's in the cage." I pointed at myself and waved. He stopped dancing and waved back. His eyebrow shot up to just under his hairline.

His focus went from me to Spencer, and then he punched his fists together a few times and flexed his pectoral muscles.

The referee called Remington and Spencer to the center of the ring and gave them instructions for the fight. I couldn't believe Spencer was going through with it. Had he flipped his lid?

After the instructions, the men went back to their corners.

"Change your mind, Spencer," I urged. "Don't do this. I don't want to see you disemboweled. I don't want to see your nose punched into your brain."

"Gee, Pinkie, your confidence in me is heartwarming. How about the other guy? Aren't you worried I'll disembowel him?"

I looked over at Remington. He was focused but relaxed, poised to strike, like a king cobra. Or a really good-looking leopard.

"No," I said. "I think he'll be fine."

"Mouth guard," Spencer said.

"What?"

"Mouth guard! Mouth guard!"

"No need to get pissy," I grumbled. "What's a mouth guard?"

Spencer tore through the tote until he found a

mouth guard. Meanwhile, the referee told me to exit the cage with my supplies.

"I know what I should do, Spencer," I said, before I left the ring. "I could trip you. You'd only break a leg."

"Get out!" Spencer shouted, pointing toward the exit. It took me three trips to get everything out of the ring. I thought I was done after two trips, but Spencer reminded me about my purse.

The bell rang, and Spencer charged Remington, who seemed apprehensive about pulverizing his boss into dust. He merely fended off Spencer's attack, adopting a defensive posture instead of actually trying to win. It was a great relief. For the first time that evening, I didn't think I would be a witness to Spencer's murder.

I decided to make myself useful and organize the tote while I waited for the round to end. I had figured Spencer wouldn't last a round, but now that Remington was taking it easy on him, Spencer would need his water and maybe the Vaseline, and I would have to be able to find them.

But the round was shorter than I had thought, and when Spencer went back to his corner, I wasn't ready for him.

"Stool," he mumbled through his mouth guard.

I took the mouth guard out for him. "What?" I asked.

"The stool," he repeated.

I ran out again and got the stool. "There you go," I said, patting it. "Right where you need it."

Spencer huffed and puffed and tried to catch his breath while he sat. "Water," he panted.

"Oh, yes, of course," I said, but then it was too late. The bell rang.

"Are you kidding me?" he asked. I put his mouth guard in his mouth and left the ring with the supplies. I was getting the hang of being a corner man. I managed the supplies in one go.

"Spencer, I got it all out in one trip this time!" I yelled from outside the cage.

Distracted by my voice, Spencer turned toward me. It was a mistake. Caught off guard, Remington landed a punch on Spencer's jaw. I heard the crack over the noise of the crowd, and I screamed.

Spencer flew to the floor, landing headfirst. Remington gave me a pointed look, shrugged as if he was apologizing but had a job to do, and joined Spencer on the floor, where he put him in a bare-naked choke hold.

It was sexier on TV. In person, I merely watched in horror as Remington choked Spencer. There was nothing exciting or thrilling about it. Spencer suffered in silence, while the life was literally sucked out of him. I watched Spencer's chest rise and fall and rise and fall. I feared that if I looked away, he would stop breathing.

*Stop the fight before his last breath,* I prayed. *Stop the fight before he dies.*

They did stop the fight, and Spencer continued to breathe. They ran him back to the changing room on a stretcher and laid him on the table, where a doctor diagnosed him as alive and breathing.

Then they left me alone with him, because there was some other gravely injured fighter who needed attending. I leaned over his face.

"Do you want some water?" I whispered. "Do you want some Vaseline?"

Spencer moaned and stirred.

"The doctor said you were alive. Don't prove him wrong."

Spencer opened an eye. "Ouch," he said.

"You're alive," I said.

"At this moment I'm not sure I want to be," he croaked.

"Where does it hurt?"

Wordlessly, he pointed to his forehead. I bent over and softly grazed his forehead with my lips. He was warm and salty. I tasted life on him, strong and resilient.

"Better?" I asked.

"It hurts here, too," he said, pointing to his cheek.

I kissed his cheek, allowing my lips to stay a little longer on his skin.

"And here," he said, pointing to his lips.

I touched his lips with mine, and I felt the familiar electric zing through my body that I felt every time I touched skin with Spencer. He tasted clean, hot, like he was bathed in fire, and maybe he was. I was heating up nicely, too. It could have been a by-product of our chemistry, a connection I couldn't deny, even if I wanted to.

He welcomed my kiss, opening his mouth, and I pressed deeper, slipping my tongue inside. His arms wrapped around my body, and his fingers combed through my hair. Time slowed, and the room disappeared. I felt an almost uncontrollable urge to join him on the table and take the kiss as far as it would go, but something—either common sense or ridiculous prudishness—stopped me, and I broke from our embrace.

"There, all better?" I asked him, my voice coming out deep and hoarse.

Spencer thought about that for a minute. "No, I still hurt," he said. "Here."

He pointed down low, below the belt of his trunks. I slapped his arm.

"You are five years old," I said.

"No, I'm feeling all grown up right now," he said. "And you can't blame a guy for trying."

It took a while, but Spencer managed to get upright, cleaned, and dressed. Besides a black eye, he didn't look like he had almost been killed in a cage in front of thousands of people. I helped him with his shoes, and he clipped his gun onto his waistband.

"Spencer, why did you do this?" I asked.

"Because I'm five years old, remember?"

"No," I insisted. "Why did you fight Remington? Don't you like him?"

Spencer looked me dead in the eyes. "No," he said after a moment. "I don't like him at all."

"He's not a good cop?"

"He's an excellent cop," Spencer said.

After a moment of silence, he added, "I didn't do too bad tonight."

"You were great."

"I mean I didn't die. I'm still walking. My balls are still on the outside of my body."

"All good things," I agreed.

"You didn't have faith in me, Pinkie."

"Shows what I know. You're a born cage fighter."

I opened the door for him, and we walked out into the hallway. "You're not such a bad corner man yourself, Gladys."

"Don't call me Gladys."

# Chapter 15

*Body odor, bowel movements, bellyaches, bosoms, and burps. Lots of "B"s or TMI? Relationship "experts" will tell their clients to stay clear of these embarrassing little topics, but I say: What the hell, get in there and air your dirty laundry. One man's shmata is another man's Dior Couture. Talking about the gas he's got from eating stuffed cabbage might make a woman run for cover, or she might say, "My burrito is backing up on me." TMI can be A-OK.*

**Lesson 56,**
**Matchmaking Advice from Your Grandma Zelda**

I WENT to bed with a smile on my face. For once, I had no new injuries, no one had tried to kill me, and my clothes didn't smell of bear. Besides, I had kissed Spencer, and it didn't end with him passing out or saying something reprehensible. Sure, he did try to get me to kiss his doodad, but I took that as more of a joke than anything else.

I felt like we had started something, and it didn't make me panic. After all, Spencer was hot, he could be fun, and if he really was over his womanizing ways, he could make a good boyfriend.

It had been a long time since I'd had a boyfriend.

Holden hadn't been around long enough to be a real boyfriend, and since I hadn't heard from him since he'd left town, it was doubtful we ever would be a couple again.

Spencer had dropped me off at home and gone back to his house to sleep off the aftereffects of a bare-naked choke hold. I slept like a baby and woke up early, at six. The house was quiet.

Ruth was in the kitchen, reading the paper. "Oh, hi, Ruth. How are you feeling?"

"You mean besides the fact that I'm homeless, jobless, and carless?"

"Uh—"

"There's a fresh pot of coffee. Your grandmother went outside to smell the wind."

I found Grandma in the backyard, looking up at the clear sky in her blue housecoat and slippers.

"Brr, winter is coming quickly this year," I said. "What are you doing out here so early?"

"The wind's changing."

"Uh-oh."

"Changing back, I mean," Grandma said. "Got to get ready. Lots of damage to repair."

We were halfway into a bagel and our first cup of coffee when the doorbell rang. Doris Schwartz, Grandma's old client, was at the door. Her eyes were red and puffy, and her bouffant hairdo had lost its pouf.

"Is Z-Z-Z-Zelda here?" she blubbered. Her nose ran, and she wiped it on her sleeve.

We sat her down in the kitchen and gave her a cup of coffee. She blew her nose on a napkin.

"Didn't get the flu shot this year, Doris?" Ruth asked.

"Oh, Zelda, everything's gone to hell in a hand-basket," Doris said, ignoring Ruth.

"I know," Grandma said.

"I thought I had found love. Luanda matched me with a beautiful twenty-six-year-old model." I choked on my coffee and Grandma slapped me on the back. "He had a lot of energy," Doris added.

Grandma rolled her eyes. "Doris, the last thing you need is someone with a lot of energy, not with your sciatica." Sciatica and the fact that she hadn't seen twenty-six since before I was born.

"Doris, have you been lobotomized?" Ruth asked. "You have as much business with a twenty-six-year-old as I have." I pictured Ruth with a twenty-six-year-old, and I giggled into my coffee.

"I'm a very vibrant woman, Ruth," Doris shot back. "Anyway, he went with me to the barbecue at the Golden Age Senior Center. They have it every year to raise awareness for hip-replacement surgery." Grandma nodded. "And he had too much to drink and insisted on coming home with me."

I didn't like where her story was going. "Maybe I should leave," I said.

"I should have left when Doris started blubbering," Ruth said.

"No, stay, *Gladie*," Doris said. "I need my friends around me now." This was the longest conversation I had ever had with Doris, but I was touched that she counted me as a friend. "So he came home with me, and, well, we went to bed."

I squirmed in my seat. "Have another bagel,"

Grandma told me. I smeared some cream cheese on half an onion bagel and took a bite.

"And he fell asleep," Doris continued. "Fell asleep on my face."

"On your face?" I asked.

"On your face?" Ruth asked.

"Couldn't get him off me until he woke up this morning to throw up." Doris started blubbering for real, big heaving sobs that made her nose run even more and melted the lipstick off her lips.

"That's rough," I said.

"I'm not done," Doris said. "There he was, equidistant between the bathroom and the kitchen, and he chose the kitchen. Threw up all over the kitchen sink. Grossest thing ever. Zelda, I'm matched up with a sink puker!"

"A sink puker," Ruth said. "I wonder what he does in the toilet."

"A sink puker," Grandma repeated, shaking her head. "That fraud Luanda. Look at the damage she's done!"

After a few more graphic details about the sink-puking, Grandma promised to take over Doris's love life and gave her permission never to date the twenty-six-year-old sink puker again.

"The worst thing is that you got no sleep last night," I said.

"Oh, that's nothing new," Doris said. "I've been an insomniac all my life. I never sleep at night."

Grandma and I locked eyes. I knew what she was thinking, because I was thinking the same thing. The solution came to me like a bolt of lightning. "Harold Chow," I mouthed, and Grandma nodded.

Doris would be perfect to make sure Harold the sexsomniac didn't run through town in his sleep, naked and on the prowl.

I felt a sense of accomplishment, knowing Doris and Harold would find happiness together, even though it wasn't officially my match. The day was progressing well, and I was in a better mood than I had been in weeks.

After I had showered and dressed, Ruth insisted that I drive her on her errands, since it was my fault her shop had been destroyed. I was starting to believe it really was my fault. Besides, I felt sorry for her, even though she was a mean old woman.

"I have errands to do, too," I said. "We can make a day of it."


"I DON'T see why we have to do your errands first," Ruth complained. We were driving back from Dave's after I had dropped off my bag of bear clothes. He promised to do a rush job with my shearling coat. The weather had definitely turned cold.

"Keep an eye out for Luanda," I said. "I think I've figured out a way to get her to lay off Uncle Harry."

"If you'd let me go at her with my Slugger, she would lay off the whole town. Take me to Tea Time now. You think you can do that without driving the car into it?"

"I wasn't the one driving!"


A GROUP of construction workers was waiting for us at Tea Time. I parked carefully across the street, and we walked over to meet them. Ruth inspected the contractors like a general with her troops. She didn't seem to be overly pleased with them.

"Not a day over two weeks to complete the job or I don't pay you, and you work around me. I'm opening up today," she said, without even introducing herself.

She handed the head contractor a check, which must have had enough zeroes to soothe his concerns, because, without saying a word, he pocketed the check and ordered his men to start working.

Ruth stepped through the rubble into her shop, and I followed her. Inside, it was Iraq circa Shock and Awe. The wall had exploded inward. Most of the tables and chairs were destroyed, and china cups and saucers littered every surface.

"How can you open up?" I asked. "There's no wall here. Most of your stock is gone."

"I don't care," she said. "I want my life back. I've had enough of your kind." Ruth didn't explain what my kind was exactly, and I didn't ask. I was happy she was reopening Tea Time and getting back to normal. It was another sign that the wind was changing back.

"Starting tomorrow you come here, not to Cup O'Cake," she told me. It was an invitation, a request in command form.

It was hardly a sacrifice to give up Cup O'Cake. Even though they had great stuff to eat, I was starting to get a stink off them, and I was ready to go back to my regular coffee place.

"Can I order my usual?"

"Latte?" she asked, clearly affronted. She thought about it a moment. "Goddamned coffee drinkers. When will you realize tea is the way to go?" She kicked at a piece of rubble. "All right, fine, but don't expect me to like it."

"I'm sort of relieved, Ruth. I don't think Mavis and Felicia like me anymore."

"That family is weird," Ruth said.

"Family? Mavis and Felicia are related?"

"No, Mavis and Arbuthnot. By marriage."


**MY SHEARLING** coat was done when I returned to Dave's an hour later.

"You sure get your share of wildlife," Dave said.

"I used to be a member of Greenpeace."

"I have a customer who's a PETA member. His clothes smell like cat, but you're my first bear customer."

I slipped the plastic off my coat and tried it on while Dave attended to other customers. "A crazy bitch threw spaghetti sauce all over my shirt," one customer explained. "Soul mate, my ass."

Three women were in tears over their silk shirts. "He wanted me t-t-to—" one cried.

I stepped closer, trying to hear what he wanted her to do, but I couldn't make it out through the crying. The other two women were horrified by whatever she said, and they added their dating nightmare stories.

"Excuse me," I said. "May I ask you if you were matched by Luanda Laughing-Eagle?"

"That woman! If I ever see her again, I'm going to wring her neck!"

The man with the spaghetti sauce turned toward me. "I'll give you twenty bucks to tell me where she is. I have a score to settle with her."

Grandma was right. There was a lot of damage to be fixed. Luanda had left disaster in her wake.

"Aren't you the Burger girl?" one of the women asked me. "Related to Zelda?"

"Yes."

"I should never have fired her. She knows what she's doing. Luanda is a hack."

I smiled. The day was getting better and better. Everything was falling back into place where it should be. Like magic.


I DROVE through town, intent on enjoying some Apple Days ambience now that the wind had changed. It had been a shame to miss even one day of what the town did best.

I parked on Main Street. The construction workers were busy hauling rubble away from Tea Time. Ruth was hanging a YES, WE'RE OPEN sign on the lamppost outside her store. I waved at her, and she sneered back at me. Everything was back to normal.

I called Bridget and Lucy from the pay phone outside the drugstore and invited them to Saladz for lunch. Lucy jumped at the chance to go out, but Bridget took some convincing.

"I don't know, Gladie," she said. "The men are out there."

"No, the men are in your phone, Bridget. You need to turn off the phone."

I sauntered down the street toward Saladz. I passed the apple-head-doll store, the pub, which advertised apple wine, the home-goods store with the apple-scented candles and soaps display in the window, and the jewelry shop, which specialized in silver charms shaped like apples.

Daisy from the ice cream shop was sweeping in front of her store, getting ready to open. "Hey, Gladie," she greeted me. "Haven't seen you in a while. I've got delicious apple ice cream with a crumble topping just waiting for you."

"I'll bring Bridget and Lucy after our lunch," I promised her.

"Good. You, I welcome. But no more couples. We've seen the most bizarre dates lately. Tragic."

I was early for lunch, so I decided to take a walk in the little park on Main Street. There wasn't a cloud in the sky, and my shearling coat was protecting me from the cold. I took a seat on one of the park benches, and movement in one of the bushes caught my eye.

I jumped three feet in the air, maybe because I'd so recently had a run-in with a bear. But it was doubtful a bear had made it all the way into town and was hiding in a bush in the park.

The bush kept shaking, then a swath of lavender material peeked out. "Oh, my God," I breathed.

I pushed the leaves of the bush aside. There, hiding with her butt in the air, was Luanda Laughing-Eagle.

"What are you doing in here?" I asked.

"Hiding. What the hell do you think I'm doing?"

I grabbed hold of her hips and yanked as hard as I could. "No more hiding for you, missy," I said. "We need to talk."

She held on to the bush for all she was worth. "Please, Gladie, don't. They're after me."

I managed to extract her from the bush. She looked horrible—dirty, sweaty, and molting. Her feathers had migrated south, sticking to her filthy clothes.

"Of course they're after you. You made terrible matches. It's bedlam out there."

"I did what the spirits told me to," she said, sniffling.

"Your spirit-talking days are over, Luanda. You suck at spirit talking."

Luanda wiped her nose on her sleeve. "That's not true. I'm going to prove it. You'll see."

"Are you going to lay off Uncle Harry now?"

Luanda's eyes rolled back in her head, and she moaned. "I have found Harry Lupino's soul mate. I cannot stop true love," she said in a haunting baritone voice.

I dug through my wallet and took out a hundred dollars of Harry's money. Sometimes you have to pay to play. Sometimes it takes money to make money.

"Here, spirit talker." I handed her the money. "A hundred dollars. It's all I've got. Lay off Harry."

Luanda grabbed the money and stuffed it in her cleavage.

"Fine," she said in her normal voice. "The spirits are telling me Harry's not ready for love."

"Smart spirits."

Luanda crawled back into her bush.

"You can't stay in there forever," I said.

"Just until I turn this around. Go away before you draw attention to my bush."

WE TOOK a seat at a table by the window. Lucy was impeccably dressed, without a hair out of place. She was the picture of poise and class, but I knew her well enough to sense her tension below the surface. Days of anxiety over Uncle Harry, two car accidents, and a kidnapping had taken a toll on her.

Meanwhile, Bridget's sojourn in Pervertland had completely altered her appearance. She looked like she had been run through a car wash and hung out to dry. Her skirt and blouse were more wrinkled than not and buttoned on the wrong buttons, making her appear lopsided. Her hair was poufed out on one side and flat against her head on the other. I doubted she had slept last night.

Bridget took one last phone call as we sat. "No, I don't mind fudge packers. I'm a big chocolate lover. Would you like me to sign you up for the National Organization for Women? Hello? Hello?"

"No luck yet?" I asked.

"No wonder women earn only eighty cents on the dollar. Men are pigs," she said.

I ordered an Apple Days Cobb salad and an apple iced tea. Lucy ordered the Chinese chicken salad, and Bridget the pancakes.

"I have news," I announced when we got our drinks. "Something to toast." We raised our glasses. "Luanda has given up on Uncle Harry. He is officially free from the witch and her spirits and never again has to contemplate marrying Ruth Fletcher."

Lucy screamed and hugged me. "Thank you, Gladie. How did you do it?"

"Let's just say I'm a genius unmatchmaker. After lunch I'm going over there to tell him."

"Oh," said Lucy, fixing her hair.

"You want to come with me, Lucy?"

"I have work."

"Poor Uncle Harry," I said. "So lonely."

"What?" Lucy asked.

"Yeah, he doesn't let on, but he's in that big house without anyone to love, if you don't count Lurch and the two Cujos. He's probably ready for love in his life. Commitment. Not Ruth Fletcher, of course, but someone else to love."

I studied Lucy to see if she was catching on or if I was being too subtle.

"I hear Doris Schwartz is single," Bridget said. "She just had a bad breakup with a young guy. She might want to go older now."

Lucy shot Bridget a nasty look.

"My grandmother already matched Doris," I told them. "I was thinking somebody more his speed, classy, someone he knows already."

"I'm not sure I appreciate you trying to match Uncle Harry, Gladie," Lucy said. "We just got him free from Luanda."

I almost banged my head on the table. Getting through to Lucy was no easy task.

"Sorry, Lucy. I'll forget it."

"Do you hear that?" Bridget asked.

"What, darlin'?" Lucy asked.

"Those men. Their voices sound familiar." We listened for a minute. Three men at the neighboring table were talking about football and toe fungus. "Oh, my God. Oh, my God," Bridget whispered, covering her eyes with her hand. "I know those voices, those men. One of them asked to beat the cheeks and take a ride on my donkey express."

# Chapter 16

✦ ♥ ✦

*The devil's in the details. You've heard that bubbe meise before? Well, it's true, dolly. But people are scared of the devil, and they don't want to get too detailed about the details. I have the reputation of just knowing things, of being a big-picture person. It's true that I'm a big-picture person, but in my big picture are many tiny little details. Don't let the details pass you by. You can't have a big picture without details, dolly.*

**Lesson 34,**
**Matchmaking Advice from Your Grandma Zelda**

LUCY WENT off to work, and since Bridget had no car, she agreed to go with me to Uncle Harry's. I convinced her to turn off her phone and just relax for the afternoon. Five minutes into the ride, she slumped against the car window and fell asleep, snoring softly.

As we got closer to Uncle Harry's, I started to fantasize about what I would do with my money. Sure, I'd had to pay Luanda a hundred dollars to get off his back, but I would still have more money than I had had in months.

Kirk Shields, Uncle Harry's security guard and my fellow kidnappee, stopped us at the front gate. "Hi,

Kirk," I said, rolling down my window. "It's me again. How are you?"

"Fine. You're not on my list."

"I know, but I'm here on business. I have good news for Uncle Harry."

Kirk called the house to announce us. I noticed his phone hand was bruised and cut.

"Ouch," I said. "That looks like it hurts."

He slipped his hand into his pocket. "It's nothing. Accident," he said, and waved us through.

"When the workers rise up, this will be the first house to go," Bridget said, seeing Uncle Harry's mansion for the first time.

"They'll have to get past the dogs," I said. We could hear the dogs through the doors, growling and snapping their teeth. "Don't show fear."

Uncle Harry's butler answered the door and let us in. I held my breath as we squeezed by the growling Rottweilers. "Hey there, Legs, how's it hanging?" Uncle Harry greeted me in his living room. The last time I was there, a fireball was hurtling through it.

I introduced him to Bridget, and we took a seat on his gigantic couch. Bridget was looking around as if she was memorizing the location of the doors for the eventual revolution and invasion of the proletariat.

"Give me good news, Legs," he said. "The witch has shown up here three times since I saw you last. She woo-woo-wooed for hours. I still have a headache. I'm contemplating moving."

"I have good news, Uncle Harry. I unmatched you. Luanda is going to leave you alone now. You're free."

I threw my hands in the air to illustrate his freedom. He jumped up off the couch and hugged me. Then he poured himself a glass of brandy and gave me a handful of hundred-dollar bills.

"What a relief," he said. "She was worse than Eddie Two-Fingers. You're pretty good at your job. I'm impressed."

"Well, technically, unmatching people is not my job."

"Pity, 'cause you're a natural."

"Do you mind if I ask you a question?"

"You can ask, but I don't promise I'll answer."

"In all your dealings with land development and construction, did you ever come in contact with Michael Rellik?"

"The kidnapper? Yeah, sure. He made a bid, but we didn't take it." Uncle Harry lit up a cigar and took a puff.

"Too high?" I asked.

"No, his background wasn't clean, something about a fire in Orange County."

"In Orange County?"

"Yeah. Strictly speaking, he wasn't a local. Moved here a couple years ago. Why do you ask?"

There was a clicking in my brain, like cogs were moving into place. "What's the story about the fire?"

"Legs, are you snooping again?"

I shrugged my shoulders.

"Some people died," he explained. "There was a rumor about the electrical wiring. My associates and I don't need that kind of trouble."

Uncle Harry already had questionable associates and opposition to his development plans by Mrs. Arbuthnot and other members of the community. If anything went wrong with the construction, Uncle Harry's future prospects were finished.

"That's odd," Bridget said. "He seemed like a very good contractor. The house we saw was beautiful."

"That may be, little lady," Uncle Harry said. "But I wouldn't turn the lights on, if I were you."

"May I ask you something else?" I continued.

"About the kidnapper?"

"No, about your security guard."

"You interested in him? I thought you and the chief were an item," he said.

My face got hot. I thought back to our kiss, to Spencer risking his life in the cage. For what? To prove something to himself? To me? To impress his girl? Was he sending me a message through his actions because it was impossible for him to verbalize it?

"No, we're not an item," I told him. "And I'm not interested in your security guard. I mean, not in that way. I was just wondering what you know about him."

"Former cop. Clean record. As far as I know, he shows up on time. Other than that, I don't care. Is that all, Legs?"

"One more thing: You're taking Lucy out for breakfast tomorrow morning."

"What?" Bridget cried. "He is?"

"Yes, it's time. Don't you think so, Uncle Harry?"

Uncle Harry stubbed out his cigar and smiled. "Technically, is *that* your job?"

"Lucy is an intelligent, kind, generous, beautiful woman, and you would be lucky to go to breakfast with her," Bridget said, her hackles up.

"Yes, it's my job, but Lucy is my friend, so this is on the house," I added.

Uncle Harry smiled. "Lucy Smythe," he said, like he was tasting her name in his mouth. "That might be a good idea, Legs."

"I have those on occasion," I said.

I JABBED the screwdriver into the ignition and started my car. "I have a great idea," I told Bridget.

"About Lucy?"

"No."

"About the snooping?" she asked.

"Yep, about the snooping."

I PARKED in the hospital's lot.

"I thought we were going to the morgue," Bridget said.

"Actually, there's no official morgue in Cannes. Usually the bodies go directly to the mortuary or to San Diego if they need to be autopsied. They set up a makeshift morgue in the basement for Rellik, though, since Remington was here," I said.

"A morgue in the basement," Bridget repeated.

"I know. Gross. It's all my fears combined into one ball of terror." I counted on my fingers. "Dead person, diseases, murder, closed spaces, really mean nurses, and toxic cleaning products. That's why I brought this."

I held up a bottle of beer that I had pinched from Uncle Harry's house.

"I'm going to get just enough buzzed not to freak

out, because getting put on a seventy-two-hour psychiatric hold is another one of my fears."

"And mad cow disease," Bridget said.

"Mad cow?"

"Yes, there's a mad-cow-disease scare at the hospital, too."

"How contagious is that?" I asked. "Can it travel through the vents?"

"I think you get it from eating hamburgers."

My hand flew up to my mouth. "Oh, my God," I said. "I ate a hamburger yesterday."

"Maybe now's a good time to break open the beer."

"Oh, you want some, too?"

Bridget eyed me. She was haggard and slightly greasy. Dealing with sex fiends who didn't share her feminist convictions had taken a toll on her.

"Of course I'll share," I said. "Do you have a bottle opener?"

It took us fifteen minutes to get the cap off the bottle. The half a beer didn't give me the buzz I was hoping for. But I did succeed in managing my freakout by pretending I was going for an expensive facial. That way, I could explain away the mean nurses and the toxic cleaning supplies.

It was harder to get to the basement than I had envisioned. We needed a special key for the elevator to go down to that level.

"'Personnel only,'" Bridget read aloud. "Now what?"

What would Nancy Drew do? I wondered. Would she give up and go home? I was pretty sure she wouldn't let a key get in the way of her and a makeshift morgue. I shuddered. Maybe Spencer was right.

Maybe I couldn't help myself. Maybe I was a sicko meddler who needed professional help, or at least really good prescription pills.

"Bridget, we have a right to get down to that morgue. Power to the people."

"I'm all for power to the people," Bridget said, "but I'm not sure that includes breaking into a morgue to inspect a dead man."

"In the movies, they steal doctors' uniforms from the linen closet," I said. "We could do that."

"That wouldn't help with the elevator," Bridget pointed out.

I drummed my fingers on my cheek. "There's probably no key in the linen closet," I said.

An orderly approached us. "The elevator's not working?" he asked.

I racked my brain, trying to think of an excuse for why we were there. I didn't want him to get suspicious, didn't want to draw attention to us. If we were caught, we would be sent off to jail, and I can't pee in front of other people.

"Uh," I said.

"It's working," Bridget said, "but we need to go down to the basement, and we don't have a key."

I almost punched her. She didn't know the first thing about stealth reconnaissance missions. To be fair, neither did I, but I did know that when confronted by the enemy, lie, lie, lie.

"I have a key," the orderly said. "I'll get you down there." He pushed the DOWN button, and the elevator doors opened. Once we were in, he put the key in the slot and turned. "Push the minus one, and it will take you right there," he said, smiling, and hopped out of the elevator.

The doors closed, and we started our journey down to the basement. "People are too trusting," I said.

"I hope he doesn't get in trouble," Bridget said.

"I mean, we could be terrorists."

"If he gets arrested, I'll make sure he gets good representation," Bridget continued.

We arrived at the basement, and we stepped out. The hallway was abandoned. No alarm went off; no cops were there to arrest us.

"The security is pathetic at this hospital," I said. "Perhaps we should report them. I don't feel safe at all."

"Which way is the morgue?"

"Just follow my panic attack. Better than the yellow brick road."


WE ALMOST missed it. Michael Rellik's body was being stored in a small, nondescript walk-in cooler at the end of the hall. His black body bag lay on a shelf.

"We're going to need more beer," I said.

"If I believed in the supercilious constructs of the Judeo-Christian tradition, I would say his soul is already in heaven or hell, and the only thing in this body bag is an empty vessel," Bridget said.

"It's awfully cold in here," I said, shivering.

"That's so that his flesh doesn't rot."

"I definitely should have pinched a second bottle of beer." I took a deep breath. "Okay, how about you unzip and I look. Deal?"

"Deal." She unzipped, and I took a look.

"They sewed him up," I noted.

"That's from the autopsy. What else do you see?"

"Five little holes."

Bridget zipped him up, and we jogged back to the elevator.

"Did you find what you were looking for?"

"I don't know," I said, but I couldn't deny that a theory was forming in my brain. "Do you mind if we make another couple stops?"

I drove out of the lot, and Bridget checked her phone. "Twelve messages." She sighed.

"Delete them without listening to them, Bridget."

"What if they're calling to hear more about Gloria Steinem?" she asked.

Poor Bridget. She was the last suffragette standing.

I DROVE to Gold Digger Avenue and parked in front of a gray-and-white ranch house. I knocked on the door, and Jim Farrow answered. He was middle-aged, trim, with long hair and a beard. He was head to toe in denim. "What do you want?" he demanded.

"Hi, Mr. Farrow. I'm Gladie Burger. I found your dog on the mountain."

"Come on in," he said.

Farrow's house was tidy and modest. He offered us coffee and invited us to sit at his kitchen table. "I loved that dog. I know it's stupid for a grown man to love a dog, but she was something special."

"Very well behaved," Bridget said. "You brought Paws over to my place once. She was sweet."

"How did she die?" I asked.

"The police think she was poisoned. Why would someone do that to her? For kicks?"

"We thought she died normally and you buried her up there," Bridget said.

"No, we were walking in the Main Street park, and she took off. She does that sometimes to say hi. She's very social. *Was* very social."

"Who was she saying hi to?" I asked.

"I don't know. She disappeared. I didn't think anything about it for a while, and then I looked for her in her usual haunts."

"She had haunts?" Bridget asked. Farrow's dog had a more active social life than I had.

"The cheese shop, the hardware store, like that," he explained. "I even checked my last work site, but she wasn't there."

"Where was your last work site?" I asked.

"The old Terns house." The house across the street. The Rellik house. Time stopped in Farrow's kitchen, as we all reached our own conclusions.

"That bastard," Farrow said after a minute. "He killed my dog."

"Wow. He poisoned Paws while he had us locked up," Bridget said.

It was a good theory and probably right, but I was stubbornly seeing things differently. We finished our coffee and left Farrow's house.

"That is so sad," Bridget said. "He's going to be lonely now."

"You could give him your number."

"Not funny, Gladie."

"Let's go for a walk," I said. "Check out the neighborhood."

We didn't walk far. Cup O'Cake was only a few houses down from Farrow's. The shop was experiencing an after-lunch lull, and we were the only customers. Nevertheless, Mavis and Felicia gave us the cold shoulder. Gone were the effusive customer relations and free cupcakes.

"Maybe we should go to Tea Time," Bridget whispered to me. "I heard Ruth is up and running but you have to bring your own cup."

"I'm not running away with my tail between my legs," I said, continuing with the dog theme of the day. "Order for us."

She ordered two ham-and-cheese paninis and a box of cupcakes to take home.

"Is it me?" Bridget asked me. "They must have heard about the sex calls. People can be so judgmental!"

"They didn't hear about the sex calls," I said. "It's not you; it's me. They don't like me."

"How can they not like you? You're so likable. I like you."

"I like you, too," I told her. "You know, despite the sex calls."

Bridget took a bite of her panini. I was surprised to realize I wasn't hungry.

"Maybe I should get the number changed." Bridget had deflated, like a balloon a week after a party. "I'm not doing any good. They're very persistent. And numerous."

I nodded. "There's no shortage of horny men in this world," I agreed. "And they're reluctant to give up their perversions." I was an expert on horny men not giving up their perversions. I had worked at an adult bookstore in Butte for one memorable evening.

"This is the best panini I've ever tasted," Bridget said.

"I've gained three pounds since I discovered this place."

"You'd think they would have more customers. Where is everybody?"

"It's usually busier," I said.

"I like it this way," Bridget said, and slumped down in her chair. "Relaxing. No craziness."

The door slammed open, knocking the little bell onto the floor with a clang. Luanda danced in with a flourish, her shoes hitting the floor like *Lord of the Dance*. Her soggy feathers stuck to her face and back, and her layers of skirt were filthy.

"I am Luanda, and I speak to dead people!" she announced.

"Yes, we've been introduced," I said.

"Oh, my. Oh, my." Mavis swatted Luanda with her tea towel. "Shoo! You're traipsing dirt into my store."

Luanda grabbed the tea towel and yanked it out of Mavis's hand. "I have an announcement," she said, her voice deep and ghostlike. She put her arms up like she was going to hit a home run.

"I know who murdered Michael Rellik!"

I gasped, and so did Bridget, Mavis, and Felicia.

"The spirits have imparted their knowledge, and I will make the announcement today," she continued.

"Okay, we're waiting," I said.

Luanda woo-woo'd and danced in a circle. "Two hours," she sang. She pointed at me. "You be there," she commanded. Then she went around the shop, pointing at everyone. "You be there. You be there. You be there," she repeated. She floated back to the door.

"Where?" I shouted, as she was leaving.

"Your grandmother's house, of course," she said, and ran off like a crazy, soggy, New Age bird.

"Do you think she really knows who the murderer is?" Bridget asked me.

"Probably not, but when the hordes arrive, we'd better be there to help my grandmother, not to mention to protect Luanda from her."

I paid and took the box of cupcakes with us. We drove back through the historic district. Bridget turned her phone on and began to listen to her messages.

"Is this what men want?" she asked me. "All these unconventional acrobatics? All this dirty talk?"

"I have no idea what men want," I said. "Maybe it's not unconventional or dirty. Maybe we're behind the times."

"No, that can't be it," Bridget said.

What did men want? Were they merely testosterone jelly wrapped in a skin suit? I thought I had understood Holden's intentions. He had been devoted and loving, but I hadn't heard from him since he left town, and, in my book, those weren't the actions of a man in love. Although it could very well be that it was dangerous for him to contact me and he was only trying to protect me.

Spencer was even more complicated. An avowed womanizer, yet he swore he was turning over a new leaf. And our kiss said something: Affection. Devotion. Friendship.

I knew in my heart that I was finally ready to give

Spencer the benefit of the doubt, to allow our relationship to grow in whatever way it would.

I realized I had been holding my breath, and I let it out, exhaling slowly.

"Is that Spencer?" Bridget asked, pointing toward Saladz.

I slowed the car as we passed by. There on the sidewalk was Spencer, playing mouth hockey with a too-tall, too-thin redhead. It was bad enough that he was back to being a player, but playing with a thinner, younger model was unforgivable.

I skidded to a halt, made a U-turn, and drove up on the curb next to the happy couple.

"Bridget, hand me the box of cupcakes," I said.

I stepped out onto the sidewalk with the box in my hands. For a brief moment, I thought maybe I should remain calm, cool, and classy, maybe I should get back in the car and just forget about Spencer and what a traitorous jerk he was.

Then the brief moment passed, and I opened the box and beaned Spencer in the head with a cupcake. The fact that half of it landed in his girlfriend's hair extensions was just an added benefit.

Spencer looked up as if it were raining cupcakes, but then he spotted me, and his face turned from shock to anger and back to shock again.

I threw another cupcake.

# Chapter 17

✦ ♥ ✦

*It's all about motivation, bubeleh. The who, where, what, and how are interesting, but as matchmakers we need to investigate the why. Why does someone want love? Why is someone attracted to someone else? Why can't they find love on their own? Why did they come to us for help? The why gives us insights that can answer more questions than just the why. Why? I don't know, but it's important.*

**Lesson 60,**
**Matchmaking Advice from Your Grandma Zelda**

THE SKINNY girl ran for it down the street. I lobbed three more cupcakes and hit Spencer square in the face. I was on fire. I couldn't miss. I was the Incredible Hulk of cupcake throwing, my body turned superhuman from an uncontrollable rage.

Unfortunately, I had bought only six cupcakes from Cup O'Cake, and they ran out quickly. Spencer wiped his eyes clean with the hem of his shirt. He was madder than hellfire, but not madder than me. I looked for something else to throw at him.

"Are you kidding me?" he yelled in my direction. "Brand-new Armani!"

I growled at him. It came out less like the Incredible

Hulk and more like PMS, but he got the picture. We were drawing a crowd. A lady came up and handed me a plate.

"Go after him," she urged. "Show him who's boss."

I tossed the plate, but my aim was off and it narrowly missed him, crashing against a lamppost instead.

"What the hell?" he shouted. He marched over and leaned down so his face was nearly touching mine. "Have you finally lost all your marbles?"

"I lost my marbles last night!"

"Last night? What happened last night?" he asked. "Oh," he said, finally recalling the details of the night before.

"I will never ever talk to you again!"

"Is that a promise?"

"Better yet," I yelled, "I will continue to talk to you! But I will never ever flirt with you again!"

Spencer grabbed my arm and tugged me toward his car. "Okay, that's it. We're moving this conversation somewhere else."

"This conversation is done. I have no more to say to you," I said, crossing my arms.

"Oh, Pinkie, if only that were really true."

"What are you doing?"

"Handcuffing you," he said. "Just until I get you calmed down."

I fought against him and tried to get free, but he put the handcuffs on me and squeezed them tight. "Ow! I'm not going to calm down if I'm handcuffed!"

Out of the corner of my eye, I saw Bridget approach.

"I want a lawyer!" I called out.

Spencer shoved me into the backseat of his car. "You don't need a lawyer, woman. You need a straitjacket."

And then we were gone, driving west out of the historic district, Bridget standing at the curb, her mouth open. He finally stopped when we were far out on a dirt road near the mine. It was abandoned except for us, and the sun was beginning to set.

He pulled me from the car. "I'm going to take the cuffs off you now," he said. "You think you can refrain from taking a swing at me?"

"I'm not barbaric."

"Pinkie, you gave me a wallop with the cupcakes. It's like you're the Girl with the Dragon Tattoo. Next you'll be getting a nose ring. Are there brass knuckles in your purse?"

He took the cuffs off my wrists, and, true to my word, I didn't take a swing at him.

"So, what's this about?" he asked.

"What's this about? The skinny girl. You were kissing a skinny girl."

"And you don't like skinny girls?"

"You know what I mean."

"No, I don't. Enlighten me."

He was insufferable. He was worse than his usual smirking, smug self. He was actually bewildered, unsure of why I was upset.

"You said you were off women for a while."

"The moment ended," he said. "An opportunity presented itself. Pinkie, I'm a healthy man."

"Are you in love with her? Is it serious between you two?"

"I just met her."

"And so you throw everything away for a woman you just met?" I asked.

"Throw what away?"

"You told me you were off women," I insisted. "You were done with your womanizing ways. You lied to me. You are a big, fat liar!" I was nearly frothing at the mouth. I was seeing red. If there was anything at all I could have thrown at him, I would.

"Pinkie, I'm not fat."

"How dare you lie to me like that! How dare you go back on your word!"

Spencer waved his hands in the air. "Hold on, hold on. This is none of your business. If I want to see a woman—skinny or not—I will see her, and it's none of your business. It's my business; it's her business. Not your business. You understand? It's between her and me and my manhood, if you catch my drift."

"But—" I started.

"No!" He wagged his finger at me. "I'm a grown man. I don't answer to you."

My throat got thick, and my nose ran.

Spencer raked his fingers through his hair. "Don't start that," he said. "That's playing dirty." I sniffed and wiped a tear away. Spencer growled low in his throat.

"It is too my business," I croaked.

"How is it any of your business?"

"It just is."

"How? Tell me how."

"Because—" I started, but stopped myself. I didn't want to give him the satisfaction. There was no use having a heart-to-heart with Spencer Bolton. He didn't have my best interests at heart.

"You know, Spencer, you've always been a mystery to me."

He smirked. "I get that a lot."

"But the mystery is solved. I know exactly what you think of me."

Spencer's eyes grew enormous. "Of you?"

I went back to the car, and Spencer followed on my heels.

"Were we talking about you?" he asked, concerned.

"Take me home."

"What do you mean, what I think of you?"

"I'm in a hurry, Spencer. Luanda is coming over to point her finger at the murderer."

"I might have misunderstood," he said, and ran around the car, sat in the driver's seat, and put his key in the ignition. "Really, I think I missed some of our conversation. Can we recap?"

"Drive," I said.

GRANDMA MET us in the driveway in her best Vera Wang knockoff and Jimmy Choos. "Get in quick," she urged us. "I need help setting up. They're about to invade."

"Who's invading?" I asked.

"Everybody. The phony baloney told everyone to come." She pointed at Spencer. "She said you would arrest them if they didn't come."

"What did you mean, think of you?" Spencer asked me, as we entered the house.

We set up the folding chairs in the parlor and were

putting chips and dip on the coffee table when Lucy and Bridget arrived.

Lucy studied Spencer. "I heard you got pastried, darlin'," she said. "I heard you almost choked to death from icing up your nose. Did Gladie give you that shiner with a cupcake?"

"No, Remington gave him that last night," I said.

"Spencer, may I see you privately about sex talk?" Bridget asked Spencer.

"Uh," he said. Spencer looked around, as if he was searching for a means of escape, but when Bridget beckoned him to follow her to another room, he went.

"You'll never guess who called me," Lucy said when we were alone. I thought I could guess pretty easily, but I let her tell me. "Uncle Harry asked me out for breakfast tomorrow morning."

After one phone call, Lucy was back to her normal self. Gone was the panic-stricken, anxiety-ridden Lucy, and in her place was the put-together Lucy I was used to. Something told me Ruth no longer had to fear when Lucy was behind the wheel. She would never drive through Tea Time again.

Grandma walked in, carrying a plate of brownies. "Meryl dropped these off on her way to the dermatologist to get her skin tags removed," she explained. "She was sorry she was going to miss the show."

"Very nice of her," Lucy said, taking a brownie. "Who else is coming, Zelda?"

"The new detective just parked around the corner, and the entire team from the panic rooms is walking up the driveway right now," she said, putting the plate of brownies next to the bowl of guacamole. "All except Ruth. She told Luanda to get stuffed."

"I heard that four of her disgruntled clients chased her down the street today," Lucy told us.

"It's only the beginning," Grandma said. "I feel sorry for her."

"She almost destroyed your business, Grandma."

"That's true, but her future is dicey, dolly. You know what Luanda needs? Love."

I thought Luanda needed a prescription for a good antipsychotic.

While Grandma welcomed Mrs. Arbuthnot, Mavis, and Felicia, I made myself small in the corner. I wasn't feeling the love from them lately, and I didn't want to try to make polite chitchat.

Next up was Detective Remington Cumberbatch, who was even more massive in Grandma's old parlor. He nodded to the ladies and took a place standing next to me in the corner. Heat wafted off his body in waves, hitting me right in the pelvis.

"How are you feeling?" I asked him. After all, he had spent the last evening in the cage.

He smiled in answer. Remington was a man of few words. He didn't need them. His biceps did all the talking.

Luanda floated in next. She had changed her clothes and was wearing layers of red taffeta and a new crown of feathers on her head.

"I am Luanda—" she announced in her loud sing-song voice. "Hey, where is everybody?"

"The two men you invited are on their way," Grandma said.

The two matchmakers locked eyes. "Zelda Burger,"

Luanda breathed. "Prepare yourself to be amazed this evening."

"Luanda, I'm always amazed. I'm amazed right this second, talking to you."

Luanda seemed pleased by Grandma's backhanded compliment. She took a seat. It was the first time I had ever seen Luanda relax. She scooped up some guacamole with a chip and took a bite.

Mourning the loss of my cupcakes, I took a brownie and offered Remington one. To my surprise—I had assumed that with his body he never ate anything that tasted good—he took it. We stood in the corner, eating our brownies and waiting for the rest of Luanda's guests.

"I lead a strange life," I said.

Spencer returned with Bridget and shot Remington and me a withering look. "Let's get on with the show," he ordered. "I have a town to protect and serve."

As if on command, the two men that Grandma had spoken about, Frank Richmond and Kirk Shields, arrived. Frank was still black and blue and swollen.

Neither of the men looked happy to be there. In fact, the room was full of sourpusses—except for Grandma, who was thrilled to be the number-one matchmaker with a third eye in Cannes once again, and Lucy, who was dreamy-eyed about, I assumed, her impending breakfast with Uncle Harry.

"What the hell, Chief? How dare you threaten us with arrest," Frank Richmond growled.

"Let's get this straight: I can threaten you with whatever I want," Spencer said, taking a brownie. "But I didn't threaten you with arrest."

There was an audible cracking noise, as heads

snapped toward Luanda. In response, she rolled her eyes back and woo-woo'd.

"You know, I don't mind her half as much now," Lucy said, sidling up next to me.

Frank and Kirk decided to leave and not hear any more woo woos, but Mrs. Arbuthnot convinced them to stay. "Let's hear her out. Otherwise we'll never be rid of her," she said, with her imperious tone and pursed lemon lips.

The guests settled in for the show. Grandma squeezed between Remington and me. "Poor Luanda," she whispered.

"Poor Luanda has taken in three-hundred-thousand dollars with her PayPal account in the past three days. I'm arresting her after her show," Remington whispered.

"What?" I asked.

"Fraud," he explained with a wink. "She's got a rap sheet longer than my arm. Her real name is Bonnie Ratner."

"Actually, her real name is Tracy Lewis," Grandma murmured. "Poor Tracy."

I knew the look in Grandma's eye. It was the big-project eye. Grandma's big projects were legendary. She had completely changed people's looks, loves, and lives with her big projects.

"You don't think she's a lost cause?" I asked Grandma.

"She's lost, and she's a cause," Grandma whispered. "My favorite two things in a match."

"Michael Rellik, kidnapper and flipper, is here with me now," Luanda singsonged in her ghosty voice.

"I can't believe Ruth decided to miss this," Lucy said. "Zelda, you got any popcorn?"

"Bird is on her way, and she'll make some," Grandma said.

"What happened to the juice?" I asked.

"She was going pretty good," Grandma said. "Grinding vegetables morning, noon, and night. Then she sort of snapped last night at the store. She had her basket of leafy greens at the register and, without thinking, grabbed a kid's Pop-Tart right out of his hand. It's been downhill since then."

"I've been there," I said.

Luanda shushed us.

"Sorry," I said.

"You go right ahead, Luanda," Grandma said. "Tell us what the dolphin wants."

"Huh?" Luanda asked.

Bridget's phone rang, and she answered it. "Call me back in a few minutes," she whispered into the phone. "I understand your love stick is about to blow, but if you can't hold it that long, so be it." She clicked off the phone. "Sheesh. Sorry, Luanda. Go ahead."

Luanda seemed to have lost her train of thought.

"For the love of God," Mrs. Arbuthnot shouted. "Michael Rellik was talking to you!"

Luanda did a quick woo woo and slipped back into her ghostlike voice. "Michael Rellik is here now," she announced. "He seeks revenge against his killer."

A chill went up my spine, and I shuddered.

"He tells a very interesting tale," Luanda continued. "Of brute strength and murder."

"Get on with it," Mrs. Arbuthnot snarled. "I have a meeting to get to tonight."

"Michael was angry, angry at the world. That's why he locked us in, but he wasn't going to hurt us. He had no plans to kill us," Luanda said.

Frank snorted. "Oh, yeah? Tell that to my face."

"He shut us in and ran for the hills. What he didn't know was that his murderer was following him." Luanda was getting into it now. I had flashbacks to campfire ghost stories from the one summer I'd attended Girl Scout camp.

"Michael Rellik's attacker chased him through the grove and cornered him at a tree," she said, her voice rising with the excitement of the story. "Rellik raised his hands to surrender, but his killer was merciless. He took out his gun and shot him three times. Bam! Bam! Bam!"

"Except that he wasn't shot, and he wasn't killed in the grove," Remington whispered to me.

Luanda mimed the murder, clutching at her heart with one hand and raising the other hand to the heavens. "He didn't die right away. He fought valiantly, clinging to life." Luanda choked and gasped. "But he could not win in the end against the vile lead invaders. Finally he succumbed and died."

Luanda's hands dropped, and her head lolled to the side. After a second, she straightened up and looked around with a bewildered expression on her face, as if she was waiting for her applause.

"You forgot something," Spencer said. "Michael Rellik's killer. Who is it?"

"Isn't it obvious?" Luanda asked.

"Not to me," Spencer said.

"Detective Remington Cumberbatch, of course," she said, as if speaking to a kindergartner. "He killed Michael Rellik in cold blood, and he'll kill again if given the chance."

# Chapter 18

✦ ♥ ✦

*Once I had a match, and every word out of his mouth was completely wrong. I mean, the opposite of true. It got to the point that if he said down, I knew the truth was up. In that way, he was actually the most honest person I've ever known. Reliable. I mean, I could count on him to be wrong. Where others saw a worthless putz, I saw consistency. Find the worth in your matches, dolly, and you will be a better matchmaker for it. Meanwhile, know your own truth. Otherwise, you'll believe these putzes, and then you're royally screwed.*

**Lesson 92,**
**Matchmaking Advice from Your Grandma Zelda**

TIME STOPPED in Grandma's parlor. The oxygen was sucked out of the room from the communal gasp that occurred with Luanda's bombshell.

Remington seemed to grow taller and stronger, the perceived threat he represented increasing. And he had a gun.

"Don't just stand there—arrest him, Chief," Frank Richmond said.

"I'll help you take him down," Kirk Shields offered.

To his credit, Remington remained calm and cool and didn't say or do a thing.

"Detective Cumberbatch didn't kill Michael Rellik," Spencer said.

"How do you know? You didn't interrogate him," Mrs. Arbuthnot said.

"Detective Cumberbatch," Spencer said, "did you kill Michael Rellik?"

"Don't hate me 'cause you ain't me," Remington answered.

"What on earth does that mean?" Mavis asked.

"It's slang," Felicia said knowingly.

"That's good enough for me," Spencer said. "Anybody have anything else to add?"

Luanda woo-woo'd.

"Except for her," Spencer said. "I'm tired of her."

Grandma cleared her throat. "Gladie has something to add."

Time stopped again. I choked on my brownie.

"I do?" I squeaked.

"Oh, my God," Spencer groaned, and raked his fingers through his hair.

Grandma took Luanda's hand. "Come sit next to me, honey," she said. She gave me a little push to the center of the room. "Go ahead, dolly, tell them what you know."

I wondered what I knew. I tapped my forehead. Not much in there. I had some suspicions, however, and if I squidged my eyes they turned into theories.

"I don't know anything, Grandma."

"Start at the beginning," she told me.

Spencer raised an eyebrow. "This is your chance, Miss Marple. Start with 'You may be wondering why I've asked you all here.'"

I took a deep breath.

"It all started with cupcakes," I said.

"It always does," said Lucy.

"Mavis and Felicia are friends who own Cup O'Cake, which is a new shop in town. Really, really delicious, by the way," I told them with a smile. "And Felicia was nice enough to lend me a book, which Spencer threw into a canyon," I continued.

"That's not exactly what happened," he said, after Felicia shot him a dirty look.

"Anyway, I noticed a stamp in the book from a school in Irvine, and Felicia had told me she used to be a teacher. Mrs. Arbuthnot, it turns out, is also new to Cannes and is related by marriage to Mavis."

"What is this? Protracted introductions?" Mrs. Arbuthnot spat. "What does this have to do with Rellik?"

"Sorry," I said. "Anyway, it turned out that all of us were invited on a tour of the house across the street at the same time. I think that was a mistake. I think Mavis, Felicia, Mrs. Arbuthnot, Frank, and Kirk Shields were supposed to be the only ones invited on that tour. We were an afterthought." I pointed to Remington, Lucy, Bridget, and Luanda.

"Rellik was very excited about his flip," I continued. "He was nearly done, and then he showed us to his real pride and joy, the panic rooms."

"Oh, my God, this is boring," Mrs. Arbuthnot said. "We were all there. We know the story."

"Bear with me," I said. "It's unusual to have a basement in Southern California. When I asked Rellik about it, he said, 'Rellik Construction aims to please.' Who was he trying to please? It made me think that he already had a buyer in mind, someone who'd ordered the panic rooms."

"Oh, shit," Spencer said, catching on.

"When Rellik locked us up, I assumed the other room was the better panic room. It had furniture. But when I saw Frank Richmond's face and heard about how Rellik had terrorized you all, I knew that we had been lucky in our panic room. We only had to suffer being plastered and having too little oxygen."

"Don't forget he hit Spencer over the head," Bridget reminded me.

"I'm getting to that," I said.

"When we finally got out, we saw how Frank had been beaten up and, of course, that Rellik had disappeared. Why? Where had he gone? Perhaps he had heard Spencer and Remington break out of the room. The metal made a horrible sound. He would have realized he couldn't take them on, even if he had a gun. So he got a big head start. Ran for the hills."

"Makes sense," Kirk Shields said. "You put two and two together nicely."

"I thought it made sense, too," I said. "Picture perfect. My only question was, why did Rellik kidnap us? But that could be easily explained by assuming he was crazy. Then I stumbled on Rellik's body." I looked at Kirk. "You wanted to know who my source was, who led me to his body, but I really just stumbled on him. It was an accident."

"She does that all the time," Bridget explained. "If there's a dead person around, Gladie will trip over him."

Lucy nodded in agreement, and Spencer rolled his eyes.

"After I saw him, my question changed from why did he kidnap us to who killed Michael Rellik and why."

Lucy perked up. "Yeah, why?"

"It didn't look like he had a partner. He was working alone. So I thought it had to be revenge."

The parlor was filled with possible suspects. Heads turned as we all scanned the potential murderers. A lot of people wanted revenge against Michael Rellik. After all, he had kidnapped us. I scooped some more guacamole with a chip and ate it in one bite.

"All of us would have liked revenge against Rellik, but unfortunately there were no suspects," I said.

"Why not?" Lucy asked.

"Because we were all locked in the panic rooms at the time of death," Remington said.

"This is better than *Castle*," Lucy said.

"It's a little unusual not to have any suspects. Isn't that right, Chief?" I asked Spencer.

"Just continue on, Pinkie."

"I kept thinking about something my grandmother said to me: 'Nothing is as it seems.' She meant Luanda, but it related to the murder. So I changed my question from who killed Michael Rellik to what exactly happened in those panic rooms."

"The spirits are calling me!" Luanda announced, and stood up.

"Not now, dear," Grandma told her, and yanked her down by her dress.

"The first thing I know is that I was locked in a panic room. The second thing I know is I heard screams from the other panic room, and you guys called for help. The third thing I know is that Spencer was thrown into the panic room with a head injury."

"Are you going to count all the things you know?" Spencer asked.

"What did Rellik hit you over the head with?" I asked him.

"I don't know. He hit me from behind. I never saw him coming."

"It must have been the same thing he used to beat Frank," I said. "Frank, what did Rellik use to beat you up?"

Frank was quiet for a long time. "His fists," he said, finally.

"Oh, shit," Remington said.

"Rellik was killed with a nail gun," I revealed. "But he didn't have any injuries to his hands, which he would have had if he'd beaten somebody. Was he wearing gloves when he did it?"

"Yes," Mrs. Arbuthnot said. "He was wearing gloves."

"That explains it," I said. "Here's the thing, though: When we were freed, Lucy introduced herself to Kirk, and he shook her hand with his left hand."

"Gladie, it's perfectly acceptable to shake with the left hand. We shouldn't discriminate. We should applaud the breaking of traditional barriers," Bridget told me.

"I agree," I said, even though I didn't know what she was talking about. "Some of my best friends are lefties. But yesterday, when we were in Cup O'Cake together, Kirk signed his bill with his right hand. And then I saw it at Uncle Harry's this morning. His right hand, I mean."

Kirk's hand slid behind his back, but not before we saw the cracked, bruised knuckles.

"You used to be a policeman, right?" I asked him. "I thought it was odd that a cop would retire so young to become a security guard in the middle of nowhere. And I was sure Uncle Harry wouldn't hire a disgraced cop. He has to trust the people who work for him. So that leaves retirement.

"You came to Cannes to seek revenge against Michael Rellik. You devised a plan. And you killed him," I stated.

Mavis stood up. "This is crazy nonsense. You have no idea what you're talking about."

"Be quiet, Mavis," Kirk said. "She's right. I killed him. I confess."

"But there were five holes in Michael Rellik's torso," I said. "Five." I pointed at Mrs. Arbuthnot, Mavis, Felicia, Kirk, and Frank Richmond, and counted. "One, two, three, four, five."

"Oh, shit," Spencer breathed.

"What?" Lucy asked. "This is way over my head. I thought you said there were no suspects. He was killed when we were locked in the panic rooms."

"Yes. When we were locked in the panic room," I said. "But they were never locked up."

"Gaslight," Bridget whispered.

"Exactly," I said. "It was a ruse. Smoke and mirrors. We were led to believe they were locked in, but, really, they had locked *us* in. We never saw Rellik close the door. Spencer never saw Rellik hit him. All we know is that we were locked in, they made noise in the other room, and, when we escaped, Rellik was gone."

"Oh, shit," Grandma said.

"In reality, Rellik was being murdered with five nails in his chest," I said.

"That was me," Kirk said. "I killed him."

"I thought, five is an interesting number," I continued, ignoring Kirk. "Why five? If it's revenge, did Rellik do something bad five times? But I turned the puzzle inside out, and one nail gun shot five times by one person became one nail gun shot by five people one time each," I said, out of breath. I gasped for air. Grandma handed me a lemonade, and I gulped down half of the glass.

"Yep, you've got the gift," she whispered to me. "You're doing a great job."

I felt a wave of shyness and a building anxiety. I didn't have the gift. I didn't know anything. What was I even talking about?

"Everyone in the other panic room," I continued. "You all killed Rellik together. You probably killed him on the tarp outside the room and dragged him out of there. Quick and clean."

"Oh, Lawd, they did! They all killed him! We were in one room, and they were in the other room, killing him!" Lucy exclaimed. "Why, Gladie? Why?"

"Revenge," I said. "Rellik caused a house fire in Irvine, and people died. Irvine is the common thread with everyone in the other panic room. It should be easy to get the details of the house fire, but I have the feeling Mrs. Arbuthnot and Mavis were related to the family. Related by marriage, mothers of the couple, paternal and maternal grandmothers of the children, I'm guessing."

Mavis nodded and swallowed a cry. "It wasn't revenge."

"Be quiet, Mavis. Don't say anything," Mrs. Arbuthnot commanded.

"It was justice," Mavis continued, ignoring Mrs. Arbuthnot. "He got what he deserved."

Mrs. Arbuthnot broke down in deep sobs, wailing like an injured animal. Mavis and Felicia gathered around her and hugged her. Her sobs were contagious, and soon all five of Rellik's murderers were crying together.

It stayed like that for a long time. It was more than grief; it was a sort of cleansing.

"He killed a family of four," Frank Richmond explained. "He was hired to change the electrical wiring, but he never did."

"He had a huge outfit," Kirk explained. "Hundreds of houses at once, flipping, remodeling, and he never inspected the work. He just ordered the slipshod crap from off-site and raked in the profits."

"My daughter, son-in-law, and two grandchildren," Mrs. Arbuthnot said. "All perished."

"I was the only one to survive." Mavis showed me the scars on her arms. "My room was on the bottom floor. My son, his wife, and the children, all dead."

They were all affected by the deaths. Felicia was the little boy's special-education teacher; she had worked with him one-on-one since he was a toddler. Frank was the father's business partner and best friend. And Kirk was the cop on duty that night, who found the bodies and couldn't accept that Rellik would not be punished.

Rellik's crime wasn't limited to the four deaths and

the house fire. He could count five more victims, those forever changed by the unjust tragedy.

"They charged the workers but never the big boss," Mrs. Arbuthnot said. "He got off. The authorities said his paperwork was in order, but we know it was all him. He was responsible for our loss."

Spencer took out his handcuffs.

"Don't you see what we did was just?" Frank asked him. "We righted a wrong. We are the good guys."

Spencer listened quietly. I could tell that he was swayed by their pain. I was, too. Up to a point.

"Good guys?" I asked. "Even if we completely discount the fact you murdered a man in cold blood, you still locked us in a panic room, you tried to plaster us to death, and you could have killed Spencer when you knocked him on the head. And, on top of that, you killed a helpless dog, probably because he came for a visit at the wrong time and you didn't want his owner showing up. Have I forgotten anything?"

The five murderers answered me with shocked silence. It was probably the first time they had realized that, in their zeal for justice, they had indeed become the bad guys.

"We're sorry," Felicia squeaked. It was the confession that I was waiting for—not a lot of words, but a confession nonetheless. "But you're wrong, Gladie. We didn't track him here. We all moved here to be away from our memories. We didn't plan this. We were just trying to get on with our lives."

"The idyllic town of Cannes, far away from crime and murder. Mavis moved first, and we all followed," Frank said wistfully.

Spencer chortled. "I guess you didn't count on Gladie living here."

"We were trying to heal," Mavis said. "And then Rellik came to town. We couldn't believe it at first. He didn't know us from a hill of beans, of course. That's how far removed he made himself from our tragedy, like it was nothing for him. He hadn't bothered to even know our names. Can you imagine, Gladie?"

No, I couldn't imagine. "So you all conspired," I said.

"It was easy," Mrs. Arbuthnot said, with more than a hint of pride. "You complicated it by showing up at the tour, but the panic rooms were a happy accident. We had more than enough alibis with you there."

I was getting a little peeved. "And the plaster? And Spencer's head? I understand the ideas of revenge and justice, but not the way you did it. Murder, attempted murder, kidnapping. You murdered a man and you terrorized innocent people."

"You heard Miss Marple," Spencer said. "You're under arrest." He and Remington cuffed the men and waited for backup to arrive.

Meanwhile, I snuck out and went upstairs to take a nap. Having the gift was exhausting. I was asleep before my head hit the pillow.

# Chapter 19

✦ ♥ ✦

*We're in the love business, not the breakup business, but often one follows the other, bubeleh. Smooth break-ups are bad enough, but bitter breakups are like cancer, spreading and eating the life essence as it grows. Let me tell you, if I had a nickel for every time a bitter man or woman held up a liquor store, joined the circus, moved to Utah, or had their genitalia pierced, I would be a very wealthy woman. A matchmaker is helpless when faced with a bitter breakupper, dolly. There's nothing you can do but let them ride it out and go as crazy as they need to.*

**Lesson 90,**
**Matchmaking Advice from Your Grandma Zelda**

I WOKE hours later, disoriented but well rested. My room was dark, and my clock said it was 10:00. I was strangely wired, and I was sure there was no way to go back to sleep. I took a long shower and let the hot water beat down on me until it ran cool.

My mind raced a mile a minute. I thought of Mavis and Felicia, most likely behind bars at that very moment. I still had Felicia's book, and now I would never be able to return it to her.

Mostly I thought of their pain at the deaths of their

family and friends. Their loss must have been terrible for them to seek justice the way they did, to turn violent and not care who they hurt in the scheme of their revenge.

I knew something about loss. I had lost my father at an early age, and his death altered my grandmother and my mother and, by extension, me. Instead of avenging his death by hurting others, however, they had decided to hurt themselves, to be self-destructive in different ways.

I dried my hair and put it up in a ponytail. I dressed in jeans, a long-sleeved T-shirt, a bulky V-neck sweater, and boots.

Grandma had gone to bed, and the house was quiet. I took my shearling coat out of the closet in the entranceway and bundled up. It was the perfect night for a long walk, cold, with a sky full of stars.

At the end of the driveway, I took a right toward Main Street. White twinkle lights were hung on every store and tree, a reminder that we were heading into the holiday season. A few tourists were walking on the sidewalks, as well. They stopped to look in shopwindows and raised paper cups of hot apple cider to their lips.

I couldn't deny I lived in an idyllic setting, peaceful and beautiful, even if I did find more than my share of murders. I had lived in Cannes for the last five months, which was the longest I had lived in any one place since I'd left home when I was sixteen years old.

My commitment issues battled with my general contentment at living here on a daily basis. I had made only a handful of matches and one unmatch, which wasn't a staggering success. Still, Grandma seemed pleased with my progress and insisted that I had the gift, whatever that was. So I supposed I would stay on a while longer and see where the matchmaker business took me.

My love life, however, was a total bust. Holden had vanished, and Spencer would never change his womanizing ways. I felt a kernel of loneliness in the pit of my belly that wouldn't go away. It was my way of living with loss, with the failure of my so-called relationships with Spencer and Holden.

I kept walking until I found myself at the easternmost corner of the historic district, on Gold Digger Avenue, in front of Cup O'Cake. The shop was dark, and a CLOSED sign hung in the window.

A wave of guilt joined my loneliness. "I should feel good," I said out loud. "I did good today."

I felt a tap on my shoulder, and I turned to see Remington. "Out for a walk?" he asked. "Me, too. Funny how we both wound up here."

Remington wore a black peacoat, jeans, and boots. He smelled good, like soap. He was a breathtaking man. He exuded power and strength and something else. Gentleness.

"I might feel guilty," I said.

He put his hand out for me to take. "Come on," he said. I put my hand in his, and we went up Gold Digger Avenue, walking the perimeter of the historic district. His hand was warm and dry and held firm.

With each step, my loneliness left me, and my guilt receded into the corners of my mind. He stopped us at a café and led me to an outside table.

The waiter took our orders—cider for Remington and coffee for me and a slice of apple pie to share. A cool breeze blew my hair out of its ponytail, and Remington ran his fingers through it, lifting it off my face.

His eyes were large and dark and wholly fixed on me. I sensed desire, but I also sensed that he wouldn't demand anything I wasn't prepared to give. I enjoyed his company, even if he wasn't a big talker. He was easy to be around. Comforting. And I was in no hurry to finish my coffee and go home.

I retied my ponytail and dug into the pie. "You were pretty impressive at the fight last night," I said.

"So were you."

I laughed. "Yeah, right."

"No, I mean it. I've seen first-time corner men pass out. I saw one throw up on his fighter."

"I wanted to do both of those things," I said. "But I held it together so Spencer wouldn't kill me."

At Spencer's name, we grew quiet. I knew that Remington had questions, but he let them rest unanswered. He put a few bills under his cup and stood. He put his hand out and helped me up.

We continued our walk, but this time he wrapped his arm around my waist, pulling me against him. The last of the shops were closing, and the streets were devoid of tourists, or anyone else for that matter.

Then we stopped. "Where are we?" I asked. But I knew.

Remington released my waist and took my hand again, giving it a little squeeze. He pushed open the door to his apartment building, and we walked up the old staircase to the top floor. He unlocked his apartment, allowing me to enter first.

The décor was alternately nerdy fella and cool

*Fast & Furious.* A leather couch, coffee table, and big-screen television were surrounded by weight-lifting paraphernalia and *Star Trek* memorabilia.

Remington faced me and unbuttoned my coat. He slipped it off my shoulders, folded it over the arm of the couch, and laid his on top of mine.

The muscles in his back rippled as he moved, pushing against the material of his shirt. I felt a slow burn travel from my head to my toes. He turned sharply, as if he felt the change of temperature in the room. He studied my face for a moment and then, most likely seeing the emotion there, took my hand and pulled me into his bedroom.

The song "Love the One You're With" played in my head. Out in the recesses of my mind, I searched for Spencer. I had wanted more from him, a confirmation from him that I was special, that he wanted more from me than just a roll in the hay. And also . . . what? That he wouldn't grow tired of me and move on to his next conquest.

And here I was in the bedroom of a man I didn't know anything about except that he was beautiful and wanted me tonight. Beyond that, he made no promises, and I didn't care. In his arms, the loneliness and fear vanished. I was safe.

Remington wrapped his arms around me and held me against his broad chest. It felt so good to be held like that, completely desired. He brushed my cheek with the back of his fingers and cradled my face in his hands. His eyes were fathomless, deep and impenetrable. I gasped, taking in needed oxygen.

He leaned down and captured my lips with his. More than a kiss, something strong passed between us, as if we were sharing our essence. I ached for more and took a step toward him.

He deepened the kiss, exploring my mouth with his tongue, and I groaned with desire. The kiss went on and on and the world fell away. Remington's bedroom, apartment, the town, all the demands on me and feelings for others—all washed away within our kiss.

I was transported.

Remington made quick work of our clothes and carried me to his bed. He parted my legs with his knee and settled himself between them. He was ready, and I realized I was, too.

"You are quite possibly the most beautiful woman I've ever seen," he said.

"Right back at you," I croaked. He was hard everywhere. Granite. A complement to my soft flesh, which gave way to welcome him.

I kissed his neck, settling on his pulse, which was going at a pretty good clip. His mouth searched lower with little kisses until he found my breasts. He teased a nipple, making me writhe under him.

Despite my protests, he lifted himself off me, but my protests stopped suddenly when he began to make love to me with his mouth. I started to tremble.

"You are so good at that," I breathed.

"You are so good," he said. "I can't get enough."

He slowly brought me to climax with his tongue. Wave after wave of pleasure hit me, and I drowned in it, thoroughly satisfied.

Wordlessly, he moved on top of me again and fit himself into me. I lifted my knees, bringing him nearer. He held me close, as if he was afraid I would run away. He thrust in and out, and my hips arched upward as another climax built in my body.

I was attracted to him, but my body's reaction was more than attraction. Here was my moment to heal, to let go of doubt, to forget anxiety, to totally succumb to another and be washed clean. Reborn.

After, he covered me with the blanket. He watched me as I dozed on and off on my side. He let me rest for about ten minutes and then he kissed my eyelids, my forehead, my ears.

A person can go for years without thinking about their earlobes. Then one day a gorgeous man sucks on them, and they become the favorite body part. Ditto the underarms, small of the back, and toes.

Remington Cumberbatch was very talented with the whole sex thing. "That's your influence on me, Gladie," he insisted.

"For someone who doesn't say much, you're a really good liar."

"There are no lies in this bed," he said, and made love to me all over again.

The second time was significantly more athletic. We covered pages six through fourteen of the Kama Sutra, and I surprised myself with my increased flexibility. I figured it was because we had warmed up before.

Remington hopped out of bed and came back with a towel, which he used to dry me off. "Water," I begged. "Please. I have no fluids left in my body."

"Well, we'll need those," he said with a smile.

"We will?" I asked, but he was already in the kitchen. I heard the clanking of ice. He brought back two glasses, sat on the edge of the bed, handed me one, and drank from the other.

"Better?" he asked.

"Yes," I said.

He took my empty glass and placed it on the nightstand. "I like your hair like this, like you've been used."

"I *have* been used."

"I have a secret," he said with a twinkle in his eye.

"Uh-oh, here it comes."

"I'm going to tell you, but I need you to swear to secrecy."

I stuck three fingers in the air. "Girl Scouts' honor, unless it's disgusting, because then I tell everyone."

"I'm only telling you because I think you're Twinkie-worthy."

"I'm what? Is Twinkie the name for you-know-what?"

"Come on." Remington tugged my arm, helping me out of bed. We walked hand in hand, naked, to the kitchen. "Remember, top secret," he said.

He opened the cabinet above the refrigerator. The inside was stuffed with Twinkies boxes.

"Jackpot!" I yelled.

Remington took out a box and walked me back to bed. He handed me a Twinkies package. "You're the hoarder of my dreams," I said. "If you have a cabinet of Oreos cereal, I'll marry you."

Remington opened a second package of Twinkies. "Interesting. Marriage for cereal. A lot cheaper than a diamond ring."

"Are cage fighters allowed to eat Twinkies?" I asked with my mouth full.

"I'm expecting to work off more calories later tonight."

"You are? Will I be there?"

"That was the plan. Hey, you want to dance?"

"Can we dance naked?"

"Like there's any other way," he said.

We didn't dance for long. Two naked people rubbing up against each other while they sway to the music makes things move along pretty quickly.

AFTER OUR fifth time, I realized I had discovered the best diet ever. Bird could juice all she wanted, but she would never get the happy results I got eating Twinkies and bonking with Remington. My jeans were looser on me when I put them back on, and even my boots were slightly bigger on my feet.

The sun was rising, and Remington's bedroom was infused with a red glow.

"This was a lot of fun," I said.

"More than a lot of fun."

"Five times more than a lot of fun," I agreed. I tried to run Remington's comb through my hair, but it was no dice. I had a rat's nest on my head. "This is going to be a long walk of shame."

He offered to drive me home, but I was in the mood to walk and breathe in the early morning and prolong the evening as much as possible.

"Excellent. I want your hair to announce to the whole town that Remington Cumberbatch fucked you good."

He kissed me within an inch of my life and sent me out the door, dizzy and euphoric.

I was so high from my sexcapades that I walked through town without realizing it. It wasn't until the smell of coffee hit me in front of Tea Time that I woke up and became aware of my surroundings.

Plastic sheets hung down as a makeshift wall, pleated in the middle to create a doorway. Inside, Ruth had made amazing progress. The rubble had been cleared out, and new tables and chairs filled the space, as if nothing out of the ordinary had ever happened at Tea Time.

Ruth was behind the bar, cleaning it off with a wet rag.

"Latte, Ruth," I called, waving a five-dollar bill.

"Holy crap, you have been fucked good!" she pronounced.

"No, I haven't," I said, smoothing out my hair with my hand.

"Oh, please," she said.

I leaned over the bar. "Okay, I admit it. I'm flying high."

But then I crashed to the ground in a pile of guilt I hadn't been expecting. All because of two little words.

"Hi, Pinkie."

# Chapter 20

✦ ♥ ✦

*When it rains, it pours, dolly. It's either feast or fam-ine. That's just the way it is. It's some sort of cosmos, karma meshugas that I don't understand. Either we have a million matches to make and I don't know which end's up, or the house is quiet and I'm twiddling my thumbs. But just because the world is feast or famine, you can still ride down the middle with a sensible meal. You got me? Moderation in all things, if you can swing it. Don't get overwhelmed. That's not the way to end things.*

**Lesson 65,**
**Matchmaking Advice from Your Grandma Zelda**

"OH, IT'S the cop," Ruth said to Spencer. "But *your* hair looks fine."

"Huh?" he asked.

I smoothed my hair down. "What are you doing here?" I asked. The black eye that Remington had given him was turning yellow.

"Looking for you. I couldn't sleep."

"Neither could I."

Ruth put my latte on the bar. "Here, let me get that," Spencer said, and paid my tab. "May I sit with you?" he asked.

Guilt wormed its way through my entire body. I was eaten up by it. Spencer being nice to me after I'd just marathon-boffed his underling was going to send me to confession, and I wasn't Catholic.

"I think we were talking over each other yesterday," he said, "and we had a misunderstanding."

"On the contrary, the discussion wasn't even necessary. You told me everything you needed to tell me when you were kissing that woman."

"I get it," Spencer said. "You were jealous."

"Get over yourself. I was not jealous," I lied. "I'm just tired of your behavior, especially after what happened between us."

"The kiss."

Bird pulled back the plastic and walked in to Tea Time. "Ruth, a box of scones, on the double. I'm detoxing from the juice fast." She tapped her shoe on the floor, then spotted me and pointed to my hair. "What are you doing here? Don't you two have any shame, showing up here with sex hair?"

"What?" Spencer asked.

I smoothed my hair down, but it was no use. I had sex hair.

Spencer stared at me, and I stared down at my shoes. I could practically hear the cogs moving in his brain. "I see," he said finally.

I wanted to crawl into a hole. It wasn't that I was ashamed or embarrassed. It wasn't that Spencer didn't deserve to suffer a setback in his love life. It was the way he was looking at me that made me want to hide. Like he would never pop a root beer with me again.

Spencer made a show of checking his watch. "I need to be getting to work," he said.

"I'll see you later."

"What? Yeah, sure."

He walked out in a daze and never looked back. To my horror, I burst into tears.

"Dammit," said Bird. "Here, have a scone."

Three scones later, I had told Bird the whole story. "He'll come around," she assured me. "And if he doesn't, you have the hot nerdy fella."

But I wasn't sure I wanted the hot nerdy fella past our incredible night together. Somehow I had to win Spencer back—not that I'd had him before.

I was about to leave when Bridget came in with a smile from ear to ear. "I got one," she announced, seeing me. "A convert. He called, asking for the usual. You know, if I would suck his balls, that kind of thing. And when I brought up Hillary Clinton, he was actually interested. He let me finish talking and forgot all about his balls."

"That's great," I said. "Does this mean you'll get the phone number changed, or are you going to try to get more converts?"

"I'll think my days as a phone-sex operator are over. But I haven't felt this good in months, not since my crisis of non-faith."

Bridget's good mood was infectious. I almost forgot about Spencer, and I ordered another latte to enjoy while Bridget told me all about the glass ceiling. After a couple of hours, Bridget left, and when I was about to leave, Ruth stopped me.

"I'll be over later to get my gun," she said. "In the meantime, tell your grandmother not to turn on the oven."

"You hid your gun in the oven?" I asked.

"I figured a murderer would never look in there unless he wanted to bake a cake or something."

With my euphoria and afterglow calming down, my exhaustion took over. I couldn't wait to get in my bed and sleep the day away. I was happy for once not to have any matches to make.

What a week. I had gone through just about every human emotion. There was nothing left to surprise me. Even if aliens landed in front of Grandma's house, I wouldn't be surprised. If rabbits hopped up her driveway, singing the national anthem, I wouldn't be surprised. I was beyond surprisable. I was officially jaded.

But then I was surprised.

"Look who's here!" Grandma called from her driveway, as I walked up the street.

The tall man standing next to her turned to see who Grandma was yelling at. I was so surprised, I almost swallowed my tongue.

He ran down the driveway, scooped me up, and spun me around. "I'm back," he said.

"Holden," I breathed. "What a nice surprise."

And then I was surprised again.

"And look who else is here!" Grandma called, sounding much less pleased.

The front door opened, and a tall blond woman came out. She had aged badly, her face riddled with cigarette-induced wrinkles. She held a glass of something alcoholic in her hand, even though it was early in the morning.

"Mom? What are you doing here?" I asked, shocked to my bones.

"I'm moving in. You got any smokes?"

# Acknowledgments

The author would like to thank all the usual suspects: Junessa Viloria, fantabulous editor and confidante; Alex Glass, ever-patient agent to the stars and Elise Sax; Gina Wachtel, favorite publisher; Beth Pearson and the Ballantine copyediting team, keepers of the comma knowledge; all the fellow writers of the planet; Loren Birkett, who introduced me to a sink puker; and my kids.

See how it all began . . .
read on for an excerpt from
*An Affair to Dismember*
the first book in Elise Sax's Matchmaker series.

# Chapter 1

✦ ♥ ✦

*When you first start out, you're going to ask people what they're looking for. This is a big mistake. Huge. They want the impossible. Every woman wants a Cary Grant with a thick wallet who doesn't mind if she's a few pounds overweight. Every man wants a floozy he can take home to Mom. See? Asking their opinions only leads to headaches you could die from. Take it from me, I've been doing this a lot of years. Nobody knows what they want. You have to size a person up and tell them what they want. It might take convincing, but you'll widen their horizons, and they'll thank you for it. Eventually. Remember, love can come from anywhere, usually where you least expect it. Tell them not to be afraid, even if it hits them on the head and hurts a lot at first. With enough time, any schlimazel can turn into a Cary Grant or a presentable floozy.*

**Lesson 22,**
**Matchmaking Advice from Your Grandma Zelda**

THE MORNING I found out about Randy Terns'
murder, I was happily oblivious. I was too busy to

care, trying to make heads or tails of my grandma's matchmaking business. Nobody actually mentioned the word "murder" that morning. I sort of stumbled onto the idea later on.

That Thursday I sat in my grandma's makeshift office in the attic of her sprawling Victorian house, buried under mounds of yellowed index cards and black-and-white Polaroid pictures. It was all part of Zelda's Match-making Services, a business I now co-owned at my grandma's insistence as her only living relative and what she called "a natural matchmaker if ever I saw one."

"Gladie Burger," she had told me over the phone three months before, urging me to move in with her, "you come from a long line of Burger women. Burger women are matchmaker women."

I was a Burger woman, but I had strong doubts about the matchmaker part. Besides, I couldn't decipher the business. It was stuck in the dark ages with no computer, let alone Internet connection. Grandma fluctuated between staging workshops, running group meetings, hosting walk-ins, and just knowing when someone needed to be fixed up. "It's an intuitive thing," she explained.

I pushed aside a stack of cards, stirring up a black cloud of dust. I had been a matchmaker in training for three months, and I was no closer to matching any couples. To be truthful, I hadn't even tried. I wiped my dusty hands on my sweatpants and stared at the giant mound on her desk. "Grandma, I'm not a matchmaker," I said to her stapler. "I've never even had a successful relationship. I wouldn't know one if I saw one."

I had a sudden desire for fudge. I gave my stomach a squish and tugged at my elastic waistband. My grandmother was a notorious junk food addict, and I had slipped into her bad habits since I moved in with her. Hard to believe I was the same person who not even four months ago was a cashier in a trendy health food store in Los Angeles, the second-to-last job I had had in a more than ten-year string of jobs—which was probably why Grandma had twisted my arm to move to Cannes, California.

I decided against fudge and picked up an index card. It read: *George Jackson, thirty-five years old.* Next to the note, in Grandma's handwriting, was scribbled *Not a day less than forty-three; breath like someone died in his mouth.* Halitosis George was looking for a stewardess, someone who looked like Jackie Kennedy and had a fondness for Studebakers. Whoa, Grandma kept some pretty old records. I needed to throw out 95 percent of the cards, but I didn't know which 5 percent to keep.

Putting down the card, I stared out the window, my favorite activity these days. What had I gotten myself into? I had no skills as a matchmaker. I was more of a temp agency kind of gal. Something where I wasn't in charge of other people's lives. My three-week stint as a wine cork inspector was more my speed.

A man and his German shepherd ran down the street. I checked my watch: 12:10 P.M. Right on time. I could always count on the habits of the neighbors. There was a regular stream of devoted dog walkers, joggers, and cyclists that passed the house on a daily basis. Not much changed here. The small mountain town was low on surprises. I tried to convince myself that was a good thing. Stability was good. Commitment was good.

With sudden resolve, I took George Jackson's card and threw it in the wastebasket. "Bye, George. I hope you found love and an Altoid."

I tried another card. *Sarah Johns. Nineteen years old.* She had gotten first prize at the county fair for her blueberry pie, and she was looking for an honest man who didn't drink too much. My grandma had seen something more in her. *Poor thing. Art school better than man,* she had written in the margins.

I tossed the card, letting it float onto George. Matchmaking was no easy task. It wasn't all speed dating and online chat rooms. Lives were on the line. One false move and futures could be ruined.

The house across the street caught my attention. It had seen better days. A bunch of shingles were missing, leaving a big hole in the roof. I watched as the mailman stopped at the mailbox. He would arrive at Grandma's in twelve minutes. I could set my watch by him.

Across the street, the front door opened. An elderly woman stepped out and picked up her mail. She glanced at the letters and then stood staring at her front yard. Something was not quite right about the picture. I didn't have time to dwell on it, though. I had promised Grandma I would pick up lunch for us in town.

I grabbed my keys and hopped down the stairs. Outside, it was a typical Cannes, California, August day: blue sky, sunshine, and warm. Normally it didn't turn cool until October, or so I was told. My experience with the town was limited to summers visiting my grandmother when I was growing up.

"Yoo-hoo! Gladie!" Grandma's high-pitched cry cut through the country quiet. She stood in the front yard, hovering over the gardener as he cut roses. The front yard was about half an acre of lawn and meticulously groomed plants, flowers, and trees. It was her pride and joy, and Grandma supervised the gardening with an obsession usually reserved for Johnny Depp or chocolate. I doubted she had ever picked up a spade in her life. "Yoo-hoo! Gladie!" she repeated, flapping her arm in the air, her crisp red Chanel knockoff suit bulging at the seams and the glittering array of diamonds on her fingers, wrists, and neck blinding me in the afternoon sun.

"I'm right here, Grandma." I jiggled the car keys to remind her of my lunch run.

"Jose, leave a few white ones for good luck and be careful with the shears," she told the gardener. "You don't want to lop off a finger." Jose shot her a panicked look and crossed himself.

Grandma walked as quickly as she could across the large lawn to the driveway. She had a grin plastered across her face and, no doubt, some juicy bit of news bursting to pop out of her mouth. Her smile dimmed only slightly when she got a good look at my state. I pulled up my baggy sweatpants. As usual, she was immaculately coiffed and made up, whereas my brown hair was standing up in all directions in a frantic frizz, and my eyelashes hadn't seen mascara in months. I didn't see much reason to dress up because I rarely left the attic, but standing next to Grandma, I was a little self-conscious about my attire. As a rule, her clothes were nicely tailored. I listened to the soft *swish-swish* of her pantyhose-covered thighs rubbing together as she approached. I wondered vaguely if the friction of her nylon stockings could cause them to burst into flames. I took a cowardly step backward, just in case.

"I'm so glad I caught you before you left," she said, a little out of breath from either her run or the excitement over the piece of gossip she was about to blurt out. While Grandma never left her property, she somehow knew everything going on in town.

"I didn't get much done," I said. "I can't figure out what to keep and what to toss. Should I throw out everything older than ten years?"

"Fine. Fine. Listen. Randy Terns is dead. They found him yesterday morning, deader than a doornail."

I racked my brain. Who was Randy Terns? Was he the new secretary of state? Really, I had to read a newspaper once in a while. What kind of responsible citizen was I?

"That's terrible," I muttered, a noncommittal edge to my voice in case Randy Terns was a war criminal or something.

"Yes, yes. Terrible. Terrible." Grandma waved her hands as if everything was terrible. The sky, the trees, my car—all terrible. She grabbed my arm in a viselike grip and pulled herself close to make sure that I heard every word. "I'm on Betty like white on rice to sell that old run-down excuse for a house. I'd love to get in some people who will fix it up. Look at me! I'm drooling over the thought of waking up, going out to get the paper, and not having to see that dreadful lawn across from my prize-winning roses." She made air quotes with her fingers when she said "lawn."

She turned to face the house across the street. "I bet you will be thrilled not to have to stare at that falling-down roof every day!"

*Falling-down roof.* My brain kicked into gear, and I recalled the woman standing by her mailbox. Randy and Betty Terns were the neighbors across the street. I'd never had much interaction with them. And now Randy was dead. Found yesterday morning, deader than a doornail.

I hate death. I'm scared it's contagious. At funerals, I feel my arteries start to harden. Medical shows on TV send me into neurotic fits. McDreamy or McSteamy, it doesn't matter—I only see my slow, agonizing death from a terrible disease. Like Ebola or flesh-eating bacteria. Or a drug-resistant superbug yeast infection. If I found out that poor Randy Terns died of a heart attack, it would only take five minutes or so for my chest pains to start.

"Betty said she would think about it," Grandma said with disgust. "Said she has a funeral to organize and a houseful of kids. Kids. Huh. The youngest is thirty-seven. Three of them still live at home. It's time to push those birdies out of the nest, I say."

She harrumphed loudly and kicked the cobblestoned driveway with her left Jimmy Choo. Gold-tipped. Very fancy.

"Five children. Why do people take things to extremes?" she continued. "Anyway, they come and go like they own the place, moving in and out whenever they want. They're holding on for dear life. A bunch of losers, the lot of them. I didn't make an index card for any of them." She looked at me expectantly, and I nodded vigorously in agreement, even though the most I saw of the "bunch of losers" these days were some faceless figures going to and from various cars.

Grandma patted a stray hair in place on her head and continued. " 'Betty,' I told her, 'you could buy yourself a condo on the beach for cash and have enough left over to last your whole life if you sell now.' But she didn't have time for me. You know, Gladie, that house is one of the biggest on this street. And it's got a pool."

Grandma let out a big why-are-people-so-stupid sigh. Then she slapped her forehead. "I almost forgot! I have news about the house next to ours, too."

Geez. I really didn't want to hear that another neighbor had died. I would need therapy.

"Don't look at me like that, Gladie. It's good news. Jean the real estate lady told me there's been a bite on the house next door." She nodded to the house on my left. "A big bite. A whale bite. A . . . a . . . what's bigger than a whale? Whatever it is, it's one of those bites. Anyway, I can't talk about it yet. Might jinx it. Won't you be happy to have that house filled?"

I was only dimly aware that the house next door was empty and for sale, but my real estate ignorance would be sacrilegious to Grandma. The town was her business, and it was supposed to be mine now, too. A couple of speed-walkers made their way past us, distracting us from talk of houses and death.

"Daisy Scroggins," Grandma called out, flapping her arm at one of the speed-walkers. "You are the sweetest thing. How could I resist homemade chocolate chip cookies right out of the oven?"

The speed-walker, who I assumed was Daisy, stumbled in surprise. "How did you know I baked—" she started, but stopped herself midsentence. "I'll be back in fifteen minutes with a plateful, Zelda. It's the least I could do."

Grandma leaned into me. "Her daughter's wedding is next month," she whispered. "That was a tricky one, but in the end I convinced her to go for the plumber with one leg. She's never been happier, of course."

I had a familiar feeling of dread. Grandma's shoes were hard ones to fill. When the moment came, would I know to fix up someone with a one-legged plumber?

Jose let out a bloodcurdling scream. He jumped up from the rosebushes, clutching his hand. It grew redder by the second and started to drip.

"What did I tell you?" Grandma shook her head and clucked her tongue at him.

"I cut off my finger," he yelled, his eyes wide with terror.

"No, you didn't," Grandma insisted. "It's just a scratch. Good thing I told you to be careful. Let's go in, and I'll wash it." Jose followed Grandma into the house, holding out his hand in front of him as if it was a snake. I took that as my cue to hop in my car.

I drove a block before I realized I didn't know whether to go to Burger Boy or Chik'n Lik'n. I could have gone to Bernie's Rib Shack, my grandmother's favorite, but it was in a strip mall next to Weight Wonders, and I didn't want to face any dieters while getting an order of baby backs. I decided on Burger Boy because it was the closest and had the quickest drive-through.

My grandma's house was one of the oldest in town and located right in the center of the historic district on Cannes Boulevard near Main Street. The houses were a mishmash, most built in the haste of new-found money during the gold rush in the nineteenth century. The gold had run out pretty quickly, but people stayed on to enjoy the mountain views. The town had never grown to much of anything, topping out at around four thousand people.

I drove south out of the historic district toward Orchard Road, where just beyond, hundreds of acres of apple and pear trees stood as a beacon to all those who came up the mountain for the town's famous pies.

Burger Boy was at the corner of Elm and Park, a few blocks before the orchard and across the street from Cannes Center Park. The park had been established about 150 years before in a wise attempt by the town's founders to preserve and protect the natural beauty of this little corner of Southern California paradise. It was a huge expanse of rolling hills, sage-brush, and eucalyptus trees. It used to have a lovely gazebo in the center with park benches all around, where they held weekly concerts and regular picnics. Then, in the late fifties, a few bored and prudish housewives caught some couples kissing on the park benches, and they lobbied to have the benches removed. It was decreed that the park should be used for brisk exercise and that lounging on benches and in the gazebo would only lead to trouble and moral decay. The gazebo fell into disrepair. Gone were the kissing couples, and with them went the concerts and picnics. Today, brisk exercise was relegated to the historic district and the little park on Main Street. Cannes Center Park welcomed mostly skateboarders and teenagers searching for a little excitement in the bucolic small town.

Across the street from the park, Burger Boy had location, location, location and a killer dollar menu. It was a gold mine, a favorite of locals who did not particularly enjoy pie or tea.

An explosion rocked my car, jolting it forward a few feet before it slowed to normal. "Whoa, Nelly," I said, patting the dashboard. "No more car farts. I need you a while longer." I called them car farts. My mechanic called them a cataclysmic end to the catalytic converter. He had grumbled something to me about being one car fart away from total destruction and probable death, but I couldn't afford to fix it. Besides, it ran fine as far as I was concerned. It was a 1995 silver Cutlass Supreme, and I had gotten it for free when I worked at a used car lot for one month. I loved it, even though it had more rust than silver paint, and the interior was ripped, with foam poking out in tufts.

I rolled into the parking lot past a group of skateboarders hanging out in front, their skateboards leaning up against their legs as they packed away burgers, fries, and shakes. I followed the drive-through sign, winding through the parking lot toward the talking Burger Boy. I opened my window, and the smell of french fries hit me like nectar to the gods. Really, happiness was truly easy to acquire if you're honest with yourself. Maybe I could start eating right tomorrow.

Burger Boy's mouth was open in a big smile, and I yelled in its direction. "I would like two Burger Boy Big Burgers. No pickles. Extra cheese, please. Two large fries, and a Diet Coke."

There was a long silence, so I tried again. "I would like two Burger Boy Big Burgers, please!"

"Dude!" a voice shouted back at me.

"Yes, I would like two Burger Boy—"

"Dude! It doesn't work!"

I leaned out the car window and tried to look into Burger Boy's mouth. The voice sounded much clearer than usual, but I still didn't understand what it was saying.

"Hey, dude. Like, the drive-through doesn't work, man." A skateboarder rolled up to my car, a shake still in one hand.

"Didn't you hear me? I've been yelling at you for, like, forever."

His shorts hung down well past his knees, and he wore a T-shirt that announced the price of beer bongs. "Dude, I just thought of something," he went on. "If I didn't say anything, you would still be talking to the Burger Boy. So trippin'." He thought this was riotously funny and got so caught up in his own giggles that he didn't hear me when I said thank you and backed out of the drive-through lane.

I was disappointed about the drive-through, but I still had to get lunch. I was careful to lock up my car before I walked to the front door, passing the four skateboarders deep in conversation. Their attention was drawn to the sky.

"Dude, like, I think it's an eagle, man."

"No way, dude. It's an owl."

"I don't know, man. It's pretty big."

"Dude, it's been up there, like, you know, forever."

"Oh, man. It's been up there since last week at least. Maybe it thinks it's a tree or something."

"Cool."

I looked up. Sure enough, an owl was perched on top of a telephone pole. I don't normally notice wildlife, don't know much about it, but two years before, I had had a job typing up a doctoral thesis on the endangered Madagascar red owl, and now I was staring up at one on a telephone pole at Burger Boy.

"Check it out. An eagle is up there," one of the skateboarders said, pointing it out to me.

"Actually, it's an owl," I explained.

"Oh, dude. She so burned you. I told you it was an owl." This came from the beer bong skateboarder, who I figured had held on to a few more brain cells than his friends.

"It's an owl from Madagascar," I informed them.

"Cool."

"It's not supposed to be here," I said. "It's highly endangered, and it's nocturnal. I don't understand what it's doing here."

They looked at me with empty stares. I had the strongest urge to knock on their foreheads to see if anyone was home.

Two things were certain: the four great geniuses were not about to help the endangered owl, and if I didn't help it, I would be responsible for driving the Madagascar red owl that much closer to extinction.

I sighed and dialed information on my cellphone. A minute later I was on the line with animal control, which proceeded to pass me to seven different offices around the state before I got to wildlife management. They said they couldn't get someone out here due to budget cuts and would I be so kind as to shoo it off or get it down.

"Get it down?" I asked.

"Yes. If it's too weak, just go up, grab it, carry it down, and take it over to animal control. We'll handle the rest."

"What if it has rabies or something?"

"Ma'am, birds don't get rabies. Just throw a shoe up there or something. It will fly away. It probably is enjoying the view."

The wildlife person hung up, and I stood there a moment, looking at my phone. Our tax dollars at work. Sheesh.

"We have to shoo it down," I told the skateboarders.

"What? With our shoes, man?"

"You know, shoo. Like, shoo fly," I said. "But in this case, with our shoes. Throw your shoes up there to shoo it away. We have to make sure it's okay."

The beer bong guy was the first to take off his shoes, and the rest followed. I guessed he was kind of their leader. They threw their shoes up at the owl in unison, and I shielded myself from the onslaught of laceless, skull-embossed sneakers as they made their way back down to the ground. I looked up, and sure enough, the owl was still there. He hadn't even blinked, which made me think he was in distress of some kind. Possibly more distress than what I was feeling at being stuck with a bunch of pothead skateboarders having to save an endangered species because my government wouldn't fund its budget properly.

"Okay. Well, that didn't work," I said. "So one of you is going to have to go up there and get it down."

The guy who had thought the owl was an eagle looked at the telephone pole and whistled. "I don't know, dude. Can't you get electrocuted or something touching one of those poles?"

"No, no. This is a telephone pole. There's no danger with a telephone pole," I said. I was almost sure there was no danger with a telephone pole.

"I'm not much into climbing, man," said the beer bong guy. And that seemed to clinch it for all of them. Without saying goodbye, they put on their shoes and rolled off into the park.

I waited a moment to see if some nice passerby would pass by, and then I kicked off my flip-flops, grabbed the pole, and started climbing. I got about halfway up before I got stuck on a metal doohickey and started screaming.

I was surprised and impressed that it only took about seven minutes for the police to come. Cannes was a very small town, and I didn't know it had so many police. Two squad cars and an unmarked car with a flashing light on its roof drove into the parking lot. I was amazed I had garnered so much attention.

"What the hell do you think you are doing?" one of the policemen yelled up at me.

"I was trying to get the owl," I shouted down with as much dignity as I could muster.

"Get down immediately!"

"I can't. I'm stuck on the metal doohickey."

I was stuck. Stuck, and nothing was going to get me to move. I was sure any little movement would precipitate my plunge to earth. I sat on the metal ladder rungs, my legs wrapped around the pole in a death grip. My pants leg was punctured all the way through by the metal thing, my fear of heights had suddenly kicked in, and I was sweating so much that a nice slippery coat covered my body from head to toes.

I looked down at the policemen, who were deep in conversation. Four were in uniform, but one was dressed in plainclothes, an expensive suit.

A couple of minutes later I heard a siren and saw a giant hook and ladder fire truck come my way. Presto chango, they had a ladder against the pole, and a big fireman was climbing up to me.

"Don't worry, miss. I'll help you," he said.

"I was trying to get the owl for the wildlife management department. They have budget cuts," I told him.

"Happens all the time, miss. Come on. I got you."

He put his arms around me and gave a little tug, and the ripping sound from my sweatpants could be heard across state lines. I pulled back, trying to minimize the tear, and my elastic waistband gave way as I fell upside down, my pants pulled down to my knees, my pink Victoria's Secret special three-for-fifteen-dollars boy's-cut underpants out for everyone to see.

I heard snickering from the group below, which now included not just the police and the firemen but the entire staff of Burger Boy. In a moment of lunacy, I waved to them.

The fireman carried me over his shoulder down the ladder. Once on firm ground, I pulled up my pants.

"You have to get the owl. It's distressed and endangered," I told the fireman. He nodded and went back up to retrieve the bird.

The policeman in the suit approached me. He was tall. His thick, wavy dark brown hair was perfectly cut and combed, his chin was shaved down to the last whisker, and despite a manly Gerard Butler kind of face, he looked like he was not averse to using moisturizer and the occasional clay mask. He had largish dark blue eyes and thick eyebrows. He arched one of those eyebrows as if he had a question.

"Yes?" I prompted.

"Cinderella?" he asked, his mouth forming a smile, revealing white teeth.

"Excuse me?"

"I was thinking you must be Cinderella." He held up my flip-flops. "I found these. They're yours, right?"

I put my hand out, and he placed the flip-flops in it. "I guess that makes me Prince Charming," he said.

*Ew.* Who did he think he was? I had just had a near-death experience.

He stood with his hands on his hips. His suit jacket was pulled back a bit, and I could see his badge and gun.

"I was trying to save the owl. It wasn't my idea. Wildlife management told me to do it," I said.

He smiled and cocked his head to the side. "I don't usually come out for these kinds of things, but I heard the call come out about a woman up a telephone pole and had to see for myself. I'm not complaining, though, and neither is anybody else. Sergeant Brody over there says you have the finest rear end he's ever seen."

"Well, I'm sorry I wasn't up there longer to give everyone a better view."

"Don't worry about it. They all took photos with their cellphones," he said.

A deep heat crawled up my face, and my ears burned.

He studied me a second. "Hey, don't feel bad," he said, a smirk growing on his perfectly shaved face. "The town has cut back our overtime allowance, so the men have been pretty down. You just made everyone's day. I heard one guy say he hasn't felt this alive in twenty years."

One of the firemen approached us with the owl in his hands. "I got your owl," he said. He tapped it, making a hollow sound. "Plastic. It was put up there to scare away the pigeons so they wouldn't crap all over Burger Boy. I took it down so we don't have to go through this again. Although"—he winked at me—"I wouldn't mind the experience."

"But it looked so real," I moaned.

Prince Charming took the owl from the fireman. "Here," he said, presenting it to me. "You should have it."

"Thanks, but no thanks." I walked to my car and opened the door with a loud creak. Prince Charming was on my heels. He threw the owl behind me onto the backseat.

"Think of it as a souvenir."

I felt I needed to explain myself to him, and I hated myself for it. "I was just trying to be proactive."

"You were being a Good Samaritan," he said.

"I'm not like this normally."

He gave me another annoying little smirk. "I'm thinking there isn't much normally in your normally."

I gave him a sufficiently snotty look back and started the car. "I don't think you're Prince Charming at all," I said.

He smiled from ear to ear. "Nice car."

The Cutlass chose that moment to let rip its biggest car fart ever. I tried to retain my dignity, although I was guessing it was a little late for that. Besides, how dare he make fun of my only means of transportation? I was about to send back a zinger when he patted the roof and turned on his heel. "Bye, Pinkie," he called, waving as he walked.

I took a long, healing breath. The day had been a big lesson for me. I would never wear elastic-waist pants again.